*Recent Titles by Clare Curzon*

ALL UNWARY
CLOSE QUARTERS
COLD HANDS *
THE COLOUR OF BLOOD *
GUILTY KNOWLEDGE
NICE PEOPLE
PAST MISCHIEF

*\* published by Severn House*

# THE COLOUR OF BLOOD

# THE COLOUR
# OF BLOOD

## Clare Curzon

Severn House

M
2012500

This first world edition published in Great Britain 2000 by
SEVERN HOUSE PUBLISHERS LTD of
9–15 High Street, Sutton, Surrey SM1 1DF.
This first world edition published in the USA 2000 by
SEVERN HOUSE PUBLISHERS INC of
595 Madison Avenue, New York, N.Y. 10022.

British Library Cataloguing in Publication Data

Curzon,   Clare
    The colour of blood
    1.   Detective and mystery stories
    I.   Title
    823.9'14 [F]

    ISBN 0-7278-5596-4

Typeset by Palimpsest Book Production Ltd.,
Polmont, Stirlingshire, Scotland.
Printed and bound in Great Britain by
MPG Books Ltd, Bodmin, Cornwall.

# LUCY

# One

It was growing dark. I heard a street call from below. There came the tap of a cane and lamplight suddenly slanted up, printing a barred square of ochre over the dingy wallpaper beside me. It startled me into further consciousness.

Barely fifteen minutes had passed since I'd come alive, and I knew no more about myself than in the first few seconds. Until the baby cried.

It sounded feeble, yet demanding. So, even weak as I was, I had to get up from the chair and go across to lift it. Lift *her*; because somehow I knew it was a girl child. And I knew she was mine because my breasts were heavy and swollen. At her crying the milk had instantly begun to flow, soaking the bodice of my cotton blouse. The skirt was stiff where something had spilled. Both were stained with red.

I knew then a more urgent compulsion: something fearful. I had to check on the bedroom. The image hung on from my nightmare. I had dreamt that a man lay on the floor in there, bloodied and dying. I hugged the child close and went through.

This time he was quite dead.

It had been no dream before. The blood, in parts crimson like a fresh cut of beef, was elsewhere crusted and blackening as it congealed. He lay differently, as if at the last he had tried to crawl away.

And in a sense he had succeeded. What lay under the window, twisted and cold, was no longer "he" but "it". The man was no more.

I felt unaccountably freed. The sense of guilt would come later.

3

He must be a stranger, because I had felt no pity at sight of him. Yet he had known me. He had turned his glazing eyes on me with such bitterness and tried to speak. "So, Lucy, at last you have—" and then he had choked on blood, which spurted bright from his gaping mouth. And in the dream which had been no dream I had staggered out, left him there to die alone.

Lucy: so I was Lucy. That could be so.

Vague memory was stirring in my mind. But Lucy who? The question itself overwhelmed me with such emotion. It seemed that finding the answer must be the very reason for my being.

Who? *Who?* And who had fathered this child of mine moaning so pathetically to be fed? Was she half-orphaned when that man had finally died?

I returned to the empty fireplace, sat and began to feed the baby while I tried to get my mind together. And already dazed, then soothed by the rhythmic pulling at my nipple, I must have fallen wearily asleep.

What haunted my dreaming mind was a continuation of that rich, deep crimson, but no longer a fearsome colour. It flowed out in a heavy, supple fabric: my velour winter coat, new for Christmas when I had been eight or nine years old.

I awoke with a start as the baby spluttered, but now with sudden shock I was back in present reality. I was no longer a child, but a sick and wretched woman; not running free in Stakerleys' vast spread, but a sort of prisoner in the squalid quarters I had awoken to not long back. Yet that past time held a part of my fogged mind trapped in it like a bubble in glass. Why, from all the lifetime of Lucy Sedgwick, should that particular day have returned to me now? It seemed there was something shameful that linked me to that time, and yet I could not see what.

I was aware how on the point of near-death one's whole life can pass through the mind in a moment. Was I so ill then, that a part of my childhood had returned? Actually dying?

The sense of apprehension was fast overcome by anger. I refused to go out so feebly, but would force myself to action of whatever kind it took to make a stand.

It was fully dark by now. The square of lamplight from outside shone in brighter on the wall, the rest of the room almost invisible.

4

It could be well after eleven. I must be mad to have sat on here without trying to work out what to do, where to go. Not that I'd get far, feeling as I did, only half alive, my head floating off, somehow free of the body it was supposed to control.

I searched around for fresh candles but there were none. Only in the downstairs kitchen did I find a guttered stub, stuck in the neck of a bottle that stank of stale beer. There was a flint lighter by the sink and I set it to the wick.

Now, seen in some detail, the place looked more wretched than before. Wallpaper up the stairs, torn and bubbled, surely had creatures lurking under it, embedded in the pitted plaster revealed over half the area. The sitting-room was more than dingy; it was soot-grimed and greasy. In the bedroom – for I forced myself to enter it again and search – the few pieces of furniture held no clothes that could be mine. In a drawer I found a greyish, patched sheet, which I tore into strips and used to clean and cover the baby afresh. Her own clothes, although soiled, seemed of fairly decent quality. My own were the same.

I had been brought to this place. There was no other explanation. I could never have come by my own choice. And where were we? Still I had no memory of the journey, nor of the circumstances leading to it. I could not properly remember giving birth, yet I had to have been through that agony, and recently. Also it seemed that I had some elementary knowledge of how to care for the small creature.

Because of what lay in the next room it was vital that we leave at once. The dead man had suffered violence. His killer could come back.

It might even be thought by anyone finding me here in this state that I was responsible, since my sleeves and bodice were stiff with dried blood.

Yet, not knowing what awaited me outside, how could I risk leaving so late at night in so squalid a neighbourhood?

At the small window I bent to survey the alley below. It was narrow and crooked. Rain shone on puddled cobbles under the only street light. A row of ancient houses opposite leaned close and frowning, their front doors opening straight on to the gutter.

5

One or two windows showed dim lighting through thin curtains hung haphazardly.

Nothing moved. No face showed anywhere. It was a neighbourhood of secrets. But perhaps from behind some unlit window I was being watched. If I left now in darkness would anyone speak of having seen me arrive? And how long could the dead man lie here unnoticed before someone came to check on the stench of putrefaction? By then I must be safely away. But run where, at this late hour?

The tiny baby, sated, was sleeping soundly. I tucked her more securely in the woven straw crib and looked about for my belongings. There was nothing that seemed mine. What had I been expecting?

I had to sit again because the room spun and my head had a ligature-like tightening around. After a few minutes with my eyes closed I steadied and the pain was reduced to a quiet, rhythmic pumping.

The candle's flame flickered. While it still lasted I must find somewhere to relieve myself. Downstairs I unlatched a back door crudely fashioned of rough planks which gave on to a small walled yard. The earlier rain had ceased and a few stars showed through. There was a little privy with a cracked, stained basin. I left the door open to save me from the stench.

Upstairs again, I removed the crib from the table and took off the fringed chenille cloth. It would have to serve me for a shawl. Over my head and tied at the chin peasant-wise, it would at least cover my noticeable hair. Even in my confusion I knew it essential that I shouldn't be remarked on. Perhaps I acted from shame, finding myself in such degrading circumstances – I who pride myself on controlling my own life.

With the crib nudging against my thigh, I descended the stairs and let myself out into the alley. I was aware of a distant hubbub which I had heard in the walled yard without properly observing. But now it was louder. I turned towards the direction it seemed to come from, and at a twist in the alley came on a lighted street with pedestrians. This was no country village I found myself in, but a large town with shops and traffic, both horse cabs and motors. Perhaps somewhere half-familiar?

I crossed over and walked for some minutes without any intention but to get as far as possible from that hideous place I'd awoken in. Afraid that like a snowblind traveller I might go in circles, I took right then left alternately at each street end. But my strength was ebbing and the child so heavy. The rough string handles of the basket cut into my hands.

I leaned against the wooden shutters of a shop. From inside there escaped a pungent smell of fruit and green vegetables which turned my stomach. My foot slid on the squelchy softness of a rotting carrot. I remembered then: Covent Garden, and first being walked through the vegetable market by Uncle Geoffrey as a child. Ahead, surely that was the heavy portico of the parish church of St Paul? So I was in London, not far from the Royal Opera House itself. At least here I'd some notion of the layout of the streets.

The same smells hung on the air all around, only now the frantic bustle was stilled, the porters gone home, the stacks of wicker baskets put away. For a few hours of darkness it would stay so, and then the day here would start up again, early, before first light. The farm carts would roll in, the bustle and crowds increase – and no one would notice me. Until then I could curl up in a doorway and sleep some of my strength back.

Beyond that no plan offered itself. "Sufficient unto the day is the evil thereof."

The baby – had I no name for her? – woke me once, demanding to be fed again, and then I became aware of others sleeping, as I did, in the open. There was restless movement in other dark corners, a grumble or two and a low cursing, the clink of an empty bottle rolling on flagstones.

Twice a shuffling figure approached, peering at me as I suckled the child. One, stenchy, snivelled and moved away. The other stayed bending over me and I feared that he would mistake me for a street woman and force himself on me.

This bundle of clothes put out a hand, but recoiled in alarm as I whipped out the knife and pointed it threateningly. It was only a poor, horn-handled thing, but the blade was honed away to a stiletto. I seemed hazily to recall finding it in the dirty kitchen.

"No, miss! I mean no harm. Just to see the babby, like. I had one meself time back but the Lord took him, poor scrap."

It was a woman, and a countrywoman from her voice. I'd not expected such a one in these circumstances.

"Here," she said, producing an apple. "I'd kept it for me breakfast, but like as not your need's greater. Mebbe there'll be another come along. Some of them porters have pity on us homeless and spill a thing or two on purpose, like. Are you hungry, lass? You must keep your strength up or your milk'll go dry."

I grabbed at the wrinkled apple, wiped it on my skirt and devoured it, bruises and all. Till then I had barely noticed that the nausea stemmed from pangs of hunger, so much else about me feeling wrong. It seemed only civil then to make room for her alongside.

She hesitated. "I've got a little cart. If I leave it, it'll get took for sure."

I struggled to move the child from one breast to the other, but the effort left me breathless. "Here," the woman scolded, sorting me out. "You shouldn't be on your own."

I thought she'd gone away, but then I heard the trundle of wheels on the cobbles and she was back with her cart, to take the place beside me on my step.

I slept again fitfully, vaguely conscious of her drawing the baby away and settling it again in the straw basket. I awoke to find her still close, but recoiling to one side as a large, rough-featured man stepped over me to gain entrance to the shop. "Stay, stay, girl!" he urged. "There'll be no one through again for a while. Time enough to move on when some customers turn up."

A faint, smoky light was showing over the rooftops and I shivered at the chill air, stiff and cramped as the woman helped me to my feet. I limped behind some piled boxes to relieve myself and felt grateful it was summer: I doubt either I or the little one would survive this sort of existence in the cold.

Shutters were being removed and a steady flow of workmen appeared, to bring out crates and barrows as the first carts delivered the day's provisions. It was time to move on.

"My name is Lucy," I told the woman. "What's yours?"

"Mabel. Mabel Walters." Now that the light was better I could see she was poorly dressed in what had at least been respectable clothes. On her head she wore a small black straw hat pinned over a straggle of pepper-and-salt coloured hair. Her tanned face was lined but she could have been no more than thirty-five or -six years old. I had seen many village women of her sort and I felt I could trust her.

"You don't belong here," I said. "What made you come to London?"

She told me she'd been widowed. Her husband, a farm labourer, had died, so along with him she lost all right to their cottage. Although she'd worked twelve years as laundry maid at the farmhouse, the new man's wife was to take that over as well as her home.

"So you were turned away with nothing?"

"My few bits and pieces are in the push-cart. But the farmer's wife was kind. She gave me a pair of cockerels she'd killed that morning and a great basket of turnips and carrots. So when the vegetable wagon set off for London's Covent Garden I thought to beg a lift and make some money here myself."

That had been five days back and by now she was low in funds, out of produce and quite out of love with the capital city.

"I have enough left for some bread and a few flowers," she said simply.

"Flowers?" What kind of precious taste was this for someone faced by starvation?

"I buy them cheaply here, then take them to better neighbourhoods and sell them for more. That way I keep going from day to day, for it would shame me to beg for my keep or sell myself. You're welcome to come with me if you feel strong enough to walk. The sight of you with your little one may move people to pay us more."

"Do you know no one in London?"

"Not a soul but the poor derelicts I've met hereabouts."

"Well, I do." My mind was made up. In no condition to stand on my dignity, I would steer her to the Sedgwick house in Eaton Place and see whether any of the servants there recognised me. It seemed unlikely, however, because once they reached a certain age they were normally pensioned off or sent to lighter duties at Stakerleys. Still, if I made myself look moderately respectable they might give me work. Indeed, as a modern-day Prodigal Daughter, "fain would I have filled my belly with the husks that the swine did eat." But hiding my identity from my family, if I could.

I directed Mabel towards Charing Cross and while she took up a stand there with her portable flower stall and the crib beside her, I went boldly into Lyons Corner House, covering the bloodstains on my bodice with the shawl ends. At that hour there was only a cleaning woman in the Ladies Room, and three others who had come in for the same purpose as myself. But they were *filles de joie*, although there was little gaiety about them then under their glitter and feathers, bedraggled after their night's performances. They clearly formed a sort of sisterhood, suspicious of me as a threatening outsider who might want to share their trade. It was probably my baby's presence that saved me from their spite.

I made myself as clean and tidy as could be without brush or comb, and steeled myself for the journey on foot.

Always before, I had travelled these streets by carriage or motor and the distance had seemed nothing. Now my fear was that even if Mabel's stock lasted as far as Belgravia, I might not complete the journey alive.

In St James's Park I had twice to sit on an empty bench only to be accosted by a passing gentleman who mistook my intentions. Meanwhile Mabel had continued straight through to wait at the Palace end, for fear of arrest by park-keepers as an unlicensed street vendor.

I caught her up and pointed out the direction we must go. We were surely more than half way there, but this last part, past the Royal Mews and Hobart Place tested me horribly. Arrived at the familiar street, I supported myself along the iron railings and collapsed exhausted on the top of the basement steps. While Mabel bent to wipe my damp forehead I heard the front door burst open above us and hurried footfalls making for the pavement.

Expecting some ill-tempered footman dispatched to see us off, I was dimly aware of a polite male voice requesting a buttonhole of Mabel.

"Edwin?" I marvelled, not meaning to say it aloud. But he had caught the whisper. Then he was bending over me, his cane and gloves on the flagstones alongside. Mabel stood beyond him, mouth agape and holding out a single rosebud.

I felt his fingers explore the edge of the shawl and then my hair was exposed. "It *is* you," he marvelled. "Lucy, we've been so anxious for you ever since . . ."

Ever since the police had released me, having insufficient evidence to hold me further. Ever since I'd fled, so that they shouldn't take me in again. That much at least I remembered, although everything that had happened since remained in a sort of fog.

He had questions for me but enough sense to see I could answer nothing then. The whole scene began to spin about me and his voice came from afar, sending Mabel to knock for admittance and have servants come to help. I felt him lift me and had a close glimpse of his earnest young face, the chin sparsely pricked by the beginnings of soft golden hair.

My little brother a grown man, or nearly so. It was absurd. I heard myself begin to laugh, distantly, and then knew no more.

While the next few days were for me a procession of wakings and sleepings, Edwin saw to everything: provided a physician to treat me, a wet nurse for the baby and a neat uniform for Mabel, having mistaken her for my personal maid.

When I told her we must explain to him what a good friend she'd been to me, she begged me not to. "I'd be happy, miss – ma'am, I mean – I'd be honoured if you'd let me stay in your service. I badly need a job, and I would truly do my best to please you."

So I didn't disillusion my brother – whom I'd always found easy to deceive – and even informed him loftily that Mabel's wages had been unpaid for the past two months and he should now put this to rights.

My great concern was that no news of my presence should escape outside the house. I feared some fresh investigation could set the police looking for me again. Edwin explained that fortunately my stepfather was abroad in the Far East and Mama taking the waters at Baden-Baden, having suffered a setback in her usually robust health. Edwin himself was the only member of the family in residence, on holiday from Eton. He had set his father's lawyers the task of finding me, and now I had surfaced on my own. I felt sure of his discretion, but the servants were all new to me and had no special reason to be loyal.

"Baden-Baden?" I questioned. "So we are good friends again with the Germans?"

He tapped his chin with the silver tip of his cane and answered sombrely, "So it seems. Whoever officially won the war, it's clear that in effect all of us have lost. Europe is impoverished, and at home here the streets are still full of unemployed men who have served our country bravely, and many of them permanently suffering as a result. Among our own kind there is a deal of partying and wildness, but there's a sort of desperation under it, except for those who've profited from the war."

I struggled to sit up against my pillows. "Oh Edwin, whatever happened to that limitless golden world we once knew?"

"Perhaps it was fool's gold. Otherwise it wouldn't have tarnished so easily and fallen apart. The world only seemed innocent because we were innocent ourselves then, seeing it through children's eyes. But don't you remember how concerned our parents were? – how constantly Papa spoke in the House to try and get injustices dealt with, at home and abroad?"

"Edwin, I do believe you've gone political," I jeered.

"It's part of growing up. One's eyes come open. You'd do well to take life more seriously yourself."

"You're chiding me! Reminding me I'm senior to you."

"Twenty," he said thoughtfully. "And now a parent in your turn."

It sobered me. Soon would come the inquisition: perhaps even a demand to know who the child's father was. If he asked, must I confess I wasn't sure? And there was more about which he must be eaten up with curiosity: had his half-sister in fact murdered her husband, as the police suspected?

I shivered. If I could now be traced back to that squalid little house where I'd recently left an unknown man dead of stab wounds, what conclusions would they draw on either crime? None to my comfort, that was certain.

On my second day there, Edwin had business elsewhere and only entered my room to explain he would be away for most of the day. He blushed when I warned him not to keep the lady waiting. I had only meant it in fun, and it almost shocked me that he was old enough to be drawn into the ancient game between the sexes.

The following day I insisted on getting up, with Mabel dressing me. There were some frocks of mine from way back which fitted loosely. For all that I'd always liked bright colours, their cut made them drab. Even with shortening they missed the modern post-war look.

I spent the morning reading the newspapers but found nothing personal to alarm me. After lunch I slept a little and then sat a while in the garden. When Edwin returned before dinner I dared to ask whether he'd heard more about the inquiry into Julian's death.

"Nothing recently," he assured me, pouring sherry carefully and carrying it across to me. "But assuredly it grinds slowly on. There's a sort of inevitability about the way the police operate. After the first fuss there comes a lull. The matter goes out of one's mind and then – unexpectedly – they're back, repeating the self-same questions and nodding solemnly and writing down all we say. Then they're away again, until next time. You remember how persistent they were about that dead Italian?"

"What dead Italian?" I shot upright, spilling my sherry and mopping at it furiously to cover my confusion.

"Oh, years ago. When we were small. Someone found his body in the grounds at Stakerleys and the police kept coming back, to question the servants and guests."

I did remember then. First the local man had come, then a second time with a sergeant. Finally the sergeant with an inspector from Aylesbury. His face had the reflective pallor of parchment, with tiny, hard eyes inset like a pig's.

We children had been sitting on the stairs when Mama came by to be interviewed. She had corrected my grammar over some remark I made just as the man opened the library door and overheard. I'd been mortified. Since then I'd suffered much more at the hands of the police than that slight indignity. Just a week or so back they had treated me with cold suspicion. The war had a lot to answer for: there was far less respect shown now for the gentry.

I remembered only vaguely the fuss there had been at the earlier crime. "I was eight then. You would be only five, Edwin. Fancy you remembering. You say the man was Italian? Are you sure? I only knew he was foreign."

"Definitely Italian. I overheard the inspector talking to his sergeant. He pronounced it 'Eye-talian'."

I was conscious of my heart thudding away inside. "I don't suppose you ever heard what the dead man's name was."

"Actually I did. Being a quiet child, I was often overlooked when the servants gossiped. Now, what was it? Something quite short. No, I'm afraid it's gone, Lucy. That is stretching my memory rather far, you know."

"Do you think you'd recognise it again? Was it Gabrieli, by any chance?"

"No; I'd have connected that with Rossetti. Like one of his forenames, you know. It's the way my mind works, linking things up. I get a better hold on new facts that way. I did it even as a little chap. Whatever his name, it can't have connected with any interest of mine at the time."

"What a funny fellow you are, Edwin. All that going on inside your head and nobody knew. No wonder you were always so slow to answer. I used to call you 'the Dreamer'."

"And your name for little Rupert was 'the Great White Slug'."

"Horrid of me. I should have kept it to myself. But that was my first impression of him as a baby."

"Perhaps you were a little jealous of him."

How percipient. As a child I'd taken no thought for my brother's opinions, being so full of my own and my passions. And my greatest jealousy then was over him, because he would in time inherit his father's title, eventually Grandfather's and become Earl Sedgwick.

I felt as if I saw him now for the first time. And the once-important years that had made me senior seemed to have dissolved. At sixteen, Edwin had become a man as I was a woman.

He was turning his wine glass between his fingers, studying its engraving of vine leaves, then looked at me squarely. "Why did you suggest the name Gabrieli – for the dead Italian?"

Did I trust him, respect his new image enough to answer him truthfully?

"Because," I said slowly, "that was our mother's name the first time she married. It should have been mine, but your papa had it changed."

"I never knew."

"It was never mentioned."

"From discretion, I suppose. For fear of wounding Papa's feelings."

"From secrecy, I've always thought."

"So when did they tell you?"

"They didn't. I was left to discover the name in an address book at my grandmother's house."

He was silent a while, stroking his chin with the soft golden down on it. His long, Sedgwick chin. "So you are half-Italian, Lucy. How extraordinary! But why, when I mentioned the foreigner who died in Stakerleys' grounds, did you imagine that might be his name too?"

I took my time to answer. "Because that man was murdered. I feared there might be some connection with my missing father – I feel murder is haunting my life. That Italian was the first of them."

Edwin frowned. "And your husband the second. Is that what you mean? Why should you regard them as a sequence?"

"Is it just coincidence then? I feel they both involve me personally." I couldn't suppress a shudder.

"Lucy, that's nonsense. You know it is, with all those years between. My dear, you're still confused." He came across and knelt by my chair, taking me into his arms.

Goodness knows what he made of my silent shaking. He hadn't seen, as I had, that third, bloodied body I'd left behind in the squalid little house somewhere south of Covent Garden just a few days before. Surely Death was shadowing my footsteps.

And, terrifying above all, there hung over me this new fear of something hideous having happened – for which I had been

15

responsible – in the recent lost days before I found myself again.

"There is so much I don't know." Then, lest it should sound too ominous I added pettishly, "People have always concealed things from me."

Edwin gave a wry smile. "I could complain a little of that myself. I am waiting hopefully for you to tell me about the time when you went missing," my brother said gravely, "and how you come to turn up here unannounced and in such a sorry state."

"I can't," I admitted, succumbing at last to womanly helplessness; "since most of it I've no memory of at all."

# Two

W hile I tried to explain, Edwin listened, holding my trembling hands in his own and shaking his head at the more perplexing parts of the story.

"You seem to have strayed on to dangerous ground," he said at the end, "but our first consideration must be to make sure you have the best medical care."

"Because I lose my memory? Would you have me certified insane?"

Was my brother my enemy? I snatched my hands away. He reached for them again.

"Nothing of the sort, Lucy. But, until now, I'd assumed you suffered from no more than fatigue and exposure. It's possible, even likely, that your sickness is due to some recent injury, and the memory-loss stems from that. It can continue sometimes for a considerable period, as I understand it, and then be recalled by some incident which hinges on the lost circumstances."

He continued to amaze me, this little brother I'd dismissed so easily before. "Where did you gather all this medical information? Are you intending to follow Uncle Millson in his career? I can't imagine that will please your father. Isn't he warming you a seat in the Lords as an Independent politician?"

"It's possible to be of use in other ways as well," Edwin said almost drily. He sat silent a moment.

"What most interests me at present is the study of the psyche, which is becoming of enormous importance, especially when frightening experiences cause physical symptoms. But the opposite's true as well, because the mind runs parallel with the body. We must also look to the body for its effect on the mind.

"All I have so far is a very general knowledge. It's early yet to be sure which particular discipline I shall want to specialise in, but when my education's done I certainly intend to choose my own career rather than have one handed to me on a silver plate."

"A gold plate, Edwin, one embossed with the Sedgwick crest, so that you can go on in the family tradition, and your sons' sons' sons after you to the umpteenth Earl Sedgwick."

He looked at me sadly, seeing inside my heart. "Are you still so bitter about Papa, Lucy?"

Damn him for his acuity. I mooched across to the window and treated him to my back view. "Not so bitter as I was. He really doesn't deserve it. I'll admit he's a good man. And by now I know well enough there's few of those in our world."

I swung round to face my brother. "No, what I find hard to bear is being grateful to him for his years of patronage, wiping out the name I have a right to, making me a mock Sedgwick. To be honest, I can't forgive him his bloody loving-kindness. And you're just such another, Edwin. It keeps reminding me I'm made of different stuff."

"If you say so."

I stomped back to his side. "What were we talking about? Yes, your career, after your education's 'done'. Education's never *done*," I said bossily. "If you've a real interest in the psyche that's one fact you must surely accept. I know that I'm learning all the time – from my mistakes – even if the facts learnt then elude me!" My laugh was a poor cracked thing.

He smiled and squeezed my fingers. "Of course I accept that. I see you're still a stickler for others' accuracy, and whatever your predicament you've not damaged your sense of humour. I was talking of my formal education at school, and later at Oxford."

I skipped back to the subject of psychology, more earnest now. "I don't intend letting anyone pry into my mind, Edwin. There are things in there which I'd want kept decently locked away."

"Which might not be to your advantage in the end."

"Total exposure, is that what you suggest? What horror. For all that I'm uneasy about my mind's state, I'd as soon – sooner perhaps – walk naked down Piccadilly than submit to that kind of jiggery-pokery. I'm not entirely ignorant, you know. I suspect that Freud and his like are so determined to find odious creatures lurking under the stones which they turn over that they will introduce some of them there themselves."

"That's an opinion I've heard before. But would you agree just to discuss the possibility of a consultation, with someone you felt you could trust? Simply that?"

I considered a while. "Perhaps. *If* I could trust anyone enough, but I never would. No, my mind is my own and I'll keep it that way. No foreign alienists, no hypnotists, no fortune tellers."

"There's a professor at University College, an Englishman, who is thought to have some very sound ideas . . ."

"Nor learned college professors. Certainly not. I'd rather just go on from day to day with the confusion easing – as I believe it's already doing – in the hope that, as you said, the memories will return of themselves."

"That's probably what this specialist would agree with. Also offer you a little help with bringing it about for yourself. Without outside interference."

"Edwin, you sound like the man's disciple. Have you been attending his lectures? How did you escape from school to do that?"

"No. I have a friend, a post-graduate student of his at UCL, and he's shown me some of his thesis notes. He's a really splendid fellow, of our own generation. Well, seven or eight years older than me. I'd so like you to meet him, Lucy. Will you, to please me?"

"Not even a real alienist, but an unskilled amateur? What a risk you're proposing for your poor demented sister." I shrugged, smiling at his rueful expression. "Well, no reason, I suppose, why I shouldn't meet this paragon sometime, but only socially. It could even prove amusing to argue with him, if nothing else. And God knows I've little enough to sharpen my mind or claws on at present, except the problems of breastfeeding and how to regain some weight."

Edwin let two more days go by, while I strongly resisted his suggestion that he should notify our mother of my return.

"She would only rush back to England and spoil all the good effects of her own cure. And I don't wish her to see me feeble like this. I promise to be still here when she does arrive." Though

19

how I could account for myself to her I'd no idea. It was certainly something to put off as long as possible.

By now I was feeling stronger, rising after breakfast, to sit a while in the garden and join my brother for lunch. I came in through the verandah doors one morning to find he had invited a friend to join us. The young man rose from his chair and came forward to be introduced. "Clive Malcolm," my brother said.

The light from outside shone on his face, the quirky eyebrows and merry eyes a slightly richer brown than his short-cut curly hair. He was medium tall, reaching only to my brother's shoulder, for Edwin took after the lanky men of his family.

"Miss Sedgwick," the young man said, holding my fingers firmly. He seemed not to know I'd a married name; which pleased me.

There was something persistent in the way he stood looking at me, as though I should surely remember him. But I couldn't place him at all. And that troubled me increasingly throughout the meal which we three shared, because if he belonged to that recent frightening part of my life which still eluded me, then whatever experience we'd shared could hardly be a good one. Lost though it was, yet I felt certain that the occasion of our meeting – our collision – had brought disaster and misery. Why else should my mind have closed itself so thoroughly on what had happened?

It appeared he was the graduate at University College of whom Edwin had spoken. He had amusing stories to tell of student doings in Gower Street and his Bloomsbury lodgings, but the longer he spoke the more bemused I became, unable to see where he and I could possibly have rubbed up against each other. Surely I would have remembered his voice if nothing else: low, and warm like his brown eyes.

I tried to tease it from him. "You remind me of someone I knew once," I suggested, but he didn't follow it up, just smiled and said, "How sad that I should leave too feeble an impression for you to recall me in full. But in fact I fear I'm the sort of very ordinary person that comes by the bushel, quite indistinguishable from the next fellow. Perhaps I simply remind you of someone you prefer to forget?"

The first part of which was untrue. He was distinctive. I quite saw how Edwin was attracted. I could have been so myself, in other circumstances. There was such controlled vitality in his compact person, a calm strength underlying the banter, so that one could guess at the seriousness he applied to his studies. Studies of the mind, according to Edwin. Well, I'd do well to make myself scarce before he began to plumb my uncertain depths.

I needed time alone to consider his reply, which had sounded ambiguous. Had he, or had he not, half agreed that we'd met already somewhere?

But before I could make my excuses he was thanking us both and taking his leave. A servant brought his outdoor things and then as he stood smiling at the door, cap in hand, I knew for sure he was familiar. Yet, fearful that insisting on it might trigger too much unwanted memory, I turned away and let him go.

"It's curious," I said to Edwin on his return from seeing the young man to the street (an informality that must irritate the household).

"What is?"

"I had a feeling we'd met before, yet I can't place him at all."

He stood considering me. "I thought it was only recent memories that escape you. He goes back a long way. But then the meeting was brief, so perhaps, as he said, it never made a great impression on you. As a child you were not much aware of things outside yourself."

"You mean I was self-absorbed. Is that it?" True, but it stung me that Edwin, the subservient little brother, should all along have been silently watching and judging me. Now, these years later, he towered over me physically and seemed to have outpaced my intelligence.

"You have your own way of seeing things, and react instinctively. We are almost direct opposites in that. Which is why I think we complement each other so well."

He was full of surprises now that he had come out of his dreamy shell and was expressing himself. And he was right about my behaviour, always demanding, protesting, while he accepted. Perhaps as a child he'd been silenced by my loud forthrightness.

Edwin's words provided plenty for my mind to work on, but for the present I dismissed them, overlooking too how he had failed to follow up my suspicion of having met Clive Malcolm before. At least he had implied that any connection would have been fleeting, so it could hardly be of great importance.

There were grimmer problems overshadowing my conscience, and alone in my room at night, I tried to face again all that had happened in the squalid little house where I had come back to life. As I lay staring up at the shadowed ceiling I seemed to watch the re-run of a grainy film with myself within each jerking frame. Fear made it real, so that every detail returned with its accompanying emotion and confusion. The lifeless body on the floor brought back the very smell and colour of spilt blood.

The colour of blood, and a distant memory of a velour coat. The mind plays strange tricks of its own. Why that particular frame from the life of Lucy Sedgwick? Blood wasn't the only connection: there had to be some other link.

Go back and follow the action through on that late December afternoon when I was a little short of nine years old. What else had happened then that gave me a sense of *déjà vu*; even of half-forgotten guilt?

The moving picture's reel was changed. Now we were back at Stakerleys. The year was 1909.

In that particular week before Christmas, although Papa and Mama were away in London, the house had already been buzzing with hectic activity. Eight or so new servants were brought in – three from the Belgravia house and therefore almost strangers to us children. Others, local and part-trained in families of professional men in Aylesbury, were being drilled by Hadrill, with many of his usual duties being passed down to footmen and parlour maids.

Everyone was over-occupied except us children, released from lessons and temporarily between governesses. Idle hands; and if the mischief they found to do was innocent enough to present eyes, it was bound to find disfavour then.

We went treasure-hunting. In such a venture I was still leader then, always rasher than the hesitant Edwin, four years my junior. He was in any case hampered by having to drag little Rupert along by his reins. The object of our search was the hideaway of the gifts stored secretly until Christmas Eve, when they would all appear as if by magic under the decorated tree.

Noiseless as Red Indians we tracked the movements of the enemy and hid ourselves when scouting parties came our way. Crushed into cupboards or behind curtains we listened for a safe moment to emerge and continue our stealthy foraging. Once, in silencing Rupert's baby protests with my hands, I thought I had stifled the little wretch, but his colour crept back and he came awake again when I shook him thoroughly, once the interruption was over.

At last we ran the treasures to earth – or rather, to attic. There were square and round shapes, hard and soft, some that rattled and others that didn't. Most were covered in glittery paper with satin bows of silver, scarlet or gold; and a few, delivered by post, still had their brown-paper wrappings, franked with stamps showing King Edward's bearded head in profile. These last were tightly trussed with string and sealed with crimson wax.

Whether in familiar handwriting or on labels from London stores, the addresses on these parcels had a formal distinction. Most came care of our parents, but some were directed to us children by name. "The Honourable Edwin and the Honourable Rupert Sedgwick." But for me merely to Miss Lucy Sedgwick.

I was not honourable even then.

Furious at the insult, I had been unaware that the toddler was gleefully shredding bright paper and that at that very moment we'd been discovered. A positive mob of housemaids fell on us with shocked wailing and chidings.

Rupert was swept up and we were trooped off as captives to the servants' hall, there to await transfer by Hadrill to family authority. Which – since there was currently no nursemaid – was Aunt Isabelle, roused from her afternoon sleep and none too pleased with us because she'd had to dress again and have her hair repinned. I observed with disgust that unpleasantly strong perfume on her breath of which she always smelled when she was drowsy and out of sorts – so we knew to appear demure and chastened.

Not that that had much effect on her. She was all for having us dismissed to our beds except that it meant appointing someone to make sure we weren't fighting with pillows or throwing chamber pots out of the windows. So I suggested we might all put on our warm things and take a turn in the grounds, with Rupert in his little dogcart. Again she was unwilling to accompany us but had a footman ring the garden bell for one of the outdoor men to come and take us off her hands.

And so it happened that, outdoors, I was the first to see the station trap distantly approaching with Mr Warner in it, the visiting tailor who periodically came to see to our clothing. He would spend a day or two working on the lesser household's needs, being accorded a room in the attics to sleep. And on this occasion he had brought along his son Cecil to help carry his bags, because for him school was over for the term.

The junior gardener we children were handed to had been glad to quit his heavy digging and lead us out of sight of the house, where he could pull out his pipe and settle to a peaceful smoke. While Edwin wheeled the dogcart with the slumbering Rupert I sat on a gothic rock and watched the fascinating male performance of bowl-scraping, tobacco-shredding, filling and tamping.

Papa and the other gentlemen of the family smoked fragrant cigars, and I had even caught Aunt Isabelle lighting one up, but pipes were somehow more brutal: a peasant thing accompanied by ill-mannered suckings. And in its own coarse way impressive.

"Yardley," I said with my most winning smile, "won't you give me a puff?"

He was taken aback, but in the slow country way of his kind. "Well, miss, I doan' know as I should," he pondered. "Such young ladies as I know ain't given to asmokun of t'baccy."

But, however determined, I wasn't to be initiated then because a housemaid came running to fetch us, the streamers of her cap flying out behind her. I noticed the dazed way the young gardener gawked at her, and she was saucily sizing him up as if he had come seeking an indoor job.

We children were herded into Mama's morning-room and at least there it was "ladies first". Edwin's new Norfolk jacket and knickerbockers should wait upon the final fitting of my crimson velour winter coat.

The tailor was a thin, buttoned-up man with a shiny-pale, cheese-textured face like one of those scrawny saints in village church windows. He was so interminably patient that I often adopted tactics which would test his limits, to put off as long as I dared the moment of enduring his pernickety measuring and fitting. He had cold, bony fingers, almost as long as the blades of his cutting shears, and when I shuddered at his accidental touch he would instantly freeze motionless, his eyes hooded, take a long breath and then start afresh to swathe the cloth about me.

Cecil, the son, several years my senior, was different: level-eyed, assured, perhaps even a touch assertive, but in his father's presence he had that under control.

"Why are you staring, boy?" I asked him as he stood by, holding a strip of curly black fur intended for the collar.

Warner sat back on his heels, his mouth a single tight line, but Cecil answered instantly. "It's your hair, miss. So garish against the crimson. But likely it'll look better with the black in between."

I know my face then must have rivalled the brightness of my hair. The insolence of the boy to criticise me!

He smiled easily. "It's the material that's wrong, not the hair, miss. It's very pretty red hair. With such bouncy curls."

At that Warner dismissed him, and quite properly too. He should never have brought him along. Things would have turned out better for us both if only he'd stayed at home.

When it was Edwin's turn to be fitted I slipped away. Which wasn't difficult, with only the under-housekeeper present to keep an eye on us all.

Outside, I came upon the boy Cecil sitting on a step between the twin stone gryphons on the terrace. He was whittling away at a piece of whitish wood with a curved blade like a pruning knife's. He must have heard me coming but he failed to rise.

"You should stand up when a lady approaches," I told him.

He barely lifted his eyes as he said mildly, "I would, for a real lady." Then he looked fully in my face and smiled.

Because it was friendly he momentarily disarmed me and I'd missed the moment to check his rudeness. Even if he'd only meant I was too young for formal *politesse* it was still ungallant.

But then he was just a tailor's boy and doubtless unschooled in good manners.

"What are you making?" I demanded.

"If you're patient, you shall see."

I peered over his shoulder. "It's a person."

"A little girl." He was digging intricate small holes and swirls into the thing's head. "There, it's roughly finished. Do you recognise yourself, Miss Lucy?"

"Not at all!"

"I'm no artist, it's true. Yet that is a little how I see you. How do you see yourself?"

The truth was that I didn't see myself at all. We were not allowed mirrors in the nursery. Elsewhere they were hung too high to reflect anything but the gentlemen's whiskers or the ladies' bare shoulders. Yet in Mama's boudoir there was a long cheval-glass where she would check herself completely before going down to dinner. How it came into my head to show it to the boy I have no idea, but we found ourselves there, in forbidden territory.

I stood with the little wooden figure in my hand and stared from it to my reflection. The dress I wore was made of a forest green plaid, dark like pine trees against the sunlight; my woollen stockings and buttoned boots black. Again I had the shock I always suffered on seeing my right leg encased in the cruel shiny irons.

So that was how the boy would think of me: as a near cripple. It was unforgiveable that he should be allowed to stare. I watched myself transformed. Under the fiery hair my pale, narrow face flooded with angry colour. I well understood then why Mama had questioned my choice of the crimson velour. I tried to picture how the boy had seen me in the almost finished coat. The florid colour would have shrieked against my riotous hair, even with the collar of black astrakhan set between.

"Well?" he prompted, meaning nothing to do with colour, but rather wasn't the carved figurine a good likeness?

Before I could answer I heard voices in the corridor outside. Mona, my mother's personal maid. Even as the brass rings clashed with the rising of the door's *portière* rod I had thrust the boy bodily behind the long window drapes and pulled them closed.

Mona burst unceremoniously in upon me. "Why, Miss Lucy, whatever next?" she exclaimed on a note of disapproval, catching sight of me in the shadows.

I moved towards her. "I'd a fancy," I said, "to make certain everything was in order for Mama's homecoming."

"You may be sure that it is," she said sharply. "What else would I be about?" She started fussing around, shaking up cushions that were already plumped and moving ornaments a fraction of an inch, as if I might have caused havoc there. And then she went in a beeline for the window alcove where the boy was concealed.

"There's no call to shut the light out. Milady will arrive tomorrow morning before luncheon. And what's *this*, miss?"

How could I explain the horrid boy's presence, here where even I should not have been? I waited for the heavens to fall and, when they didn't, peered between my fingers at her. She was reaching up for the iron hasp and was firmly closing the casement left ajar. There was neither sight nor sound of the tailor's boy.

"You're a foolish little girl to let the cold air in," she scolded. "We'll have a hard frost tonight. And it's dangerous to play with windows this high up. Why else do you have all them bars put up in the nursery?"

She herded me out and I went back to my brothers. Later when I excused myself and ran post-haste to release the boy it seemed that everything conspired to frustrate me that day, for I found the door to Mama's rooms locked against me.

What more could I do for the wretched fellow? He should have known better than to penetrate the private part of the house. It was quite unfitting. Shut out, let him somehow climb his way down the side of the house, like Tom of the *Water Babies*. That was who he reminded me of then with his pert face and bold manner. A chimneysweep's lad who could scale drainpipes and climb like a monkey. And certainly he was no concern of mine.

The little wooden carving bit into my chest, buttoned inside the plaid dress. Tomorrow I would get rid of it.

Later, while we children were served supper, there was a fluttering among the servants and much scurrying to and fro. I

27

tried to overhear the whispers, because it seemed they had some serious concern. I hid the carving under my feather bed while I was kneeling for prayers, and when I lay waiting for sleep I tried not to think that up in the attics Mr Warner's second truckle bed might still lie empty. But though it would take the boy some time to scramble down, yet I told myself he would do it. He was that sort of boy.

Sometime during the night, after the whole huge house had been scoured without success, it seems there was a search made outside with lanterns. Someone eventually thought to bring a ladder and inspect the balustraded lower roofs that jutted from the house on its west side. And so he was found.

I overheard next morning how he had been taken down lashed to a hurdle, frozen stiff, both legs broken and heaven knows what else. It seems he came awake briefly, but he couldn't explain how he came to be there. It was assumed he'd climbed the building's stone face that far, attempted to go further and then fell awkwardly. A terrible mishap, they said. And a stupid thing to do, but boys were like that.

Later in the hall I saw the hurdle, still frosted and with dark blood soaked into the wood. Darkest crimson, and crusted black. I stared appalled at the boy's blood congealing as, despite all efforts, his life began to seep away.

Dr Millson – married to my elder aunt, Lady Mildred – was recalled from some village crisis and had him lodged in the room next to his own. It disturbed me that the boy should still be under our roof. I should have been happier with him sent to the infirmary in Aylesbury where he couldn't tell tales on me, but Uncle Millson seemed to regard his condition as some responsibility of the family's.

It left me apprehensive, which quite spoilt any excitement about our parents' imminent return. But I felt no involvement in the accident. It wasn't my fault, having simply happened.

All the same, I waited in trepidation for the outcome. If Cecil didn't soon manage to die from injuries and exposure, he would surely lump the blame on me. I'd be in terrible trouble.

I knew then he was more dangerous to me alive.

# Three

Next morning we children were watching from the nursery windows as down by the portico Mama and Papa were welcomed home by Aunt Mildred and Hadrill. There was a light dusting of fresh snow sparsely covering the hard frost of the previous night, and the brougham's wheels left black tracks in the driveway like intertwined snakes.

Mama wore a short sable cape over a dark blue coat like a highwayman's, but I could not glimpse her face under the enormous feathered hat. I would have given my ears to know what Aunt M was confiding to her but doubtless repercussions from it would reach me soon enough.

Papa replaced the tall silk hat he'd removed to alight, and he was the first to look up at us and wave a gloved hand. Then he offered his arm to Mama and they moved out of sight under the portico. How long must we wait for them to come and discover us?

I couldn't share the boys eagerness. I went sickly to sit in what had been Nanny's rocking chair while from the window Edwin excitedly described the parcels and baggages being removed from the trap drawn up behind the carriage.

We had a young laundry-maid overseeing us at the time, but she was too impressed by the magnitude of the charge to complain at my seizing the rocker. Seeing me in the chair of office, Edwin made for the fine dappled rocking-horse and rode it so high on its iron struts that the heavy wooden stand shook on the creaking floor-boards. But I knew that on a real horse he hadn't my courage. All the same, I had no fancy to take over the wooden beast then. Its flaring, chiselled nostrils reminded me too keenly of that ruder carving which the boy had whittled, portraying what he called my "bouncy curls".

29

For a supposed treat we two older children were required to take luncheon with our parents and the aunts. I went down with leaden heart, but all through the meal there was no mention of the tailor's boy and his escapade. As we finished our main course – which for us children was steamed fish – Uncle Millson appeared and took his seat with apologies for lateness. I caught Mama's anxious glance at him and the slight shake of the head with which he replied. It must surely refer to the boy's condition. But what exactly had Mama questioned: whether he improved or was beyond all hope? It was clearly a matter that wouldn't be mentioned in our presence, and about which we children were presumed quite ignorant.

When we left the table Mama detained me by the hand. Although throughout the meal I had gradually grown more confident, my spirits plunged.

"What is this I hear about you leading your little brothers into mischief?" she asked almost lightly.

"Oh, *that!*" escaped me, more in relief than with the contempt which she took it for.

"Yes, that, Lucy. I had hoped you would make good use of having no one to oversee your every move. This was an opportunity for some freedom of choice. Your leadership could have made up a little for lack of a governess at present."

"It was only a game, Mama. We went exploring." Then came a flash of inspiration. "As Uncle Geoffrey does."

"Only instead of chasing wild game to bring back, you happened on secrets we hoped to keep from you a while longer. *For* you eventually. But now you have spoilt some of the surprise. As at the opening of Pandora's box, some of the magic has escaped and flown off for ever."

After my secret invasion of her quarters it seemed so petty a thing to take me to task over. Hadn't the servants made fuss enough? As ever, I chose attack, rather than defence, and rounded on her.

"I saw the way they were addressed, those parcels from town. It really is unjust the way I'm treated. The boys are younger than me. Rupert is just tiny, but he's accorded an 'Honourable'. I don't tell any more lies than Edwin, so why should anyone make this difference, Mama?"

She froze a second, then I heard her breath expelled. "Why, Lucy; does it matter so much what people call you?"

But I knew I had somehow scored, for Papa ran his open palm down over his face and kept his eyes averted until lifting them to rebuke me for the tone of my protest.

Surprisingly it was Aunt Isabelle who smoothed it for me, though hardly, I think, to the others' liking.

"Your Mama once had no strings to her name, child. Why should you? Always remember that a young lady, if ever you become one, can acquire any title she really sets her heart on. Even Queen, if she so desires. Whereas her brothers are stuck with whatever succession supplies."

My parents had moved together, as if protectively. I was conscious of standing there alone, with the adults all ringed around me. Something about the tableau – which I seemed to see from a distance, as if outside – was inimical and filled me with unease. It came from the language of their stance, not premonition. No, if I had any leanings towards the psychic, it would surely have shown then.

But I was mollified at least, overlooking for the moment how my aunts were ladyships in their own right. I was temporarily complaisant. Since even Mama had started off plain Miss, eventually to become Viscountess through marrying Papa, there was hope for me yet. My heart was full of admiration for her, so tall and elegant, with her huge dark eyes and smooth, high-piled black hair which I so sorely envied. I determined then to amaze them all and marry every bit as well, despite my frizzy head like the burning bush in a biblical painting.

"Come, my dears," Papa said abruptly, offering a hand to Edwin and myself. "I'll see you both upstairs as I'm bound there now, to visit our poor patients."

Edwin halted in his tracks, noting the plural. "Is our grandfather unwell again, sir?"

"No, child. Happily he's in as good spirits as his health normally allows. But Nanny, as you know, is very weary and must keep to her bed. Then we have a little visitor who has suffered a sad accident."

"One of the servants' children?" I demanded coolly, knowing none were allowed inside the house.

He looked at me, considering whether to satisfy my curiosity, then must have decided I'd been chided enough for his first day home with us. "It seems that the tailor, Mr Warner, brought his young son with him, and the lad had a fall when rashly climbing somewhere outside. Your Uncle Millson has had to set his broken leg and give him something for the pain."

Only one leg, I noted. As usual the servants had exaggerated.

"May we visit him with you, Papa?" I pleaded, hoping for a chance to threaten the boy and ensure he held his tongue about my part in the misadventure.

"You shall both wait outside his door while I see if it's convenient. That was a kind thought, Lucy. Perhaps some young company may help to cheer him."

Not, I promised myself, if we were left alone together.

He wasn't sharing his father's attic among the servants under the eaves, but had been assigned a good room on my aunts' wing as if he were a real guest. I picked up the scent of disinfectant as we reached the landing, and then a hint of Aunt Mildred's Oil of Lavender. Really, they were treating him like one of us.

Papa stayed with us for the short time we were there, so I was unable to give any warning beyond as fearful a scowl as I could muster.

The boy was lying on his back with a bandaged and splinted leg outside the counterpane. It was the right one, and immediately I thought: Now we are even. He'll be a cripple too.

He was very pale, his temples badly grazed and one arm also bandaged. He could barely keep his eyes open, so heavy were the lids. Papa murmured something about poppies and mandragora: it sounded like a line from poetry.

I bent over the bed and took the boy's free hand in mine, digging in my fingernails to ensure his attention. Lazily he regarded me as if from a great distance. Then he closed one eye, opened it again and almost smiled.

It made my flesh creep that, even so weak, he could hold such power against me, and again I fervently wished him dead.

My prayer must have been granted soon after, because I heard no further mention of him. Certainly something quite sinister happened because I have no memory at all of the days or weeks that followed. I think perhaps I may have been unwell myself over Christmas that year because in mid-January Mama and Papa were at some pains to make a special fuss of me. As eldest child I was to be taken with them on their return to London. And they promised that as a birthday treat I should visit the Theatre Royal at Covent Garden. Which opened up a new world to my enchanted eyes.

In preparation for the coming evening at the Opera I was put to bed for an hour in the afternoon; as if anyone could store up rest against future demands on it. Which certainly proved impossible, because I was far too excited to sleep.

On the table by my bed lay a crimson velvet box containing the gold bracelet my parents had presented to me that morning. I took it out and lay admiring it on my thin arm. It was exquisitely formed of twin arabesques criss-crossing a fine central band and sprouting fernlike fronds set with graduated pearls. These two main strands finally met in a gold daisy shape, the petals framing a single glittering green stone, which Mama had told me was a peridot. A fine gold chain reinforced the clasp in case it should at any time come loose.

Certainly the bracelet was too large for my wrist at present, and I was able to put it on without opening the clasp. But Papa assured me I would grow into it within a year or two. We were agreed that I should wear it that night at the Royal Opera House, and to ensure its safety I was to cover it with a pair of long white gloves in softest kid, miniatures of those worn by Mama.

However, the dress she'd chosen for me was quite childish, with a bunched skirt and tight top, all in chestnut brown with a cream lace collar. Once I was dressed I thought it dull and said so.

"Dark colours pay compliments to a lady's complexion," Papa said teasingly, but he was looking at Mama in her black watered silk which glowed midnight blue as it turned to the light. She had fixed a gardenia in her piled black hair, but it was Papa who attached the other to her *décolleté* bodice and then bent to kiss above the flower.

I must have been the youngest person in the audience, which caused some little interest as I took my place. Opera glasses were turned on our box from others opposite. "Doubtless there will be comments," Papa murmured as he bowed from behind me at salutes from other gentlemen who raised their programmes. "Act modestly, child, or we shall be told that we're spoiling our eldest and she'll end a Sybarite." So I lowered my eyes as if in church and repeated the new word silently in my head so as not to forget it.

The opera was incomprehensible, enormous and brilliant and terribly overdone. Grown-ups never behaved so in real life, ranting against each other so rudely and swooning and *singing* all the time, even to shout each other down. It didn't help that the words were foreign, even though my parents whispered occasionally what it was all meant to be about.

One character alone made sense to me, a man who was barely ever off the stage, magnificent whether in thigh boots, buckler and feathered hat, or indoors, trailing the severe gown of a scholar. He had the face of a ruined angel, but at times so sad that I wept for him in the dark. And his voice came sometimes as a whisper, or roared like an angry bull. And, whichever, it pierced me. He suffered, you could tell. I felt it through my whole body.

"Lorenzo Neve," I read aloud from our programme.

Mama corrected my pronunciation. "The surname is Nay-vay. And Lorenzo is Italian for Laurence."

"He has Papa's given name then?"

"And Neve means 'snow'."

"Snow? Do they truly have snow in Italy? I thought it was very hot there."

Mama shuddered and drew the edge of her silk shawl over her breast as if some sudden memory chilled her through. "It can be bitterly cold up in the mountains of the north," she whispered.

So she had visited the country out of season. I thought no more of it then, my heart and mind so taken up with my new romantic hero, the Italian tenor and his tortured soul.

Laurence Snow: even in English it spoke meltingly. A name nearly as beautiful as the dark-featured face. And at the end, as his strong, firm arms were raised to heaven in a plea for divine mercy, I knew I was in love with this man, broken but forever noble. When I stumbled on the steps as we left they thought I was tired because of the unaccustomed late hour. But I knew it was from the torment I suffered for another.

Next day, barely recovered, I was instructed by Papa to remain behind after luncheon with them, as Mama and he had something of importance they wished to say to me.

And then without more ado he revealed the shocking truth: that he was not my father at all, but Mama had been married once before and I had come from that. He thought it was time that I should know, since already I had raised the question of a title, to which I had no legal right through him.

It made no difference to his affection, he promised; for I was as dear to him as any true daughter could ever be. He had chosen me when he chose Mama. But he could do nothing about the law of succession. The fact was, as Aunt Isabelle had said, that I would remain a mere Miss until I chose to marry into another titled family.

"Which indeed you may choose not to do," he added generously. "For there's many a good man not born to such a label – for that is all it amounts to beneath the responsibilities we inherit. Uncle Millson, for example, my sister Mildred's husband is just such a one: noble by nature if not in rank."

"But he's called Doctor," I objected.

"A title earned for himself, not passed on."

It had never struck me that when they were introduced, as Doctor and Lady Mildred Millson, there was any great distinction between their names. Now it became clear there was.

"Perhaps I can earn a title for myself then?"

"Become a doctor? Well child, why not? Some ladies do so nowadays. Though I hardly see that as your chosen future, Lucy."

In which he was right. I could never have devoted a lifetime to severed limbs and seeping wounds.

"I think you need a little time to get used to all these new ideas, dearest," my mother suggested. "I'm going to ring for Agnes to take you driving in the park. Be sure she wraps you warmly for there's a keen east wind."

She bent to kiss me. She, at least, was still my mother and I hung close a moment until she gently lifted my arms from her neck. But when Papa came close I felt a *frisson* of horror and turned my cheek away.

"Lucy?" I heard the hurt in his voice and was suddenly, fiercely glad.

I held out my hand. "Good afternoon, sir," I gave back formally. Let him suffer too.

It was decided I should be driven back alone to Stakerleys next morning, for there were purely adult occasions planned, including a formal presence at King Edward's court, in which children could have no place. A knee-breeches affair, Mama had called it.

The new distance between Mama's husband and myself was not difficult to maintain for the intervening hours, but when it came to parting and I held out my hand in a cool good-bye it was to receive not his, but the little red velvet box again.

"Open it, Lucy," he commanded.

I did so, and found it empty.

At first I believed he had withdrawn the gift from me as unworthy of such a fine jewel, but then a doubt came.

"Where is the bracelet, dearest?" my mother prompted.

After the excitement of the opera, and weary from the late hour, I had no memory of taking it from my wrist. I could no longer be sure that I had worn it for all that evening.

"Someone must have taken it," I said in a flurry of shame. Even as I lied I remembered in the interval unbuttoning the tight, hand part of the glove to let it dangle from my wrist, like some limp snakeskin half sloughed-off, while I searched the programme for my operatic hero's name. If the loose bracelet had later silently fallen off it might be anywhere.

"Someone . . ." repeated the man who was no longer my father. (No, he had never been my father. The *deceiver*, then.)

"Must we suspect a member of the household?" Mama murmured. "I know them all and believe we can trust them."

I must have out-stared her then, because she lowered her eyes and went to stand by the window. My own eyes, I have been told, are hard like green marbles in a stream bed when I choose to challenge anyone.

She turned back and came close. "Do you truly believe what you imply, Lucy?"

There was a terrible silence then, so long that I had to fill it somehow. I felt my fingernails cutting into my palms and concentrated on the local pain as I fought to hold the tears back. "I may have lost it," I owned wretchedly. "Perhaps at the theatre. I didn't realise until now that it was gone."

"You valued our gift so little?" That was Papa. No, *the man*. Couldn't he see that so much had happened in so very few hours that I was in turmoil? My empty, child's life had been burst asunder. I was disowned, half-orphaned. And at the opera I had been flooded by a fiercely new and devouring kind of love.

"It was loose on your wrist," Mama conceded. "No one can blame you for it falling off in a moment of being distracted. But to pass blame to someone incapable of proving themselves innocent: that is something you cannot be proud of. What makes you do that, Lucy?"

Well, I wasn't an Honourable like my brothers, was I? But cast off, as I felt then, I couldn't use those words. Instead I made as near honest a confession as I could, head high and scornfully defiant:

"I sometimes have a problem with truthfulness: in undoing the lies that have popped out of themselves."

It left them speechless and, realising this, I revelled in it.

An hour or so later they waved me off, I stiffly erect beside the chauffeur Busby and wrapped about with a rug, a little basket of refreshments beside my feet for the journey up-Thames. The engine had been warmed and was throbbing heartily as I was handed aboard. In a mood of defiance I leaned across and squeezed the rubber bulb of the horn. It hooted rudely and we drove away, not looking back.

Despite my outer attitude I was mortified inside, quite shamed and sure that life had taken a permanent turn against me. It was because of the boy, the tailor's son, I knew suddenly. It was my punishment because I had caused him to die. I, Lucy Sedgwick, had killed another human being, and I must be made to pay for it.

The morning was still frosted and the speed of our passage

made the air seem keener. By the time we were free of Ealing the nausea from guilt quite overwhelmed me. Rather than be sick on nothing I delved in my basket for some plain food among its contents. Which was when I discovered the bulky envelope with my name written on.

Inside it was my bracelet. The note which enclosed it explained how cleaners had found it on the floor of our theatre box, and that the management dutifully returned it with their respects.

So for a whole morning Mama had known of my carelessness – even as I tried to throw blame on someone in the house.

Of course they would have known the truth, even without the bracelet's return. As Mama had said, she could trust the servants. I was the one she must have doubts about. I who am not honourable. What would she have said if she'd known more about me? – of my part in the boy Cecil's death, for instance?

By now I knew that a chambermaid had found his crumpled cap beneath the windowsill in Mama's boudoir, so the supposition was that he'd secretly entered the room to steal, been startled at someone's approach and had escaped by the casement, to fall to his eventual death. I had overheard the servants' tittle-tattle and I'd held my tongue because Mona, who alone could stand witness against me, had by then gone to visit her mother for Christmas and stayed on to nurse her through an illness.

He'd been no thief, that boy. But my confession could hardly help him now. It was up to Saint Peter to clear his name. And to mark another cross against mine for eternity.

A headache which had threatened me for hours now suddenly tightened a leather band about my temples and I cried out to Busby to halt the motor. Before he could fully apply the brakes nausea overtook me, and I was most horribly sick all down the shiny carriage side. How I made the rest of the journey I scarcely remember, and once inside Stakerleys I was ordered immediately to my bed.

Things were so different in those days. We had different manners, different ways of addressing one another, different beliefs. We had unquestioned faith in the prevalence of goodness. Or so it had seemed to me.

It was the Great War that caused the immense chasm between past and the new present. In that only could it truly be called Great. I once used to think that the world was an innocent place and I the only rogue in it. Until the Great Betrayal. Until that day in London when I discovered I was not who I'd supposed I was; until I learned of adult deception. But there were four and a half years more before the world outside my family was to fall apart. And to my mind they went slowly.

For my own wretchedness I held *him* to blame, my non-father. But Mama too had been part of the conspiracy of silence. Yet I still needed to cling. Nine years old, I wasn't yet equipped to take full revenge. For quite a while I felt the two of us were isolated, mother and child, in an alien miasma. All her myriad preoccupations which excluded me were wounding, ate into my confidence. And that loss I tried to cover with brash impudence, so that our temporary governess complained that I was unpredictable and quite out of hand.

And then, of course, I began to wonder, for it struck me suddenly, in the company of a family invited to stay, that in losing one father I had found a cause, a quest: to discover the man who had truly fathered me. My mother's first, dead, *real* husband.

I watched Rhoda, my imposed playmate, with her own papa. He was an indulgent parent, allowing her to climb on his knee at will and even ruffle his whiskers. She was, to my eyes, quite horribly spoilt, and I detested her for the intimacies he permitted her. He became for me, briefly, a shadow of someone I'd been deprived of. I was outraged when laughingly she suggested he had grown so tall that his head had come quite through his hair at the top.

It was true he was bald, with a monk's little fringe above the ears, but he made up for that with a generous growth of sideboards and beard, and this at a time when gentlemen mostly copied the seafaring, trimmed fashion favoured by the King.

Another of our house guests at that time was an elderly bishop, round and rubicund on spindly gaitered legs, and reminding me of a robin. Despite his approachability I assumed he was very wise because I'd heard his support was needed by my spurious father for the passage of some new bill they were to debate in the Lords. It occurred to me to question him when Mama sent me to take him on a tour of the walled winter garden.

"Call me Bishop, child," he allowed when I addressed him formally, "for we're all milords and miladies with fancy titles here." And he chuckled at his own wit.

All except me, I thought: I might as well be a servant, or an in-between, like a governess.

"You were going to ask me something," he prompted kindly.

"Yes, Bishop." But now, on the point of it, it proved difficult. I had to go in obliquely. "I suppose there are still times when you marry couples?"

"Indeed I do. A very joyous duty, I find it. But surely you are full young to be requiring my services yet?" Above merry eyes his brows, like short, furry white caterpillars, mocked me, and I felt myself flushing.

"No. I'm not even sure I'll ever marry. There must be something more useful to do."

"What can be more *useful*, as you put it, than to love someone with all your heart and wish to make a family together?"

It wasn't the sort of question that requires an answer. He presumed to try to make up my mind for me. Nettled, I blurted out, "Can one marry twice – love *two* people with all your heart?"

It took him aback and he paused before he spoke again. "Not at the same time, certainly. But time changes one's feelings. Doubtless you are thinking of your dear grandpapa. I was no more than a boy myself when he first married, but I remember the lady well. Your Aunt Mildred's mother. It almost broke his heart when she died. But the years healed it over and at last he found another worthy of his love. There; has that answered you?"

Not quite, but the example he'd chosen kept him safely off recognising exactly what I was after. "So Grandpapa made do with second best?"

"That is not what I meant. Not that at all. Although his second wife, your grandmama, was much younger than he, yet they made a fine couple and were happy together. Their love was soon blessed with the birth of the present Viscount, your father, and several years later little Isabelle. Had your grandmama not been killed in that unfortunate hunting accident, I am sure that with maturity she would have grown to share some of her dear husband's quieter tastes. And so remain a blessed comfort into his old age."

My Lord Bishop was somewhat flustered, or surely he would not have given so much away. The second marriage had not been a great success. A mismatch, in fact. Doubtless they had kept a good front up, as Mama and her second choice now did. But first love was the real love of one's life, which was why now it had to be kept unmentioned, for fear of causing offence to the substitute.

I was more determined than ever to discover the story of my mother's true romance, and abruptly cut short the discussion by turning to show off the brilliant rose-hips which decorated the archways. I'd no further use for my informant, since he clearly was ignorant of my own real identity, accepting me as a Sedgwick by bloodline. Although conversant with earlier family history, he must have been absent at the later point, too taken up with episcopal matters in his distant See for our local gossip to have reached his holy ears.

Once indoors we parted, and I shut myself up alone in the nursery bathroom to consider what I knew. I had no clue at all to the past before my birth, not even my lost father's name. Only one thing came to mind: a reference my non-father had once made to excuse Mama's abruptly quitting a musical concert in our rose drawing-room. I had been sure she was in tears, and afterwards he told me, "It was the piece they played. Mama once had a dear, dead friend and he played the 'cello. It brought back memories of the past. The sweetest memories are often the saddest for us."

I was suddenly certain then that he had spoken of my father, and that one thing – as well as true devotion – that my parents had shared was a love of music. It made me determined to work harder at my pianoforte, and perhaps later Mama would let me take up a stringed instrument.

It was His Majesty who next upset the smooth tenor of life at Stakerleys. Papa – by early Spring I had returned to use of the term, since it was just a childish word lacking the precise description of "Father" – Papa, as I say, was urgently summoned by the Prime Minister and left for London at once on his own.

The King was suffering from a severe bronchial attack which was causing some alarm. The Queen had been required to break off her visit to Corfu and hurry back to his side. Along with certain other gentlemen Papa was to meet her train at the station, since His Majesty was prevented.

The following day brought a letter to say that the Royal Family had assembled at the sick-bed and that although King Edward had declared himself somewhat improved and intent on fighting the disease, it sadly seemed he deceived himself.

Within a few days, shockingly, he was no more, leaving the nation grieving.

So distressed was Mama that like a mother sheep she gathered her little ones close to her, and so we shared some measure of her sorrow. There was much discussion among the gentlemen and ladies – for we were entertaining widely at this period – of how the Queen had called Alice Keppel to King Edward's bedside at the last and they shared their grief together. They whispered of this lady as his mistress, but I couldn't see how a king could be employed by any lady as if he were a butler or a steward.

Everyone put on black. Aunt Mildred, almost savagely plunging purple lilac branches into huge vases as a mark of mourning, supposed that Prince George would make a fair enough monarch, for he appeared robust, shrewd and respectable, with some gravitas and consideration for affairs of state.

"But lacking his father's flair and endearing personality," Aunt Isabelle gave as her opinion. "Yet at least we may rejoice that God has spared us from the Duke of Clarence."

It seemed to me quite shocking then that they discussed the Royal Family as if they were ordinary mortals.

The significance struck me that I had been born at the time of the Old Queen's death, and now I had outlived her son's reign. That was something we shared, those nine years, and it seemed to have a special meaning for me.

Something very strange occurred. I never saw it, but it was described to me by Uncle Geoffrey who had been travelling abroad and witnessed it himself: an awful sign had lit the sky even as the King died. Halley's Comet blazed across the heavens, marking a terrible supernatural occasion. Perhaps it was an evil augur for our family too.

In the second week of May we children were included when the household moved to London for the royal funeral. Mrs Langrish, my newly appointed governess, took us out in the carriage, and under a gentle drizzle we drove to Westminster Hall to see the long file of people who waited to pass the late King's bier lying in state there. But we were not permitted to join it.

Papa was to attend the funeral service along with the government and all the crowned heads of Europe, driving in the cortège beside Lord Morley, Secretary of State for India.

There followed a period when everything seemed in flux and yet, to go by their faces, those who must have suffered most were austere and unmoved. I was conscious of widespread unease under the stiff observation of formalities, because the future was uncertain, the more so because a general election was due for the Commons, and although few seemed to admire Mr Asquith, no one seemed able to offer an acceptable alternative for Prime Minister. From conversations overheard I gathered he was working on the new King to approve a hotch-potch government of mixed parties. The general opinion at home was that a coalition would be dangerous, because to keep a majority and stay in power the many must keep giving in to the few.

"It cannot be wholly trusted," my false-father explained. And he should know about deceit, if any did.

Whether indeed Mr Asquith's tolerance of the Irish nationalists and suchlike had actually hastened the Old King's end I couldn't say. I gained the impression that what the Commons got wrong it would be the Lords' responsibility to put right. If it could.

From all sides we heard that this was the end of an era, and that from now on the monarch would no longer be supreme, but a foil in the hand of the people's elected representatives.

"And why not?" demanded my Aunt Mildred in one of her more suffragette moments. "What have monarchies ever achieved but envy and wars?"

She was a well-travelled, reliably sensible woman, unlike her feather-brained younger half-sister Isabelle, so I heeded her opinions. But less than four years later it would be proved to her that control by an elected government was no guarantee of everlasting peace.

Almost a year was to pass before the Coronation and in the meantime I grew older, although not much taller, and worked reasonably hard at my studies, especially music, determined to earn myself some credit in life, even if birth had denied me any. Edwin was eventually swallowed up by school, little Rupert became asthmatic, and Aunt Mildred and Uncle Millson made plans to visit Crete again to view plans for the reconstruction of a prehistoric palace at Knossos. Uncle Geoffrey was to accompany them, Isabelle having been accorded court duties which alternately dissatisfied her by their insignificance and vexed her with the necessity of attending. She complained pettishly that things would be quite changed there now and the new regime a joyless one.

Perhaps the most notable person in my life then, and certainly the most intensely provocative, was my new governess, Mrs Langrish. She had no charm, no beauty, but an abruptness I had never encountered in any gentlewoman or common person. And yet my mother chose her from among several undisputed ladies. I recall the moment when she decided.

There were three applicants and I was permitted to be present, although cautioned to silence, during their final meetings with my parents.

Mrs Langrish was the last interviewed, a dumpy, square-faced woman in her late thirties who answered all questions without expression in face or voice. Something in her story gave general pause for thought and then she remarked, "Well that is the past, whatever one cares to make of it." She turned, gathered her skirts and made to leave the room without any further words exchanged.

Mama's eyes followed her and she said gently, barely above a whisper, "It's best always to look forward, to the way ahead."

The woman had reached the door before she turned and bobbed respectfully. There was a dryness in her voice as she answered. "Unless, milady, you're waiting for an omnibus. They've a disconcerting way of coming up behind."

Mrs Langrish, we were to discover, was a dispenser of home-spun philosophy. And Mama was sufficiently amused not to rebuke her pertness. But I was later amazed to discover the choice she had made, especially since to my knowledge she herself had never in her life boarded an omnibus.

"I think Mrs Langrish will suit us very well," she told me. "She has a strong character. She will match you admirably."

"And," Papa put in, "it seems that she is a gifted mathematician, which is unusual in a woman. You could do well for yourself by studying with her, Lucy."

How little, I thought, he knew me.

For almost a year the coming Coronation ruled our lives. The ermine and velvet robes were taken out of store where they had lain for the whole of my lifetime. Even before the formalities were finally drawn up a famous artist arrived to work on a family portrait. Centrally Mama and the Viscount stood in coronet and tiara, with before them, seated, the shrivelled form of the Earl, whom I still called Grandpapa. His two noble daughters appeared a little behind, one to each side, Lady Mildred's large frame slightly drooping under the long, sheeplike head; her half-sister delicate as a Dresden milkmaid. The boys sat on a fur rug on Papa's extremity, with me on Mama's, moved farther out so as not to obscure the toes of Aunt Isabelle's pretty satin shoes.

After the initial sketch each of us sat – or stood – for the portrait in turn, Papa's head being completed first. One of the footmen would be later substituted to display the formal robes. Next, Mama's head was painted in, a professional model being hired for the rest. This was necessary because hard on the Abbey ceremony Papa must travel again to India, and this time with Mama alongside.

A new King on the throne meant that pledges of loyalty must be renewed throughout the Empire. There was to be a great Coronation Durbar at New Delhi to honour the King-Emperor George V and his Empress. It was to be a splendid and extravagant celebration, with processions on elephant back, exciting tiger hunts and lavish feasts with exotic eastern dishes.

Papa was to liaise with the staff of the Viceroy, examining the content of speeches and approving the lists of native Indians to be presented to His Majesty.

"And what will you be doing?" I asked Mama when she explained this to me.

"She will look radiantly beautiful and everyone will fall in love with her," Papa said.

"She could do that here, without crossing the globe to please a lot of foreign people."

"But that is the point – to please them there. India is the greatest glory of the British Empire. Haven't you yet learnt about it in the schoolroom?"

"We've barely started India," I admitted. "Just trading and sending out soldiers to protect the merchants from pillaging."

"You'll find there's a lot more to it than that. We will be sure to bring back photographs so that you children can share what we see," Papa promised.

But that was not what I wanted. I saw no reason for his taking my mother from me. They could be away for as long as half a year. It was a poor substitute to offer me instead a fortnight at St Leonards-on-Sea with my stern maternal grandmother, and in the company of my new governess.

But, although I knew there'd be small chance of obtaining information from the old lady directly, still there showed a glimmer of hope. Surely she, if anyone, must have about her house any souvenirs of my lost father, Grandmother being the only relation Mama had left from before she came to live as a Sedgwick at Stakerleys.

If I went carefully about it I might discover what I was too proud to ask of Mama herself: what he was called, how he had looked, whether I took after him in any way. It seemed to me that as his only child I should already have known all that, and any need to ask was somehow shameful.

When my bags were ready packed and awaiting collection by the carrier in the outer hall I unstrapped the smaller one and inserted my Covent Garden programme with the likeness of my beloved, the Italian tenor Lorenzo Neve, treasured and adored for over a year. In that way I should not be entirely alone in enemy territory.

# Four

On earlier visits to St Leonards I was always with Mama. Twice Edwin had joined us with his under-nanny, and Rupert only once while still a swaddled baby like the fat white slug I still regarded him as. But the seaside air had not suited him. He quickly developed a fretful cough and our visit was cut short to return him to the Buckinghamshire countryside.

On this present occasion even my brothers' company would have relieved the expected tedium of schoolroom transferred to Grandmama's rigid domain. Without Mama I expected there would be no paddling in the sea, skirts tucked up into bloomers just like the shopgirls who squealed at the delightful chill of salt water rippling over naked toes on warm, ribbed sand. I could not see Mrs Langrish hoisting her petticoats as Mama did in full frolic far from Society's eyes, for Mama, confident they would not criticise a Viscountess, set no store by the private opinions of Grandmama's more proper cronies.

Instead this time there would be the lone purgatory of the bathing machines, dragged out to where the sea was shoulder-deep and burly fishwives ducked one in the shocking chill. I found the stuffy smell of those enclosed cabins offensive and shuddered at the rough touch of woodwork long penetrated by brine. My woollen bathing costume would stretch as it loaded with water and I'd come out like a drowned rat holding handfuls of knitted material in my hands and anxious for my person being still decently covered. The gentlemen and ladies looked smart in cotton stripes but as a child I was condemned to wool, since there was always the fear of taking cold, even in summer.

Grandmama's rheumatism made her past taking long walks, if

ever she'd been so inclined, but Mrs Langrish was to surprise me as an unsuspected athlete. We would briskly cover the length of the promenade from Warrior Square to White Rock and thence to the extremity of Rockanore in Hastings Old Town. Or, taking an omnibus to that point (a delightful novelty), we would transfer to the lift, ascend to East Hill and follow the cliff path by the Fire Hills to Fairlight or Pett Level, Mrs Langrish carrying a wicker basket with our lunches, and I my artist's satchel.

After such a demanding programme we had earned the journey home by carrier or farm cart, and, happily, my governess would then rest in her room for an hour or more. Which left me free to pursue my researches, since Grandmama frequently spent the evenings with her cronies.

I found the photograph albums when searching for music sheets in the drawer of an adjustable seat before the pianola. This machine had at first had me marvelling at the elderly lady's skill as she rippled out some complicated piece of Mendelssohn or Brahms, her fingers and the keyboard hidden from my sight beyond a potted palm.

That her manner of swaying to the melody was unstylish – more like Thomas Gray's plodding ploughman's gait – eventually caused me to look closer. Then the deceit was revealed and I later found how to open the machine's front panels, labour over the pedals and watch the reams of perforated paper roll over the brass harmonica which expelled the air I pumped.

Why should one study so hard to become proficient in music, I asked myself, when such a simple fraud offered itself to hand? Or, rather, to foot, leaving one hand grimly hanging on and the other free to turn pages of the photograph albums. Meanwhile I convinced any distant listener I was indulging my boasted pleasure in music. It was a study I had by now given up any ambition in, revelling in mixing colours on a palette rather than scowling over finding the right harmony.

The photographs which I found were interesting but of no help to my pressing need, being of too distant a past: my mother's childhood, in pinafore and bunched hair; posed family portraits before a professional photographer's painted backcloth; one or two snaps of a shooting party which included the tall, sad-eyed man who also appeared fondling the head of a black Labrador dog. He must be Grandfather Fellowes whom I had never known. He was also one of a group of seated musicians posed in identical formal dress, as if for some amateur performance. On his knee rested a violin.

At once I was afraid of having made a wrong assumption. Was this actually the musician of whose playing the remembrance had made my mother weep? I knew she'd loved her dead father dearly, because she'd often spoken of him with great affection. So was it he who had played the cello? If one stringed instrument, why not the other?

I went so far as to ask of Grandmama but she took it amiss. "The pianoforte and the violin, that is all," she said shortly. "When your Grandfather died I got rid of them both, for they were of no use to me. They went in part payment for the pianola and some music rolls. I had a good bargain of it, being well acquainted with the Lindridge family, through their ladies being my clients."

It seemed to me she was as much excusing herself for any musical shortcomings as reminding me of her business acumen locally. Grandfather, as I knew from Mama, had been a master printer, and Grandmama had used his finances to found a successful salon as modiste and tailoress employing eventually a workroom of eight seamstresses. They had lived then at a large house behind Gensing Gardens, but on Mama's becoming a Sedgwick – Viscountess Crowthorne – her mother, by then a widow, had sold both house and business. She then moved to this Italianate mansion on Maze Hill, just within sight of the castellated bridge-house of Rider Haggard, which curiously spanned the narrow road.

I considered what I had been told. There was no need to insist, "Had there been no 'cello as well?" because Grandmama would certainly have listed it as part of her 'bargain' from the music shop. So I was safe in my assumption that it had been not Mama's but *my own* father for whom she wept when she heard his music again. I found it comforting, and next day set more vigorously about looking for photographs of a later date.

It seemed there were none of the sort I was seeking. A time gap appeared between those early faded images and those of the grand Sedgwick wedding and several later poses by Mama as Viscountess, splendid in Court Dress. Yet no written account had been kept to give the surname with which she had first replaced her maiden name. Surely there was something strange about that?

On the fourth day of our visit I was invited to spend the afternoon with a lady who had been at school with Mama, and there I expected more success. This Mrs Mallalieu had four children, a boy a little younger than myself, and three girls of six, four and three years who were identically tricked out like Alice in Wonderland, in white pinafores and with long fair hair with not a kink in it.

"I was a day-girl," Mrs Mallalieu explained over tea. "Your mother Eugenie boarded during the week because her own parents were taken up with their professions. So perhaps I knew her less intimately than the girls who shared her study and dormitory. But we were friends, rode or played tennis together according to the season.

"I became engaged to dear Henry barely a month after leaving school and we married within three months of that because he was due to visit America and wished to take me with him. By then your Mama had disappeared from St Leonards on her Grand Tour with the Honourable Mrs Isabelle Delmayne, now your aunt.

"I wrote inviting her to the ceremony but it seems she moved on so frequently that my letter never caught up in time. When Henry and I returned to England for the birth of little Walter I heard she also had wed. In Venice to an Italian doctor."

At this last I had almost dropped the scone I held while mesmerised by the account. At last, at long, long, last, I had confirmation that she had truly married! Although never admitting it to myself, there had lingered this terrible doubt that I was perhaps the outcome of some unofficial alliance. Ever since my substitute-Papa had told me I was no child of his I had feared the worst, because of the silence surrounding my true origins. I was convinced there was some shame being concealed and so I must never question my step-family.

And now it was revealed: the scandal was of no more import than the fact that my true Papa was a foreigner! Which would make me half-Italian myself, and must offend so blue-blooded an English aristocrat as Viscount Crowthorne. How very snobbish to consider the fact distasteful. And Mama, by nature more liberal-minded, had been prevailed upon to accept her new family's prejudice.

"Eat up, Lucy," Mrs Mallalieu urged in her jolly way, "or Walter will have cleared the table of the best cakes before you reach that stage. Here, try one of these chocolate meringue boats. They used to be a great favourite of your Mama's."

But my appetite for food had quite gone. I was eager only to get away and digest mentally what I had already taken in.

Walter was sent to take me on a tour of the stables and grounds, with the three little girls frisking and stumbling in our wake. He was a rather sullen little boy, overweight and disinclined to act the host. Outnumbered by so many little sisters perhaps he despised all female kind. Indeed he eyed me with disfavour and commented, "You said you were ten. You should be taller for that. I'm already four feet six myself. Papa says I'll be a fine figure of a man someday."

But never particularly civil, I thought. I gave him one of my green-marble stares and walked on without comment.

We passed through a parkland of mixed fields and woodland, mainly oaks and ash, to arrive at a mossy stone wall some eight feet high.

Using slight projections which he must be familiar with, the boy shinned up remarkably well considering his girth. His action challenged me to do the same, which I did easily, finally to sit astride the coping with my skirts tucked up about my thighs.

The view from there was splendid, gently downhill over some five miles of pasture and spinney, past the shining roofs of Silverhill and Hollington, then a dim blue haze that was St Leonards and beyond it the shimmering English Channel rising up to our eye level. Travelling here in the Mallalieu motor with my talkative hostess I had been unaware of the scenic beauty unrolling behind.

"I bet," said the boy, "you've nothing like this where you live. Inland." The last word came out with a curl of his lip.

"We have the Thames," I said as coolly as I was able.

"London's river: the most important waterway in the world."
Perhaps he would have as little geography as myself, and that
claim would silence him. For some reason it did. We slid down
to where the little girls were trying to make daisy chains, and all
trudged back to the house.

Returning to Grandmama's in the family's open carriage with
my new acquaintances, I was vexed that Walter returned to the
subject of my size. "She can't be ten," he accused in his surly
way. "She's too small."

"Perhaps in her tenth year, darling," his mother suggested.

As if I wouldn't know my own age! "My tenth birthday was
in January," I corrected them both. "I was nine the year the Old
King died. To celebrate that birthday we went to the Opera. The
hero's part was sung by Lorenzo Neve. I shall never forget it,
although it was over a year ago."

It flooded me with a special warmth to mention his name. An
Italian, after all. So now half of me had a newly discovered link
with that wonderful man. If only he could have been my father.
Yet the thought was disloyal to my real one. I should like instead
that they would be very similar. From then on, I think, they were
almost identical in my mind.

Mrs Mallalieu was frowning. "My dear, you must surely be
mistaken. To be ten you would have been born in January of
nineteen hundred and one. Which must be too soon. I think if
you were to check you would discover your mistake."

Surely not, for although nobody had actually mentioned my age
I knew it from diary entries I had made over the recent years. If I
had been mistaken, certainly Mama would have corrected me.

"How does one check a thing like that?" I demanded brusquely.

The lady waved a hand vaguely. "Oh, there must be documents
of some sort. A birth certificate. And then there are papers
registered at the Public Records Office in Somerset House."

"I am hardly likely to go to Somerset to find out," I grumbled.

"No, Lucy, it's simply called that. Somerset House is in
London, in a street they call the Strand."

Yet just as much beyond my reach at present. If she were
right and I mistaken, then I must rely on finding evidence at
Stakerleys itself.

"But in any case your Mama can put you right," I was told easily.

In fact, though, I was to turn up something useful at Grandmama's which put the age question out of my mind. One evening, upon her reticule being dropped and bursting open, I was expected to stoop and retrieve the belongings scattered over the carpet: a drawstring purse of soft kid containing coins, an étui of miniature sewing tools, no less than three faintly perfumed handkerchiefs, a folding fruit knife and a small booklet with rubbed gilt edges which contained addresses of her correspondents.

Since this last item had the appearance of some age, it struck me that it might be of use in my quest. I contrived with one foot to ease the booklet under the edge of the occasional table at which Grandmama sat, and it stayed lodged there without her notice during our game of draughts.

Praying more devoutly than was my custom and fighting off sleep, I sat upright in bed until the whole household had retired. Then I stole downstairs in the dim moonlight which slanted through a landing window, and recovered the prize.

Mama's name was first entered as "Fellowes, Miss Eugenie", with the school's address. But this was neatly scored through with a note below, "See Gabrieli". And under that name I found it a few pages later: "Signora Gabrieli, c/o The Hon. Isabelle Delmayne, Stakerleys, nr. Mardham, Buckinghamshire".

That entry too had been amended. The name was more vigorously struck through and another written above: Mrs Eugenie Gabriel. So by then Mama was a widow and had been decently anglicised.

My father had shared the name of an archangel. And I'd been deprived of it.


The days grew sultry and I was permitted to spend my last two afternoons on the sands. Before this, however, I was visited by Grandmama's doctor who removed the cruel calliper from my leg. It looked to me that the bone had grown straighter, and I was determined the harness should not be put on me again.

Beyond and below the promenade the tide was far out, leaving stretches of ochre sand and rock pools alive with transparent shrimps and tiny scuttling green crabs which hid among the strands of bladder wrack. Mrs Langrish had found a toy shrimping net from a previous visit with Mama. She kept watch from afar as I played barefoot but with my petticoats in proper order, climbing from ridge to ridge of the green, slimy-coated rocks.

On the first of the two days she soon abandoned her anxious warnings of sinking sands shouted from the little camp she had established higher up on the pebbly beach, and I observed she was in conversation with an older woman in a deck chair a few feet away. Between them a little boy of four or five with an enormous squarish head sat patiently moving pebbles in and out of a rubber bucket. On the second afternoon the same pair were there again, but now the woman had joined forces with my governess and they were sharing a flask of tea. I watched a while unobserved while Mrs Langrish was totally absorbed in entertaining the strangers.

It vexed me that she had ceased to care for me, and it was possibly no entire accident when, leaping from rock to rock, I suddenly slipped, fell sideways into a deeper pool, and ended drenched. I stomped out, blood streaming from a cut on one calf where sharp-edged mussels had sliced at the soft flesh. And still she had not seen.

Bedraggled and dripping, I marched up the pebbles ignoring their discomfort and short of one rope-soled sandshoe. My governess glanced up as my shadow came between her and the sun. Her face drained of colour at sight of my angry tears. "Lucy," she babbled, struggling to rise. Never before had I seen her so disquieted.

"You neglect me," I accused her. "I could have been swept away by the tide or lost in the sinking sands and you wouldn't have stirred. You don't care!"

Which was unlikely since the sea had barely a ripple on that sultry day and we were well away from the dangerous stretch opposite Warrior Square Gardens. Nor was it fair since she'd given up her free afternoon to accompany me to the beach.

"Here, show me your leg," ordered the older woman, the stranger. I stared back offended. She shook a linen napkin impatiently in my direction. "Sit down, girl, and let me staunch the bleeding. There's salt aplenty in the water so there's little fear of infection, I'd say."

And still Mrs Langrish stayed silent, appalled at her own dereliction of duty. "Grandmama will be most displeased," I threatened." And now my governess was not so much pale as greenish.

"Such a baby," the other woman marvelled. "What is it but a small cut? And a wetting, which is only to be expected at the seaside. Sit yourself here, miss, and I'll attend to it for you."

I was so unused to such disrespect that I found I had lowered myself beside her, next to the little boy who was staring at me with the most round brown eyes I had ever seen. Now that I was so close I could see the grotesqueness of his oversized head. He'd be an idiot, surely.

And then suddenly he smiled, reaching for a pebble from his bucket and offering it to me.

"Take it," the woman said. "He wants to be friends."

As it lay warm in my hand I found I was being briskly rubbed dry. The white napkin had been wound about my calf and safety-pinned in place. "Are you a nurse then?" I asked, astonished.

She gave a short laugh like a cough. "A grandmother. Which is much the same thing, wouldn't you say, Laura?"

It astounded me that she was so quickly on Christian-name terms with my formidable governess. And then I was amazed no longer as, looking from one woman to the other, I saw the likeness. And the shape of the child's overblown head had something of the more geometric square of the younger woman's. "He's yours," I whispered.

Now that she was discovered, Mrs Langrish had no reason to hold back. With tears in her eyes she reached for the little boy to nurse him on her lap, her head bent over him to hide her face.

She amazed me, having secrets, such an ordinary person as I'd thought her. I felt a new respect, and remembered then the day Mama had hired her. There had been something exchanged between them that I had failed to understand. A reference to the past, a sad reference. And when Mama had counselled her to look forward she had replied in that odd way about omnibuses coming up behind. Well, her omnibus had caught her up now and her past was discovered. I felt no pity, only respect, conscious of her strength in having kept so much concealed. Perhaps a little fear too.

"Does Mama know about him – your little boy?"

"Barty. Oh yes." At last she was able to speak and face me. "Your Mama is a most understanding lady. I am glad I had the courage to be open with her about my situation. Through her generosity we are all three able to – to go on."

She kissed the child on its hideous, bulging brow and handed him over to her mother. "But we must not linger here with you in your damp clothes. Come, Lucy, and we'll get you to a hot bath and a change of garments."

So that was my last day at Grandmama's. Mrs Langrish did not refer to it again. Without any great display of emotion she had suffered her mother to take the child away. When I enquired if the other two lived locally, she merely said they had lodged for a night with fisherfolk at Hastings but would return home by train that very evening. She did not offer to tell me where home might be. I was certain by then that I should not report her negligence to anyone. Certainly not to Grandmama. Perhaps one day to Mama, to explain how Mrs Langrish's "omnibus" had briefly caught up with her.

Next day we left for Stakerleys again and, although I had not wished to come, now I could hardly bear to leave behind the cheerfully thronged town with its promenade and pervading scent of sandy seaweed and magic rock pools. There was so much life here, and at home just the huge house, empty but for servants. There were experiences too that I did not want to be deprived of – one was to hang over the tunnel embankment above Warrior Square station and breathe in the heady scent of engine smoke which promised adventure and travel. I dreamed on these occasions of how, as soon as I was free, I would pack my bags and go off to find my origins. A steamer to France and overland by train to Italy. One day I would search and discover my other, un-Sedgwick family.

# Five

*July, 1921*

I was awakened by the maid drawing back my curtains to let in a hazy early light that promised another blazing day. And straight upon that came the mewing voice of my baby as Mabel brought her to my bedside.

Instantly I made a return journey through years to the present day; and from Grandmama's home at St Leonards to the Sedgwick town house in Eaton Place.

There is nothing like a small infant desperately clawing at one for food to recall reality.

"She's pulling more strongly," I told Mabel. "I'm certain she's beginning to put on weight."

Her face too was changing, less like porcelain in texture, more plumply peachlike. And in myself I was conscious of improvement too. I determined to take my bath soon and join Edwin for breakfast.

His face, when he saw me, lit with genuine pleasure. "Lucy, it's good to see you look so well."

"I am, I think. Almost recovered. I slept so soundly, remembering Stakerleys and things we had done when we were children. Not all of them reassuring, but life felt more secure then, before I had made so many mistakes."

He smiled. "And the more recent past? Has any more of that returned?"

I took it lightly, avoiding the dangerous issue. "I distinctly remember yesterday, and the intriguing Mr Malcolm who for some reason sticks in my mind."

"Dr Malcolm," Edwin corrected me.

"You say I had met this Clive Malcolm as a child? A playmate then? His name means nothing to me."

"No, it wouldn't. He changed it, or had it changed for him when he was adopted."

And was probably never consulted on the matter, just as, all unknowing, I'd had my own surname withdrawn and was made a Sedgwick by statutory agreement. "So who was he before?"

"Do you remember the travelling tailor who once brought his son along?"

In shock I instantly saw him again in Mama's room, looking back at me with his crumpled cap in his hand as I pulled the curtains across to conceal him. Just as I'd seen him stand at our door here yesterday, with the same quiet smile, the same challenging eyes, almost the same cap.

"But he died," I protested. "He fell, climbing the walls at Stakerleys, and was killed."

"Was quite badly injured." And he still has a slight limp. But he survived. Papa felt responsible and had him sent away to be well looked after. Then later when his father died and he would have had to leave school, a friend of Papa's stepped in and offered to adopt him. Bishop Malcolm. He was childless and made Clive his heir. You surely recall the bishop; he stayed with us several times in the country."

"Cecil! That boy's name was Cecil, not Clive."

"He explained that to me. Since one name was to be changed he thought he might make a thorough job of it, having always considered Cecil not masculine enough. And the Bishop agreed, since Clive was already his second baptismal name. So, anyway, you do remember him now."

I was unlikely ever to forget. And what did Cecil-Clive remember of me? Every shaming thing, I was sure. And what malicious stories had he spread about my treatment of him?

"He's a close friend of yours?" I wheedled. "You're his confidant?"

This puzzled Edwin. "What exactly do you mean? He's told me how the change came about, because I recognised him and called him by the wrong name. He was invited to Stakerleys last year, and Papa approved of him as a suitable older companion to oversee my staying in London on my own. So every vacation now we meet up, and have become firm friends. It gives me a chance to stand on my own feet and at the same time mix with some lively company with modern ideas."

"And that injury he suffered as a boy, has he ever explained what led up to it?"

"Oh, that's long forgiven him. It was a childish prank that went wrong. Every boy has done something foolish of the kind in his time. I could even recall some escapades of yours."

"Indeed you might." I spoke drily, mindful of many little meannesses I'd inflicted on poor Edwin, and very many more to the Great White Slug, Rupert. A truly hateful big sister.

"Lucy, shouldn't you be resting now?" he asked solicitously.

"No. Suddenly I feel full of energy. Do you know what I'd like most of all? For you to take me on an omnibus, shopping in Knightsbridge. Only I haven't any money, Edwin. You would have to lend me some.

"Not an omnibus. I'll get Forbes to drive us. That is, I would if you were fit enough for it, which I'm not sure you are."

"I'm sure enough for both of us, Edwin. There are things I must get for the baby. We can't leave her in that straw basket, wearing our ancient baby cast-offs."

"Yes, I see. Of course. Well, shall we take Mabel with us in case you . . ."

"A splendid idea. We'll set her up too with a complete new outfit. If your pocket-money will run to it."

"There's no need for that," he said easily. "Mama made arrangements for me to use her account at Harrods. I haven't done so as yet, but I know she'd want me to sign for anything you need."

And so we set off in state, in a new automobile I'd not seen before, with poor Mabel in her battered (but well brushed) black straw hat up front with the new chauffeur, and we two snug behind. A really magnificent automobile of gleaming dark blue with brass lamps.

And in the traffic, seeing people scramble to get on a waiting omnibus, I again remembered my old governess. It seemed that with Clive Malcolm's arrival my own omnibus had ominously come up behind while I'd been looking elsewhere.

"By the way," Edwin reminded me, "we can't go on saying 'the baby'. What name have you given her?"

None, so far as I knew, but I wasn't admitting as much to this brother who'd as good as called me blind to anything outside myself.

I grinned at him, pretending gaiety. "Eugenie; what else? Naturally I named her after Mama." And then, on a sudden inspiration, "She's Eugenie Gabriela."

The outing exhausted me beyond what I'd expected, so Edwin left me in the restaurant while he and Mabel worked through my list. When eventually they joined me, she was pink with excitement, never having seen such a magnificent emporium in her life. Nothing larger, in fact, than a village grocer's.

She was also differently dressed, in a decent donkey-brown linen coat and a beige straw hat with veiling. Edwin later explained that it was to make her a more suitable companion when we went out together, because for quite a while he forbade my being utterly alone.

My little brother forbidding me! Well in this case it didn't matter. Mabel was the nearest I had to a confidante. She at least had seen me at lowest ebb.

The goods ordered were delivered that evening and included a superb carriage for the baby; for Eugenie, as we must learn to call her. Edwin was already arranging for the gardener to have all outside steps reduced to gentle slopes to make it easier to promenade her – in which exercise I saw at once he intended to take a share, as much as anyone.

The very next day a telegram arrived from Mama announcing her imminent return from Germany.

"No," Edwin assured me, "I've made no mention of your being here. It will be a welcome surprise for her."

"It won't; because I shan't be here. I really don't feel up to facing her as I am."

He frowned, displeased. "Nonsense, Lucy. Where would you go? To Stakerleys? If so, who can I send with you? I'd need to stay here and welcome Mama."

"Edwin, there's no case of 'sending' me. I shall simply *go*. But not to Stakerleys. I'll visit Aunt Isabelle in Kent, if she's at home."

"I believe she is. There's nobody at Stakerleys at present except Dr and Aunt Millson. But it's too stressful for you to travel to Tunbridge Wells, even if Forbes drives you by motor."

"Don't fuss so, Edwin. You're quite the old woman. But yes, I should appreciate Forbes, and we'd stop at the halfway mark to refresh ourselves, so you'll have nothing to worry about."

If there was anything less pleasant than confronting Mama in my present state it would be to face Dr Millson's questions and Aunt Mildred's all-seeing eyes. They'd surely have me confined in a nursing home, as they did Isabelle whenever she overstepped the mark in the absence of Uncle Geoffrey.

"I'm not sure Isabelle's the right person to take care of you at present, Lucy."

"You mean 'take charge' of me, don't you? Can't you see that what I need is time to myself, to relax?" (Even to get to know my baby daughter, I suddenly realised.) Too much had happened too rapidly of late, so that I did truly begin to doubt my own sanity. Isabelle, if anyone, would be ideal company, totally taken up with her own affairs.

So I'd speak to her by telephone, that shining black daffodil in the study, which the housemaids venerated, keeping it elegantly polished as a household god. Aunt Isabelle was not at home, but her housekeeper gushed that she would be enchanted, truly enchanted, at the prospect of my visit. So I promptly had Mabel pack my new things, together with the baby's – no, *Eugenie's* – supplies and her own bundle. Even the enormous perambulator was wedged in the motor alongside poor Forbes, while I installed myself in the rear with Mabel, the new crib between us.

Edwin had meant well, so I thanked him sincerely. "You'll be able to breathe more freely once I'm gone," I told him.

Greylings, Isabelle Penrhydd's Kentish home was a pleasant half-timbered manor house on a grassy slope with woodland and a sizeable reservoir which her husband kept well stocked with fish. Geoffrey, an only child, had inherited the estate from his mother, the other family home being a rather grim stone fortress in Cornwall. Isabelle – whose slightest whim was Geoffrey's command – spent about half the year in Kent, and the rest, when not travelling, with her Sedgwick relations at Stakerleys.

She had never been close to her half-sister Mildred, and for reasons of her own preferred to steer clear of Dr Millson, so it seemed natural that with her brother and sister-in-law absent she should withdraw from her suite at Stakerleys.

I found her little different from before, perhaps a hint plumper in the face, leaner in the body; even stringy, with the flesh of her upper arms hanging loose in fine wrinkles as she waved them extravagantly in welcome. She had been drinking, of course. I turned my cheek to receive the brandy-laden breath.

Geoffrey kissed me shyly and then held me at arms' length. "You look as if you could benefit from our country air. How long have you been shut up in London? I find it quite unendurable at this time of year."

I evaded the direct answer. "I was enjoying Edwin's company and catching up with his impressive new persona."

"An admirable young man. He's promised to come to Africa with me when he's finished at Eton. He wishes to study the baboons. Why don't you join us, Lucy, and do some of your exciting paintings, with animals for models?"

"That's not possible, I'm afraid. As you shall see, I have my own little cub now. Or should it be kitten? It will take me a while to accustom myself to that."

They both made delighted noises at the news and I had Mabel bring the crib from the motor and put the baby on show. I observed Isabelle's corrugated brow as she tried to reckon when the child would have been born or how I'd concealed my pregnancy from Papa's lawyer when he visited me in the cells.

She soon gave up the demanding mathematics as beyond her. After all, she'd as little experience of, or taste for, babies as I. And I hadn't managed that calculation for myself yet. How could I have no memory of so dramatic and painful an event as childbirth? And yet I retained some misty knowledge of policemen interrogating me while I could not understand what they said.

"Your rooms have been made ready," Geoffrey said. "Mrs Cartwright will take you to them. Do ask her for whatever you require. Meanwhile I suggest we leave you to rest and we'll meet up again at seven thirty for dinner."

I was glad of the offer and actually slept for over an hour under the open windows. The distant lowing of cattle woke me as they trailed back to some hidden byre for evening milking. There was a calm, pale sky barely streaked with cirrhus and a faint scent of roses on the still air.

It suited me well there. I relaxed in Geoffrey's uncritical companionship. How is it that the almost-intolerably demanding, such as Isabelle, always manage to pair with the easily enslaved?

I had shown no such genius for selection myself: Julian and I had not been complementary but disastrously alike. Yet our different upbringings had set us apart in the manner in which we conducted ourselves. However far I was from being a Sedgwick by blood, yet I had inhaled their air, absorbed some of their principles indirectly through my mother.

Isabelle struck me as some kind of throwback to an earlier Sedgwick wife, perhaps one of those seventeenth century courtesans who were passed on to the aristocracy by Charles II. But perhaps my opinion of her was warped by a too vivid recollection of her rashness a few years back when Stakerleys had been a wartime nursing home for recuperating officers, and the family were supposedly restricted to the west wing. But there again her memories of me at that period were ones I hoped she had forgotten. Which seemed likely, she seeming to take no account of what had happened in the past, whether from lack of conscience or through alcoholic haze.

At dinner that first night Geoffrey asked the baby's name, was she christened, who were her godparents. I raked desperately through my acquaintances' names while I sought an answer.

"I thought to have her baptised in Stakerleys chapel," I extemporised. "By Bishop Malcolm. And I haven't asked anyone yet to stand in as sponsors. You are the first I hope will accept, Geoffrey."

He was absurdly flattered but unsure that his age left him

suitable. "I may not still be here when she's of an age to need advice."

"What are you – fifty-four?" I demanded.

"Fifty-two."

"Then you've as many years again left to support her, and I've every confidence it will be excellent advice."

He was delighted. Now even Isabelle was staring at me wide-eyed and dewy. "The child," she said weakly, "what are you calling her?"

"Eugenie Gabriela."

Her blue eyes grew enormous and a little spurt of wine escaped her mouth to roll red down her chin. Then, with no more sound than a little gasping sigh, she sank back in her chair and went out cold.

Geoffrey made shamed apologies for her, and himself carried her bodily from the room. While he was absent I had ample chance to consider the circumstances. Admittedly she had been near collapse already, but what triggered it finally was when I spoke my baby's intended names.

There was nothing in the first to surprise her: it was natural that I should choose the baby's grandmother's name. But the second – had she made the connection I had gone for? Had a Sedgwick at last confirmed that Gabrieli was my father's surname?

I must admit I felt no anxiety for her and had to pretend some when Geoffrey returned. My heart was singing because now I realised who I should all along have approached for the truth about my own origins. Isabelle knew. Isabelle had been there with my mother in Venice, had doubtless been witness to the wedding of her paid companion.

Tomorrow I would tackle her on it. And Isabelle, poor helpless addict, should tell me all she knew, if I had to hold her down and pour brandy in to get it from her.

But next morning Geoffrey was alone at breakfast. Isabelle's maid was preparing her for the journey by road to Stakerleys. We were all to assemble there for my mother's return. I could hardly insist on remaining in Kent on my own.

Geoffrey drove with me beside him, the crib at my feet. Isabelle languished with her maid in the rear. Mabel was to follow on with two other servants and our luggage.

Pandering to our supposed female weakness, Geoffrey insisted we stop at a hotel for lunch and it was there, when we retired from the table, that Isabelle referred to what was uppermost in my mind.

"So you know about Gabrieli? Il Dottore Gabrieli." She exaggerated the Italian accent. "Did you find the certificate, then?"

"The marriage one, do you mean?"

"There was your birth document too, of course. In the same drawer."

"Of Mama's bureau?" I guessed.

"Of course."

That was one private place I'd never violated, out of respect for Mama. It had been Papa's study I'd disturbed as a child, deliberately leaving evidence of my riffling through his papers, often State Papers, simply to make him admonish me, so that I'd have some secret complaint to hold against him.

It was fortunate that we'd been summoned to Stakerleys just now. At last I would get my chance and, older, I had fewer scruples. The certificates concerned me, rightly belonged to me. I had only to unlock the bureau and take what was mine. I would do it as soon as I arrived, before Mama was there to prevent it.

"Gabrieli was not a good doctor," Isabelle recalled sourly. She was waiting for some comment from me.

"I've known my father's name for a long time," I said, elaborately casual. "I learned of it as a child, from Grandmama Fellowes."

The trouble with lies, if they're to do any good – and with some truth too, for that matter – is that you get stuck with what you've said. Which was why determining the baby's exact age was so important. I had no experience of infants, and there was someone under the same roof with me now who was an expert in the matter. Make a wrong claim and Dr Millson would be taking off his spectacles to polish them and clearing his throat in a quite familiar manner. The trouble was that I had no idea how long a period was missing from my memory.

How I wished I had not choked off the physician whom Edwin had called to the Belgravia house. I should have milked him of every probable detail of the birth that I'd need to quote later. For Mama would be totally baby-obsessed and full of questions as soon as she set eyes on her small namesake.

I recalled how devoted she'd been to baby Rupert, hovering over his cradle, not allowing even Nanny to bath and change him at first. Surely that had been the source of my dislike for the new little half-brother.

Maybe it accounted in part for my strange ambivalence towards my own child too. Deep inside I felt a similar urge to smother her with love, yet I was held back – not so much by distaste as fear; even a ghostly doubt whether she could be mine, despite my body's evidence that she was. I had no sense of permanence between us, as if there were an impediment, and at some unexpected moment we would be rudely parted, whether through some fault of mine or her physical weakness.

In my disquiet I dared to invite Uncle Millson to look in on us while Mabel was bathing her. I trusted to his slow, courteous manner to prevent his leaping in with questions, and I got there first, eagerly demanding, "Isn't she quite splendid, Uncle? A healthy child, wouldn't you say?"

He knelt to dribble warm water over her pink shoulders, before Mabel lifted her out in a towel, on to my knees.

"A bonny little girl, well formed. With a lusty voice; so good lungs, one can be sure."

"She dislikes leaving the water, sir," Mabel explained. "Otherwise she's docile as a lamb."

"Hardly like her mother," I said drily.

He smiled, then came the crucial question: "How old is she?"

I smiled back, coquettishly. "You're the expert. Guess."

She was quiet now, balled in a fluffy towel, her kittenlike gaze wandering about the white walls and straining towards the light of the window. I noticed for the first time that she had no eyelashes yet, and when the two lids met they were like a clean slit in fresh raw pastry.

"Very young," he considered. "No more than two or three weeks. Indeed, if you were my patient I should never permit your travelling about as you've done. You must rest, Lucy, now that you're home."

"*Home.*" I felt tears gather, and steeled myself not to let them brim over. I wasn't a true Sedgwick, and had rebelled against the family; a once-married woman, now widowed, and a mother who should have provided the child with a shelter of her own. Yet here I was back at the only place that had ever offered me security. And warmed my heart.

He was regarding me quizzically through his wire-framed pince-nez. "Stakerleys is home to any number of refugees. I'm one myself. We are fortunate to be part of an elastic family."

I left Mabel to dry Eugenie, and accompanied my uncle by marriage – by two marriages: his own and my mother's – down to join the others on the open terrace. It had been a perfect day of moderate heat, and we all relaxed in an evening langour, sipping cool drinks and talking in desultory snatches without any tiresome effort to be witty or wise.

"I met an old acquaintance at the London house," I found myself saying. "A friend of Edwin's, Clive Malcolm."

"Another honorary Sedgwick," Dr Millson murmured.

"He spoke with gratitude of your care for him after his accident here as a boy."

"An admirable young man."

"—who is following in your profession."

"But progressing much farther than a humble village practitioner, I'm sure. Clive is gifted with a fine intellect."

"Wasn't he a tailor's son?" Isabelle demanded coolly from an aristocratic height. "I seem to remember Bishop Malcolm took an interest in him as a youngster. It caused some speculation at the time."

There was a stiff silence. "Totally unfounded," Geoffrey put in quickly. "The Bishop has always been exceedingly charitable."

Which Isabelle never was. Instinctively I knew she was setting out to be provocative, and for my benefit. Wasn't I equally an outsider, born to an unacknowledged man and the daughter of a mere tailoress?

Mildred turned the conversation by ringing for a rug to tuck round Grandfather's knees, and observing that the evening could be cool for anyone obliged to sit still.

As ever, she was devoted to her father's care. From my window I had observed her manfully struggling with his invalid chair on the rose-garden path, which had been too liberally gravelled. Always the feminist, she would have thought it beneath her to summon one of the gardeners to help.

Grandfather too seemed unchanged; present in body, but what occupied his mind was as much an enigma as last time I had been here, just after the war's end. With paralysis permiting no physical efforts, he appeared not to have aged further. When Mildred presented me to him, speaking slowly, he had squeezed my hand with his good one, and the skin round his eyes had wrinkled in a smile.

I believe he remembered me and how close we had once been, especially in the days before the boys came along. Then, I'd been told, he had pushed me in my infant's carriage along the same paths Mildred wheeled him by now. I wondered if that thought was behind the sweetly rueful glance he gave me.

Suddenly Mama was with us. We were all at dinner and had heard nothing of the motor's arrival. Hadrill was serving in a token manner, with an assistant butler on hand to cover any contretemps. To me he had always been old, but now more ancient tortoise than human. He still regarded me with a suspicious eye as if I might at any moment be guilty of some childish solecism.

Between our cheese plates being removed and our glasses finally recharged, the door had abruptly opened and Mama stood there beaming. "My dears, I'll not disturb you now. But when I've removed my hat and the dust of the journey we shall meet properly in the drawing-room."

She spoke brightly but her thinnness alarmed me. I had assumed her visit to Baden-Baden had been more social than truly medical. Quickly she withdrew.

She had been all in black. Surely not from respect for my late husband? I had never considered mourning wear for myself, since I'd never grieved. My only regret was that I'd ever married Julian at all.

I turned in alarm to Mildred. "Mama in black. Tell me she's not widowed too? Not that!"

"No," Isabelle dropped into the brief silence that ensued. "Laurence is safely on his way home by sea. Eugenie remains in mourning for Rupert. But surely you knew. You were informed of the funeral date."

"Rupert *dead*?" I'd assumed he'd been abroad with her. "But he can't have been more than twelve, thirteen. I knew nothing of this! You may have written, but I received no letter. Whatever happened?"

Everyone turned to Dr Millson who answered with eyes downcast to the table. "He was away at school. There was always a question of his delicate chest, and he was warned not to take risks or overdo his interest in sports. He contracted bronchitis which rapidly turned to pneumonia. Your Mama was able to reach his bedside only in time to say goodbye."

"I'm so sorry, Lucy, that you should have to learn it in this way," said Mildred gently. "But with her return I'm doubly glad for your Mama that you're here, with your little one to take her mind at last off grieving."

They were all looking at me now, and it struck me that none of them wore black. "So when did this happen?"

"Eight months ago." Geoffrey nodded in sympathy. "Your Papa had just sailed for India again and Lord Curzon insisted the mission should be completed. We expect Laurence home this month. Then surely your Mama will find some joy in life once more."

Stunned, I followed them to the drawing-room. I was vaguely aware that since I was last there it had been changed from rose-pink to pale green and gold, and some ornaments and statuary were new. This provided a distraction for small talk until the door was opened by Hadrill and two gentlemen came in. I turned to see Edwin, and Clive Malcolm, who limped across to stand beside me as my brother greeted the others.

"What are you doing here?" I demanded. It came out rudely. I foresaw more embarrassments with him while I was still shaken by the death of the child I'd callously referred to as "the Great White Slug".

"I never knew about Rupert," I blurted out. "Edwin should have warned me."

Clive's eyes had lost all their merriness. "He's still saddened by it. It's not a subject he would raise himself."

"But I spoke so heartlessly of Rupert! What can he have thought?"

Isabelle was frowning in my direction, trying to overhear our passionately subdued words. Clive instantly caught on to her curiosity and changed tack abruptly. "You asked what I'm doing here. I went with Edwin to meet your Mama at Dover and share the driving back with Forbes. She brought only a small bag in the motor with her. The rest will be sent on later by carrier."

The unnecessary mundane detail gave me breathing space, but I was still not prepared to meet Mama when she swept in, over-bright and her eyes still red from renewed tears.

She greeted the family almost ecstatically, surveying the room, and then for the first time recognised me standing against the wall.

"Lucy? Can it really be you? This is wonderful, dearest."

She gazed around again. "But no Julian? Too busy, I suppose. How good of him to let you come!"

I was aware of Clive firmly gripping my elbow as Mama advanced upon me. "She has never been told," he whispered urgently. "It would be too much on top of all else."

In the event it was not so difficult to keep both matters out of our converation: Rupert's death for fear of causing her further pain, and Julian's, more to save my face than to spare her sudden shock. It was little Eugenie who saved the day. On hearing she was a grandmother, Mama insisted on creeping into the old night nursery to steal a glimpse of the child.

My baby played her part superbly, lying pink and serene in sleep, her expelled breath emitting a tiny, moist popping sound from puckered, cherubic lips.

"Perfect," Mama whispered. "Oh, her darling fingers. She will be like you, Lucy. At birth you had just the same downy gold hair."

"Like my Papa, then?"

"I wouldn't—" She stopped, looked up dismayed, then put a hand to her brow.

Afraid for her, I took her in my arms, felt the shaking throughout her thin frame. We stood locked together while loud, angry sounds racked her. This new encounter with a baby had reminded her of too much.

"Forgive me, Lucy," she managed to get out. "I'm sure you will understand my weakness."

"I do now," I said fervently. "Now that I have a child of my own."

The company broke up early that night out of consideration for Mama's health. Mabel lighted me upstairs with an oil lamp and struck matches for the candles in my room. Gaslight had not yet reached so far from the town but electricity was on its way.

There was no question of her helping me to undress. A healthy countrywoman, as Mabel was, would never consider me incapable of fending for myself. Which I was glad to do. She retired to sleep in the large dressing-room off my bedroom, where a fine iron bath on moulded lions' feet was now plumbed in against one wall.

My night was disturbed by fitful dreams, which dissolved each time I awoke, until about three by the stable clock's chimes, after which I fell more deeply asleep. Then I seemed to be with Clive Malcolm and, clearly alive, he was angrily berating me for the killing of Cecil Warner.

I thrust out an arm to ward him off, but he grasped my wrist and wrenched it upwards so that it forced me closer. I felt the hardness of his chest bruising my breasts.

"You hate me for your own bad conscience," he accused, and shook me roughly for emphasis.

Then, gazing fixedly at me, he murmured, "No. You have no conscience. You had forgotten completely. You relinquished me to my fate, crippled or whatever, and went your uncaring way."

"I was sure you had died," I protested.

"Done for, over. To suit your purpose, is that it? Do you really think my death would have been the end *for you*? Haven't you learnt yet that all actions have consequences?"

"But you are *not* dead!"

"Alive enough to confront you. And wiser for what you did to me. But what are the consequences for *you* – are you become more callous because of it?"

He released my wrist, or rather discarded it, repulsing me. Yes, he was alive enough, vibrant with contempt.

And then suddenly he was no longer Clive Malcolm but Julian, my husband. His arm rose, the hand gripping a slender cane, and he was beating, beating, beating me. At which I woke up soaked in sweat, passionate with shame and anger.

# Six

As Mildred had predicted, little Eugenie proved her grandmother's salvation. Mama appeared next morning in pale
grey silk with rose trimmings. The dress hung loose, and her own
mother would have puckered her mouth at how its cut lagged
behind fashion, but it did show a willingness at last to throw off
melancholy.

I was careful not to steal her company completely from Edwin,
and we spent almost an hour together outdoors, strolling in a
foursome with Clive Malcolm, while she made some pretence of
snipping dead heads from the flowers in Grandfather's wonderful
gardens.

I was most uneasy in Clive's company, with my guilt over
our first meeting increased by the confusion of my dream. To
remove the barrier between us I knew I must raise the subject
myself, since he clearly didn't intend to. Eventually I arranged it
that we lagged slightly behind, out of earshot of the other two.

"There is no way I can adequately make up for how I behaved
to you over your accident those years ago," I admitted. "You
see, I thought you were dead, and for me that was the end of
it. After I saw you bandaged in bed you simply disappeared
from the house and no one spoke of you again. That was how
everything was hushed up in those days: the truth too ugly for
children's ears. I was a coward, reasoning that confession would
only bring unnecessary blame on myself."

Perhaps I had hoped he would treat it lightly, turn it off with
a joke, but he was totally serious.

"All these years," he said in wonderment, "I have kept that
vision of you standing before the long mirror in your mother's
room with my little whittled figure in your hand. How you stared

73

at yourself, disgusted because of the irons on your leg. And you so beautiful.

"You knew what it was to be crippled. Yet when you learned my leg was broken in the fall you felt no pity that another might suffer in the same way."

I felt my face flame. It amazed me that I could still feel shame. And then it struck me, what else he had said.

"Was I, truly? Beautiful, I mean."

"Were. Are. Total Eve."

But if Eve, a temptation then? I felt a wild elation stir in me, only to be instantly stilled. There could be nothing in this for me: he was a threat. "All actions have consequences," he'd told me in London. But no; it had been in my dream. Yet that was what Clive Malcolm would really think. His return for my cowardly action all that time ago must be disgust, and now it had caught up with me.

"Happily," he said, "it seems we're neither of us crippled any more."

"I had the irons taken off soon after," I explained. "When I visited Grandmama at St Leonards, she had her doctor remove them. She said it was for me to run freely on the beach, but really the sight of me like that offended her."

"And they were never put back. So you forgot about them." His voice became teasing. "As you choose to forget about everything disagreeable."

"If only I could!" The words were wrenched from me. All my earlier wretchedness returned suddenly anew, overlaid with this new guilt about him. I turned away half blindly but felt his hand on my arm restraining me.

"But is it true that you've lost some part of your memory, as Edwin believes?"

"Absolutely true. I wish there was more would join it!"

Mama and Edwin had turned and were coming toward us. "That's unhealthy," Clive said shortly in his soft voice. "You are willing yourself to stay ill. I should like to help you get better."

That evening we all sparkled at dinner, outshining the cut glass and silver on the table, more glittering than the chandeliers.

Or so it seemed to me. Everyone had news of their own for Mama: the Millsons a forthcoming visit to archaeological sites in Egypt which Mildred had been involved with before the war; Geoffrey relating fresh finds of insect fauna in Scotland; Isabelle's discovery of a new masseuse and a London nightclub with exotic dancers.

Edwin made a few modest claims about his progress at Eton and pressed Clive to enlarge on his researches at University College Hospital. I listened enthralled while silently praying that the meal would end before I was called on to give an account of my doings.

What could I tell them that wasn't bizarre and sordid in the extreme? – that I had been wretched in my marriage, had deceived my husband and taken a lover; that Julian had discovered, brutalised and raped me; and then, when he was found stabbed to death, I'd been suspected of his murder, arrested by the police, shut in a cell and questioned to the point of near insanity?

What fine entertainment that would be for Mama, although no news to the others who had first learnt the outline of it from the London newspapers. Geoffrey and Dr Millson had visited me and pleaded in my defence, so that I was allowed my freedom while the police built their case. Which I assumed they were still occupied with and would eventually pounce again once they learned of my whereabouts.

And meanwhile there had been that missing period, with my baby's arrival, possibly some kind of injury to me, then final re-emergence in that squalid house in the neighbourhood of Covent Garden. Not to mention a nameless man, yet oddly familiar, stabbed to death, and my clothing soaked in his blood.

Sick, Clive had thought me. Well, if not knowing the whole truth about myself was sickness, then I preferred never to be well again.

We moved to the drawing-room where an infusion of dried lime flowers was served with slices of lemon. This had been one of the German remedies Mama had been given in preference to tea, and it proved quite popular.

Isabelle was behaving herself this evening, drinking moderately and fixing me from time to time with a speculative stare.

I found myself sitting next to Geoffrey who patted my knee and declared himself quite won over by the littlest family member.

"As you know, Lucy," he said, "Isabelle and I have not been blessed with children, much though we should have loved them. Now I fear it's too late, and since you find yourself alone at present, we want you to be assured that if . . ." He hesitated, embarrassed by needing to refer to my predicament.

". . . that we will be happy to help in any way . . ."

"—if I am tried, found guilty of murder and hanged by the neck until I am dead?" I was filled with a terrible rage against him but kept my voice low for fear Mama should hear me. "You are so full of pity for me that all you can think of is to encourage Isabelle that she should adopt my child? Is that your intention? Even if the worst should happen to me, do you imagine Mama would permit her grandchild to be kept from her?"

He recoiled suddenly, gasping like a startled turtle withdrawing its head. "Has Isabelle spoken of it to you?"

"She doesn't need to. Her eyes have been devouring the baby since I first arrived."

My anger suddenly dispersed, and I took his arm. "Geoffrey, I know you are the kindest person on earth, but you must find some way to convince her that it's quite impossible, utterly unsuitable, whatever happens to me."

He looked away. "I had hoped that with a child to care for, she could – recover herself."

He meant control her drinking. Even if she managed that, there were still impediments. She was rash, impetuous, shamefully unaware of others' feelings, or wilfully oblivious to them. How could I trust her to deal wisely with my baby? Even I, the family bohemian, could recognise her shortcomings. What my little Eugenie needed, deserved, was the stability of her grandmother's love. A Stakerleys upbringing.

Poor Geoffrey, Isabelle's victim. How often, it seems, do tyrants attract the very prey their outrageousness will feed on further. As Julian had done with me. Not that I was malleable. I had fought back, and that was the conflict he thrived on, driving me in the end to God knows what lengths of violence. Perhaps, if the police were right, even to killing him.

I shuddered, appalled at my child's inheritance, the wild blood that could run in her veins. Pray God there'd be some saving grace, that she'd take after the woman she was named for.

For distraction from such disturbing thoughts I toured the house and grounds, deliberately reminding myself of incidents from my childhood, as if ghosts of a more innocent past could pull me back from what I feared I had become.

Gazing with fresh eyes, I was struck by how peculiar inherited wealth was, releasing one from the necessity to make one's own way. What compulsion was there to earn when all one needed for subsistence and comfort was here already, amassed by earlier generations? And how wonderful for me, having broken free, and suffered, and known rejection, to return and find a place still left open to slide back into. Wonderful, yes; but not enough. I needed something more.

There was still my studio. On leaving I had taken with me all my best work and materials, but finished canvases were still stacked against the walls, and in the shallow drawers were watercolour efforts: Stakerleys interiors with figures; landscapes and views of the river; snow scenes observed from the windows; close-up sunny wildernesses of meadows with ox-eye daisies and poppies, painted as I lay on the grass, while nearby little Rupert incessantly sneezed at the pollen. And dozen upon dozen of my turbulent storm-torn skies, bloody sunsets and fires.

So much the same, untouched. Yet Rupert had gone. That was the only real difference at Stakerleys. It was as if the war years, all those young men, recuperating here before being sent back to kill or be killed, had never existed. But if that time had never been, wouldn't I be unchanged too? As what, as whom?

Always it seemed that I returned to the enigma of my origins. Well, now, as Isabelle had reminded me, I had the opportunity for some research. I went to Mama's boudoir when she was away consulting with the housekeeper. Her writing-desk was unlocked and open.

The upper, toy-like drawers with their tiny ivory knobs were tidily filled with pen nibs, rubber elastic bands, erasers, pens, pencils, sharpeners, a magnifying glass, drawing pins, paper clips. The longer ones below held stationery die-stamped with Mama's name and address in blue. There were invitations and correspondence from acquaintances, photographs that had yet to be stuck in albums, keepsakes such as programmes for concerts and dramas, little tasselled cards with silver pencils attached for recording one's dancing partners from long-ago balls. She had even kept her last school reports and a letter of recommendation, "To Whom it may Concern", from Miss Court-Withington, her one-time headmistress. Glowing with praise, of course. But what I was seeking seemed to be gone.

Then I noticed, under some loose papers, the Chinese carved casket which Mama called her treasure chest. It was locked, but I found its tiny key on the ring which still hung from the bureau itself. Inside were a number of crinkly official documents concerning her two marriages, and birth certificates for us children.

I removed only the one which related to me and that for her marriage to my father. She would surely have no need for them again. Back in the studio I had time to examine them to my satisfaction. Now I had proof that my parents had indeed been married. At least I was no bastard.

Smoothing them out, I was conscious of something vaguely disturbing about the papers, but there seemed no reason for this. I had been born, as I'd always supposed, on January 14th of 1901, making me now twenty. And the birth was dated almost a year from the marriage in 1900. I could find no cause there for any uneasiness. I was Margherita Lucia, daughter of Ernesto Fabrizio Vincenzo Paolo Gabrieli and his wife, Eugenie Fellowes Gabrieli.

Not until I lay in bed that night, recalling in detail every experience of that day, did something else come to mind. Almost visibly floating before my sleepy eyes was the cream-coloured deckle-edged vellum of the testimonial offered by the old principal of Mama's boarding-school.

Surely I wasn't imagining how it been headed in that elegant italic script? It seemed impossible that so precise-seeming a person should make such a mistake. It was credible enough, in the early days of January, for one to mistake the year, writing down the date that had long become familiar, but almost unimaginable that the mind should leap ahead to a year still twelve months away. And she had written it a few days before Easter.

That letter was imprinted on my mind. I was sure of what I'd read. Miss Court-Withington had dated it, "regretting Eugenie's leaving us today", as March 24th, 1900 – almost two whole months *after* Mama had supposedly become Signora Gabrieli. Yet I knew, from her own conversation and Isabelle's confirming chatter, that the two of them had set out on their Grand Tour only *after* Mama left school and became the widowed Honourable Isabelle Delmayne's travelling companion.

It was too weird. And it made sleep impossible.

One of those dates must be incorrect, and since the two Italian certificates corresponded satisfactorily it was more likely that the English one should have been a mistake. An elderly spinster, confused in a rush of end-of-term activities, briefly losing her grip of details. Yes, it would be that.

And yet hadn't there been some doubt raised before about my age? Mama's school friend, whom I'd met at St Leonards as a child – Mrs Mallalieu, was it? – had challenged my being ten. Her wretched, oversized son had declared I was too short, and so I must be nine. Then she had reasoned somehow that he was right and I was mistaken. It had been something to do with the time between Mama leaving school and my being born. Which would mean both Italian certificates were made out in error.

Or were false.

In which case there had been some reason for a forgery, and I could well be illegitimate after all.

The indecision left me so restless that there was no cure but to get up, relight the candles in my room and submit the certificates to the most searching examination.

I held the yellowing paper close to the flame and peered through it. It then appeared that in places something had been written over the original. Turning the upper surface again to the light I suspected there was a slight difference in the quality of the ink. Colour is something I am particularly sensitive to, and I became sure of it the longer I looked.

There had been no alterations to the date or registrar's signatures on my birth certificate, but "Gabrieli" had been added *after* my mother's maiden name and "Ernesto Fabrizio" inserted *before* "Vincenzo Paolo Gabrieli".

The early hours of the morning are not ideal for reasoning, but I managed to work out that although my mother had not apparently been married at that time, yet my father was indeed this Italian Gabrieli. I rolled the names Vincenzo Paolo round my tongue and was not totally downhearted.

Next I turned to their marriage certificate, which would surely have a forged date. Yes: originally dated February 12th 1901, the final figure had been rounded into "0", thereby legitimising me on paper. But how curious: Gabrieli being available to marry Mama a month after my birth, why had he not done so a little earlier for propriety's sake?

Then I noticed a further irregularity in the written name of my father on the marriage certificate. It was, at first sight, the same as on the other document, but under "Fabrizio" I could just make out another name. The "b" and "r" were suspect, the final "zio" added in another ink which had aged differently from the first, and in which the whole of "Vincenzo Paolo Gabrieli" was also an addition.

To my horror it now appeared that not only was I proved illegitimate, but my mother, that impeccable English titled lady was, if not herself a sometime forger, at least a party to committing a serious crime.

As for my father, it seemed I had either an invented conglomerate or a choice of two; whereby I was either Margherita Lucia Gabrieli, or Margherita Lucia Fa\*\*i. Instead of clarifying the enigma, my research had in fact only served to obfuscate matters further.

"Margherita Lucia," I told myself severely, "go to sleep."

And by then I was so weary and confused that I complied without protest.

There was too much in the present that mystified me, which was probably why, keeping to my room next day on the pretext of weariness and overexcitement from our family reunion, my mind returned to the past, and particularly to that period of mixed adolescent emotions, the Great War.

Builders had already started work before ever I knew why there must be structural alterations to Stakerleys. Of course there was a war, and that was terrible; but it was on the continent. We were sending help, troops, guns. Beyond that, to my sheltered mind, it had seemed unlikely to affect our family.

Papa had been concerned that we young people should learn of the worsening situation in Europe, especially since he'd been involved in wrangling over rival interests in the Far East, spats which he'd seen as early symptoms of the coming madness.

We knew it troubled him that colonial jealousies between the Germans, French and Russians could push Britain into making dangerous choices; but, ignorant of the complex and changing network of alliances, I hadn't seen how the violent death of a Habsburg archduke while visiting Sarajevo should light the touch-paper to set Europe ablaze.

Nor did I at first understand, in the quite ordinary-seeming months that followed the declaration of war, how it must affect us at Stakerleys. Papa, as ever, absented himself a great deal, and Mama spent longer periods in London with him. Then, as news from the fighting in Europe worsened, servants gradually began to disappear, some fervently keen to "have a stab at the Hun" (as if it might be tossing hay with pitchforks). Others went reluctantly, anxious for how their families and work would suffer in their absence.

Naturally everyone who went to be a soldier was a ready-made hero. Nobody spoke of death or hideous wounding. Despite family calm, there was a buzzing excitement beyond the baize doors, which eventually penetrated the new west wing schoolroom where I laboured over Geography, History, Mathematics and French with Mrs Langrish – or music and painting with visiting tutors.

By then Literature was no longer a labour but sheer delight, as I devoured books from a list which all the family helped assemble for me. Yet, more and more, this pleasure was being overtaken by my passion for painting. I had always had a gift for sketching, and when a visiting portraitist let me experiment with his oils I discovered an almost delirious pleasure in mixing extravagant colours and daubing layer upon layer over canvas.

In the library a large wall map had appeared and Papa provided

a box of pins with coloured heads, with which we children began
to plot movements of allied and enemy troops throughout Europe
– or as much as we could gather of them from the *Morning Post*.
It made a new kind of progressive game.

We were confounded when Papa came home in the khaki
uniform of a major of the Yeomanry. He had little to say but
seemed discontented at being appointed to the War Office in
London. It had been his intention to serve in France on the
Western Front. About this Mama was rigidly noncommittal.

It was about then – probably the early autumn of 1915 – that
the family began to move into only a fifth part of Stakerleys. I
remember the afternoon when my own possessions were transferred. I had been in the kitchens helping Mildred pack and
store away our dried apricots and figs. This was a new domestic
venture to provide fruit out of season, because German U-boats
were already threatening the sea routes on which, as an island,
we relied for food imports.

I protested instantly at the interference with my comfort, and
then my aunt explained that the major part of the great house had
been offered to aid the war effort. Places were needed to lodge the
allied wounded during recovery. A staff of doctors and nursing
volunteers was due to arrive shortly. Uncle Millson, as a retired
medical man, would liaise with them on behalf of the family.

It was the first time I had come across the verb "liaise"; and
not so many months later I was to learn to my cost the more
questionable noun form – liaison.

I didn't care to be displaced, and doubtless behaved abominably
to everyone involved. The family household was further to
be constricted by Grandmother Fellowes moving in, since the
Zeppelins had started bombing the coastlines when unable to
reach London, and causing civilian casualties. Papa had decreed
it was too dangerous for her to remain alone at St Leonards.

It was to compensate for the new restrictions that a garden folly
was fitted out for my use as a studio. The dirt floor was tiled and
the bare grotto walls studded with seashells were hung with old
tapestries for warmth, the whole romantic effect – to my mind –
being that of a Crusader's tent in the far-off Levant.

Within my new realm I was Berengaria, Salome, Cleopatra, a

Hardy heroine. But above all, with vigorous determination, I was Veronese, Pissarro, Cézanne; and, most passionately, J. M. W. Turner, the great British colourist.

The medical team arrived, and almost immediate upon them the first wounded officers. Engaged in action some weeks before, they had already been patched up in field hospitals before coming on to us. I grew accustomed to seeing them wheeled about the grounds by nurses or orderlies. Some coughed incessantly, having endured gas attacks in the second battle of Ypres, and their lungs were quite rotted away. Others had hideous face wounds, empty eye-sockets, amputated limbs or were frozen into paralysis. Used as I was to Grandfather's affliction following two seizures, this was far more frightful because these were young men, some barely out of their teens.

It horrified me that if I were four years older, and a boy, I would be expected to endure what they had gone through. As it was, I would not be allowed even to study nursing yet.

I used to approach them, sit down on the grass alongside and try to talk with them; then go back and sketch them from memory. At first they seemed dumb, because we had little in common. Then they would bring out photographs of parents, fiancées, wives, even babies. These they would go on about for hours, but no one ever spoke of the war. Except one man who wept, and this so shamed the others that they sent me away and surrounded him like a barrier.

None of them stayed long. They were a renewable flow of increasing obscenity. Some, gratefully but hopelessly, were sent home where there would be little medical help since all able-bodied doctors were away in the armed services. The rest, patched up, went back to the hell they'd temporarily escaped from, reprocessed for eventual death.

I grew bitter about Papa's reasonable explanations of how the war had come about. Would the assassinated Archduke and his wife have wished for so much obscene slaughter to avenge them? Or the "Young Bosnia" zealots need such rivers of blood spilt in the name of freedom? Hadn't the Austro-Hungarians governed them well enough and maintained a stable state of peace throughout Europe? Why had Wilhelm II promised military aid to the Habsburg Empire if Russia should support the Slavs – and then turned on France? It seemed like a game on a board. None of it made sense in face of the damage and anguish caused.

And we, the phlegmatic British, had rushed downhill with all the other lemmings, going farther, being the only nation actually to declare war on Germany which was the Habsburgs' willing military machine. And this was because of our treaty with little Belgium which the Huns had needlessly invaded.

Sickened, I tore down the wall map, where the coloured pins had by now frozen in place because no one cared to make the red ones retreat. "It isn't a game," I told Edwin when he tried to stop me. He was home on vacation from Eton and seemed as fired by war fever as any of the servants. All he wanted was to be eight, even six, years older and become part of the wholesale slaughter.

We seemed to have exchanged places, he the usually docile one, I once the fighter. He marvelled at my attitude. "Wait until you've seen their suffering," I told him. "And then use what imagination you have." I ran off to the folly and threw paint on canvas: orange like bombs' explosion, and the reds of blood, the black of widows' weeds.

Such passion could have only one outlet then, and I had no conception of the fireball force that would soon burst over me. At first in a romantic mix of pity and admiration I made my childish approaches, found (as I thought) a kindred soul, and was met with tenderness.

Mrs Langrish discovered us in an intimate embrace at the folly. He was a subaltern from the Lancers, would have been fresh-faced but for a jagged crimson scar that crossed forehead and cheek, leaving the empty eye socket covered with a white gauze. He joked about Long John Silver, said he'd get himself a black patch, and a parrot for his shoulder. And quietly wept when I lay responsive in his arms.

My governess was distraught when she came upon us, apprehensive for me and appalled at what my mother would have said, had she known.

I made a deal with Mrs Langrish, slyly aware how blame

could have fallen on her for slack supervision: a promise to have no further contact at all with the patients, in exchange for her silence.

"Are you certain you have not gone too far with this young man?" she insisted. "Did you let him touch you, interfere with you?"

"I let him kiss me," I admitted proudly. "On the cheek first, then the lips."

It shook her. "Nothing more?"

What more did she expect? "Of course," I agreed: what more could there be?

At that she warned me solemnly. If I went back on my word, one single time, then she would have the folly closed to me. No refuge; no studio; no painting. And when Mama returned from London she should be told everything.

It sounded a death knell. There was no choice; and anyway poor Philip would be leaving in two days' time. I would never see him again. Mrs Langrish was to inform him of the ban on our meeting. Romance was denied me. I fancied I was hard done by and broken-hearted.

There was a further outcome from this: my studio was ruled out of bounds for the officers. Not that there weren't secret violations. Sometimes of a morning when I opened up, a scent of stale cigar smoke hung on, and once I found a lady's chiffon scarf left under the couch. Silken dalliance, I told myself; and savoured the delicious thought. I wondered how they had obtained a key. *Amor vincit omnia.* I wished them well, whoever.

Until I came upon them in the act. On a tapestry spread across the hard floor. The man unknown, his face hidden. But I'd no doubt about the other.

It stunned me: what they did; how grotesque she looked, her bare, white legs flung up, knees wide and rocking, then ankles locking about the man's naked buttocks. And such thrustings, such sounds! Hoggish grunting and a long crescendo of moans that finished in a scream of – of *delight*?

They fell apart, still sucking at each other's mouths, hands frantic in each other's hair.

Then she withdrew her face and stared fiercely into his, rolling over to cover him. "Wonderful!" my Aunt Isabelle whispered. "Again, oh again!"

I ran, as if for my life.

I had thought it a perversion. Not for some bewildered hours did I connect it with my governess's anxiety. "Nothing more?" she had persisted. This was her "more". People did this to each other. A man and a woman. Like farm animals. She had known, and she'd feared that Philip and I . . .

The idea had a horrid fascination. I wanted so much for that scene not to have happened; for me not to have witnessed it. And yet I could think of nothing else. It obsessed me.

Autumn gave way to a severe early winter. With the treacherous ice, riding was restricted for fear of injury to the few horses we had left, our best having gone to supplement the cavalry. But we did have skating, both on the Stakerleys lake and our river which meandered down to join the Chess.

For three whole days the ice stayed firm and even stood up to a brazier burning on the lake for roasting chestnuts.

Where it had frozen in eddies the surface was uneven, in swollen lumps, with the tops of rushes sticking out like a hog's bristles. Skating backwards to achieve the speed for a turn I struck one of these protrusions. My feet went from under me and I landed heavily on the back of my head, so shaking me that I seemed to hear my poor brain slosh and thwack about inside my skull. Flashes of blazing light were followed by darkness and confusion. I could hear voices but the words spoken had no sense to them.

I was told later that one of the nurses was by the river, and she had me carried back to the house half-conscious and my tangled hair sticky with blood. As I continued to shiver, my teeth loudly chattering, the nursery bath was filled and I was held upright in the steaming water while the wound was cleaned and covered. I remember drinking some spicy medicine which almost took away the pain and then I was propped against pillows in my own bed, and Uncle Millson was holding a candle against each of my eyes in turn and mumbling to someone about shifting retinas. I gathered I was to rest and be sure I'd see all right in the morning.

The room was sliding with shadows when they'd gone, but I thought I heard a chair's wooden legs scraped against the floorboards over where the window should have been. Someone watching over me. A guardian angel. It filled me with an awesome glow.

I slid lower, enjoying delicious shivers of adjustment as my warm limbs swam over the sheets' cold linen, languidly scissoring against its freshness, burrowing into the softness of the feather mattress. Then, taut and threshing, I seemed to enter some new element full of strange longing that must at all cost be satisfied. Reawakening the numbed injury, I turned on my back.

A powerful tension was arcing my spine, my small breasts suddenly so heavy that I must cup them protectively in my hands like soft warm puppies with questing little noses; noses to fondle with persistent fingertips, round and round and round in ecstatic discovery.

My hands slid away over the full extent of my quivering body, exploring the flesh, seeking the source of this thrilling disturbance. With my raised knees wide, I felt a terrible compulsive tension, and a lightning shock go through me to the very fingertips. I seemed to drown in heavy seas, and then I was lifted, cresting an immense wave, surviving, pulsing with glorious life. Sank away and knew no more.

Next day I was told that something was wrong with one eye. Which seemed perverse since it was the back of my head which had struck the ice. I put up with the pink eyeshield required for some days to keep out the light. What did anger me was to discover that a whole lump of hair had been cut off and an area shaved close in order to accommodate the bandage on my skull.

"The bump will heal in no time," I protested, "but it will take months, years maybe, to get my hair to the same length again as the rest."

I didn't care to be seen in this shaggy state, so it didn't bother me too much to be ordered to keep to my room and not exert myself.

Now and then I'd remember my confusion after the accident and whatever it was that had happened to me in bed. But I preferred not to think of it, dismissing it as a delusion, like the idea of an angel sitting in the nursery straight-backed chair to watch over me. If both had actually happened, I ruefully considered, the angel wasn't much of a guardian, allowing me to behave so.

And then, two days later, I awoke to find myself bleeding. My nightdress and bedding were stained bright red. When I tried to stand it ran in scarlet tracks down my legs.

I was haemorrhaging from inside. I knew the word, overheard in the gossip of some nurses who'd come for tea with my aunts. I could even spell it, having looked it up in the dictionary afterwards, admittedly at first under "hem . . .".

The case they spoke of had been fatal. It meant I could die.

I knew at once what my sin was, to have this visited on me.

It was uncertain how long death would take; whether it could be quickly over before I had to explain myself to anyone; or whether it would be lingering, obliging me to hide away the soiled linen and, growing ever weaker, somehow keep myself bandaged, for fear of discovery.

Or dared I openly confess, and hope there was a cure? Confession had never been my forte while there were younger brothers who could take the blame. But on this occasion it was so clearly my own misdoing. I was deadly afraid, not wanting to die, ready to make any pact with the Almighty, even as that awful old Abraham had done.

But the choice wasn't mine. I was discovered as I leant there, hands gripping the bedrail and bright blood dripping on my white feet. Mrs Langrish came in, and her hands flew at once to her face when she saw me.

"It's a haemorrhage," I said coldly, as if it were something quite normal.

And as it happened, it was quite normal. She explained it to me: that I was grown-up now. It meant I was a woman. At fourteen, able to have babies.

"But I don't want any. I *hate* babies."

The odd little woman pulled me to her and stroked my hair,

my desecrated hair, and murmured, "My dear, we should have warned you before this. I am so sorry. It's my fault entirely. Pop back into bed now and I'll fetch something for you."

"Will it stop it?"

"No. Fortunately for you. I've heard it called 'the Curse' by some women, but you'll realise in time it's just the reverse. A special kind of blessing, because it makes a woman what she is."

So I sat and fumed and hated the world which had made women the way they were. Because it seemed men were different; they got off scot-free.

And then I remembered the war: how with scant warning men could be put in uniform and made to leave their homes, ordered to kill and be killed. Which I believed then I could never do. Not kill a stranger, some foreigner I knew nothing about. Anyone I hated, perhaps. Because hadn't I already wished someone dead? – the Great White Slug; and the tailor's boy who had nearly had me discovered taking him to Mama's room all those years ago. And more recently, my Aunt Isabelle for eternally faking prettiness when I knew how hideous she could really be.

# Seven

W hen Mama returned from London alone she made a great fuss of her "wounded warrior". It was decided I must see a consultant in Harley Street about my wretched eye, so I would go back with her after she had checked on arrangements to resettle Grandmama in comfortably at Stakerleys' Dower House.

"And will you take me to some galleries?" I pleaded. "I'm sure there are many wonderful pictures still in London that I've never seen."

"That depends," she warned, and by her voice I knew that we must strike a bargain.

If the eye specialist approved, then I might be allowed to walk the galleries, but I must promise that if he forbade my reading I would comply totally and without complaining.

There was a measure of danger in staying in the capital because of the likelihood of Zeppelins coming upriver from the North Sea to drop their bombs. And recently a few aeroplanes had crossed the Channel, to remind us how near the actual battlefields were.

The greatest danger was on moonless nights with enough cloud to conceal the behemoth shapes until they already filled the black sky overhead. The Germans were constantly enlarging and refining their terrible invention, so that it could travel at ever greater heights above where the anti-aircraft guns could reach. At that time the coastal listening posts had not yet perfected equipment for picking up the throb of motors, mainly relying on intercepting messages between enemy aircraft and inadequately decoding them. The whistles, rattles and sirens too often gave their warning to civilians only after the first bombs had exploded.

It was in January 1916 that Mama and I travelled up to join

Papa at the Belgravia house, a few days before my birthday, and I was reminded of another time I had been the only child with my parents in London. Parents, yes; because at that time I'd believed I was Papa's true daughter, a Sedgwick by blood as well as name.

For my ninth birthday, in 1910, they'd given me the peridot and pearls bracelet which I'd dropped at the Opera. It had been meant as such a very special occasion, and I'd spoilt it, like so many other treats.

Now I was no longer a child, but a woman. They should see the difference. I was determined to behave well, live up to their expectations of me, keep the promise I'd made to Mama, as well as the secret one to Mrs Langrish.

Then, perhaps, without too much pain I'd get my full sight back. How could I become a great painter if I was doomed to go blind? Besides I had struck a special deal with Heaven.

I found that even the London house was partly taken over by the Armed Services. The first thing I noticed in the hall was a new board of hooks, about fifteen in all, most of them hung with a white steel helmet with initials painted on in red.

Uncle Geoffrey came out to greet us in his naval uniform. He led us into a smaller sitting-room, explaining that the salon was "under siege". He seemed utterly at home, acting host, treating us as visitors rather than the real family of the house.

Such a great traveller, because of his expeditions for wild animals, he had joined Naval Intelligence with a special interest in East African waters. Within a few days he was to leave again for Mombasa. He promised to bring me back a Kikuyu carving.

I was curious to know how he would travel; whether by sea all the way round the Cape and past German colonial territory, or from the Mediterranean southwards. But he would give nothing away, as if I had sympathies with the enemy and would blab what he told me to every stranger I met. He clearly regretted that I had even overheard where he was bound for.

So, needled by his lack of faith in my discretion, I said I hadn't much hope of the carving, reminding him he hadn't kept an earlier promise.

"What was that, kitten? I'm sure I've always tried to please you."

"You promised once, when I came back from a holiday in St Leonards, that you would take me abroad, wherever I wished. But it was a promise lightly given which you've doubtless long forgotten"

"But I do remember. You asked to be taken to Italy. In particular to Venice. A splendid choice, especially with your interest in painting."

"And we never went."

"No. I'm ashamed I never managed things better at that time. Your parents thought you still too young at ten or eleven. And then my dear wife, your Aunt Isabelle, had a lingering infirmity which obliged me to stay by her side. And finally, of course, the war threatened. Europe became unstable: not the place to find myself with a young lady to protect."

"Encumbered, as one might say." I screwed up my nose at him. "You protest too much. With so many excuses to hand, how could you have meant your promise seriously?"

"Lucy, you're determined to make a villain of me."

"No. It's not that." I struggled not to admit that I was terrified for him; that I feared I'd never see the dear man again once he sailed for foreign parts under war conditions. I shuddered to recall the Lusitania, holed and sunk last May by a German U-boat with the loss of everyone on board. Life at Stakerleys without Geoffrey's frequent visits, his many kindnesses and interest in us children, would be unthinkable; any injury to him unbearable.

"Come back safely," I begged. "And don't make any promises about it. Promises so often get broken. It's like mocking fate. Just *try* – with all your might and main – to get back to us in one piece."

I turned and saw Mama's face then, white and strained. What had I said to upset her so? I'd meant no wrong. "Mama?"

She covered her eyes while she fought to control her emotion.

"Eugenie, what is it?" Geoffrey demanded, all gentle concern.

She took his arm and let him steer her to a chair. "Nothing," she said in a low voice. "Or, rather, a memory of saying a similar goodbye, many years ago."

"To someone you loved," I guessed, "going into danger. And you never saw him again?"

Her huge, dark eyes were filled with tears. She nodded.

My father, I thought. "What happened?" It seemed that at last the subject was open. She was going to confide in me what I should have known for so many empty years already.

But she had mastered herself. Her voice was quietly controlled. "He was killed;" she said simply, "as so many before him and so many after. The terrible waste of war."

Then she stood tall, smiled sadly on Geoffrey and looked brightly at me. "But time has moved on. With all these present guests, we've put you in a different room for tonight, Lucy. Come and see how it's been arranged for you."

Downcast, I followed her up the circular stairway, and then beyond, by the back stairs, to what had been the servants' quarters. "Killed," she had said. He had not simply died: my father had been *killed*. Yet there'd been no war then in Italy. There was some mystery in it, and that was why no one ever spoke of him to me. But one day, I vowed, I would follow it up and find out. I would honour this father whom other people did not care to mention.

We were to see the eye specialist next morning, but much was to happen before then. Both Mama and I retired early, the tone of her house having become, she confided as she came to kiss me good-night, overpoweringly masculine. She joked that she had no place in an Officers' Mess.

"Or Ward Room," I supplied, out of deference to Uncle Geoffrey's naval connection.

In fact it was the presence of fliers which most excited me, two handsome young men on short leave from the RFC. Already their exploits were spoken of as the British answer to the Zeppelin threat, as they forced their tiny craft to challenge the great heights which the German "airbags" were capable of. I had seen artists' impressions of their courage and achievements, lone souls with a single Lewis gun pitting themselves against those vast rigid structures armed with powerful guns and loaded with hundreds of bombs.

I was slow to fall asleep, conscious from time to time of male voices elsewhere raised in laughter. I imagined them lounging in comfort, glass in hand; not scarred and ruined like the young men at Stakerleys, but vibrant and invincible.

Perhaps I dreamed of them, certainly I seemed still to be among them when the first crash came, and then I was fully awake, back in the attic, with my mother hustling me into a thick robe, finding me slippers, then in panic exchanging them for outdoor boots. "We must go downstairs," she urged. "I had thought we were safe. There have been no air raids for several weeks."

We descended to the kitchen, which was semi-basement and now I could hear the clamour outside: rattles and bells tolling, a hand-wound siren that wavered and screamed alternately. And above it the muffled sound of explosions. It was like a bad thunder storm, but intensified. I knew Mama had a horror of lightning and I felt the hard grip of her fingers on my arm.

"They're just our guns," my uncle reassured us, putting his head round the door. "There's no cause for alarm."

"Of course not," she agreed. "Don't worry about us."

Somewhere a telephone rang and Geoffrey disappeared. Mama followed him up to the hall and I trailed behind. He stood there, the earpiece clamped to his head. When he replaced it he looked across at Mama. "It's the city," he said. "You should be all right here. They'll try for the docks next. It's the usual pattern."

Then he reached up for one of the steel helmets, the fourth along; patted his pockets, braced himself and made for the door.

Mother said nothing, letting him go. The Admiralty had ordered him in. Clearly this had happened before and she knew her place. But her face was taut with anxiety. "Laurence . . ." she began, then stopped.

"Where is he?" I demanded. Then again," Where *is* Papa?"

"He's dining with friends, important friends."

"At the House, or Downing Street?"

"Neither." And then I understood why it was better the women didn't know where their men were at all times. "At the Law Society in Chancery Lane."

By now I had enough idea of London to realise that that could be where the bombs had fallen. "No," I said – pleaded – "he'll be safe enough, Mama. He's such a good man."

She turned on me with a brief spurt of passion. "The good men, the bad men, all together. What difference . . . ?"

She broke off, angry with herself. Roughly she gathered me in her arms. "Lucy, I'm sorry. You're right. We must keep a firm trust in God."

But, however much she trusted, it wasn't enough to set her mind at rest. I heard her calling through the house – Mama who never raised her voice – for someone to fetch a cab.

One of the officers came thundering down the stairs. "I have a motor, your ladyship. It's ready outside." He made a pantomime bow. "Commandeer me."

"If you'd be so good," she said. "All the transport in the city will be taken. I need to fetch my husband home."

She turned back to me. "Lucy, while I'm gone stay down here with Mrs Marchant, and I'll know you at least are safe. I'll be as short a time away as I can."

As she went out I recognised she still wore her day clothes under her coat. There had been no sleep for her.

The housekeeper, with her hair in curling rags, had ordered a monster pot of tea for the staff, and presented me with a tumbler of milk as if I were a toddler. She was new since I'd last stayed here so I supposed I should make allowances. "I'd like it hot, Mrs Marchant," I told her, "with a heaped spoonful of cocoa powder and two sugar cubes."

She almost sniffed at that, instructed a kitchenmaid to prepare the drink and from then on ignored me. Which suited me well. I took the hot cocoa through to the scullery, opened the door on to the garden and went up four steps to the level lawn.

The officers were all out there, in a strange mix of night and day gear. One lying flat on his back had binoculars to his eyes. Another, draped over the balustrade of the stone steps leading up to the ground floor, was waving a wooden rattle, although by now everyone within miles of London must know there was a raid on.

"Cut it out, Charles," another sang out. "Listen. There's another coming in."

The rattle was stilled. In the distance were further booms and crashes, whether from our own guns or German bombs. Then, from the northwest, steadily and with increasing menace, came the throb of heavy engines. Circling in from the Midlands.

All around us the houses were in darkness. Only searchlights encircling the capital wavered and swept the clouded sky. Then suddenly the Zep emerged, caught in their brilliance, the bow shape and under belly rounded like some great inflated sow with its gondolas hung below like milk-filled dugs. The *thing*: not a machine with men in, but some hideous impersonal force that threatened humanity!

I heard myself scream my hate at it with all the power in my lungs, shaken by a fury I'd never known before. And I wasn't alone. They were all shouting, waving their fists, cursing. From somewhere quite close a burst of anti-aircraft fire slit the blackness with tracer bullets. They fell short, but into the space between had fluttered a small white moth.

It silenced the men and then one called, "God, no! There's a fighter up. Why doesn't he fire a Very?"

"What is it?" I cried and someone reached for me, pulled me under the warmth of his greatcoat.

"It's a Camel."

Ridiculous! Camels didn't fly.

"A Sopwith Camel," someone else explained. "Peter here flies one."

The one called Peter was punching the air, willing the frail-looking craft to rise as the Zep's nose went up seeking conceal-ment in the upper cloud layer. "They haven't seen him. He's counting on that. Surprise attack."

But the gunners below had spotted the plane. The barrage fell silent and the searchlights were momentarily cut. After less than a minute's sighting, both Zep and pursuing Camel had been swallowed up again in darkness. The searchlights resumed and feverishly swept the skies, but lit only the heavy underside of cloud cover. Somewhere hundreds of feet above, in darkness, the unequal enemies would be fighting it out, killing to survive.

"You've no helmet," the officer whose coat I shared accused me.

"Here, take mine." That was Peter, the first words he ever spoke to me, careless for his own safety, smiling easily like a charming choirboy. Even to a girl like myself he looked so young, untouched.

He fitted the rubber-padded metal over my tangled curls and adjusted the strap for my chin. Briefly I smelled his hands, quite different from my own. And then, reconsidering, he marched me indoors, elbows clamped to my sides as if I were a military captive.

We sat on the stairs and examined each other in the dimmed light. This was another of the London house's marvels: electricity. It arrived with a flick of a finger, and could be as swiftly extinguished in air raids.

His was an innocent face, smoothly rounded, shining like a countryman's. Under fine blond hair that fell straight above a square forehead, the bone structure barely pulled at its cover of flesh, but under the blue eyes were mauve ditches. I explored his features minutely, fixing them for the portrait I knew I'd paint once I was home.

"Will I do?" he asked merrily.

It made me laugh. "Do for what?"

"Whatever you're on for."

I'd never had a conversation like that before and it left me unsure for a moment. Later he was to tell me I'd looked enigmatic, sphinxlike, leaving him free to infer whatever response he wished.

He held me firmly in the crook of one arm, raised my chin and kissed me on the mouth. Twice. By the second time I was passionately joining in. He was gentle when his fingers moved over me, but I responded so instantly that I'd have had him take me there and then on the stairs, but he'd more sense. And more experience; but not a lot.

We went to his room, which strangely had once been my own. I never told him then, because I was shrewd enough to realise the mistake he was making. Coming from the scullery, and wrapped in an old robe which I'd partly outgrown, I'd seemed to be one of our servants.

Even in the heat of passion I was a little nervous. "What about the others, your fellow officers?"

"Should we invite them in?" he teased. "Wouldn't that be improper?"

"I only meant won't they miss you?"

"I'm not one of them," he said with a tinge of bitterness. "They regard me as a monkey on a stick, doing tricks for them. They shout bravo since I have my uses, but privately they write me off. I'm not a toff like them, see? Not one of the *arsicrockery*!"

Well, nor was I. Perhaps that was something we'd intuitively known we shared. "But you're a pilot," I said. "That makes you special."

"A freak as well as a fake," he said. "A board-school boy who had a gift for tinkering with engines. And then dared to try them out himself."

"If you're a fake, then I am too," I promised.

"Two of a kind," he whispered. He thrust his face deep into my hair and I felt the strong beat of his heart pressed over mine.

He groaned as he entered me and I cried out with the pain of it. He seemed to check but I urged him on.

Afterwards as we lay intertwined he was wretched. "You should have told me," he said. I didn't know it was the first time for you."

"Is it always like that?" I dared whisper.

"I don't think so. Always different, I believe. But I never meant to hurt you, truly. It won't be so bad again. It's difficult for a virgin."

"What do you mean?" Virgin was a religious word. Academic sophisticate I might be, yet I was sorely ignorant of the things that mattered. But Peter, gazing at me, understood. He explained, and then part of my mind curled up like a contented cat. I was a woman now; had been so for well over a week. But no longer a virgin. I'd left that far behind me.

I crept away to my converted attic and must have been some hours asleep when Papa arrived back in daylight. He came leaping up the stairs two at a time, calling anxiously, "Eugenie! Where are you?" unable to believe she had gone out in the air raid and not returned.

I ran to my door, still in the old robe, and hung on to the jamb while the realisation flooded over me. In my lovemaking I'd forgotten much more than the air raid which had quite soon passed over.

"She took a lift in someone's car," I explained. "They went to find you. She was scared you'd been hurt in the bombing."

I saw then that he had a bandage on his temples. "Papa, you are! You're injured."

"It's nothing. A piece of ceiling came down. What time did your Mama leave? Who was driving her?"

"Soon after the first bombs. Or was it just gunfire? But ten or more minutes before the second Zep came over. One of the gentlemen offered to drive her. I don't know his name. He was tall, heavily built, with a cavalry moustache."

"Major Brockley." Papa was suddenly aware of my undress. "You shouldn't be sleeping up here. I'll have a bed made up downstairs for you."

"But it's morning already. I was just going to get up."

"Yes, I suppose so." He looked confused, had been about all night, helping to dig out buried survivors, and now was almost out of his mind with worry over my mother. "Tomorrow then. No, what am I saying? You must both go back to the country at once."

He left me on the upper landing, tore downstairs again to set up inquiries by telephone.

Mama was in hospital, unconscious, ironically having suffered a shrapnel wound from one of our own bursting shells. In a few hours they would operate to remove metal fragments from her shoulder. Her left shoulder, inches above her heart.

It was some time before I thought to ask after Major Brockley. There was an awkward silence.

"He was killed then?" I demanded crudely. If it had happened it was only right that it should be acknowledged.

"He died bravely, trying to protect Eugenie as they left the car."

Brave or foolhardy? They hadn't needed to rush into danger. I had trouble believing that so much could happen so fast; life hinging on an instant's decision, such as making a kind offer; not waiting for a cab or staying to see what happened. Instant death, while in blissful ignorance we'd made love.

Also, on the subject of foolhardiness, what about my own actions – ill-considered, or not considered at all? Yet the more

I went over what had happened on the stairs, and in my one-time bedroom, the more sure I was that that had been a crucial instant of free choice, and I had willed myself to walk on into something I knew was waiting for me. Something I heartlessly still revelled in recalling.

I wasn't dispatched to Stakerleys that day. For one thing nobody could be spared to take me. For another, Papa could think of little else than how things would go at the Westminster Hospital. He was constantly there in attendance on my mother. She made good progress, and two days after the raid I was allowed to visit with him.

I hadn't glimpsed Peter since he left me at my attic door. "At least let me escort you home," he'd insisted whimsically.

I later learned that he was caught haunting that upper corridor and been scolded by Cook, but nobody connected that with me. My bed had been promptly set up downstairs in Papa's study, and I was sternly warned to keep myself to myself in a seemly manner.

If Peter had expected me to reappear in cap and apron, serving at table or changing his sheets, he'd been disappointed. What he did see was me in my smart chestnut winter coat with matching muff and Cossack hat of creamy-brown pine martens, waiting in the hall with Papa for the car to be brought round.

"Lieutenant," Papa acknowledged him. "A fine morning again, but the wind's still chill from the east."

Peter gabbled something in return and I treated him to a monstrous wink before sailing out, leaving him, as I rightly guessed, appalled at his outsized solecism.

With Mama's return, pale but insisting that with morphia the pain was becoming quite bearable, I was allowed to circulate more freely in her company. There was a quite ludicrous scene that first afternoon when the two fliers burst into the sitting-room where I was reading and Mama was writing letters. She put down her pen and insisted they should join us in drinking tea. Peter's face was aflame and he seemed quite tongue-tied, leaving the other young man to bat the conversational ball to and fro. After a short while I made my excuses and left, going straight upstairs unobserved to wait for him on his bed.

He came in and leaned his head against the door panels before he realised he wasn't alone.

"Peter, come here," I ordered. "You really are the most awful snob."

"I?" he protested. "What do you think—?"

"—I'm doing in here? Being shameless, that's what." I swung my feet down and went towards him. "Peter," I admitted, "I'm not as bold as I pretend. Comfort me."

Which he did, to my great relief, for I thought I'd gone too far in mocking him.

"I never dreamt," he said when we were through our first fever of kissing, "that you were – who you are."

I laid my cheek against his, which was smooth-shaven and warm, smelling freshly of soap. I felt I could be frank with him as with no one ever before.

"So exactly who am I? When you claimed you were a fake, do you remember I said I was the same? I'm called Sedgwick, but I'm not a real one. Mama was married once before and I came from that. I've no noble blood at all. My real father's a bit of a mystery. He's dead. They've even taken his name away from me, and nobody cares to talk about him."

"That's sad," he allowed, but I could see he felt relief. To him his crime was that much less grave.

I squirmed in his arms. "I'm sorry you feel so guilty. I don't feel any shame at all at what we've done."

He held me a little way apart and regarded me earnestly. "Child, how old are you?"

I was furious with him. "I'm not a child! How dare you? Just because I'm not very tall! And anyway, I told you my name's Lucy. I'll thank you to call me by that."

A slow smile spread across his face, indulgent and loving. "Lucy," he breathed, kissing my brow, my temples, my hair. "Tempestuous, redheaded Lucy. What am I to do about you?"

Not a lot, I thought miserably, since Mama and I were to be packed off to the country next morning. I could believe, looking at him now, that we were meant to be together, meant to share our grand passion while life was still in us.

But I knew love was a fickle flame. There had been stories

whispered among the servants; false lovers who made promises for eternity and forgot in a fortnight. There were greater promises broken than tours of Italy or wooden carvings from Mombasa. I wouldn't extract anything of the sort from Peter.

"That rests with you," I said, and left it to him.

I visited him in bed that night and we made love fiercely, then gently. I crept back downstairs before dawn and had breakfast alone with Mama in her room. When Papa tucked us into the horse carriage that had come up from Stakerleys I saw Peter at an upstairs window watching. As we drove off he did not wave, just let the curtain fall before we were out of sight.

At home we celebrated my fifteenth birthday sombrely. There were cards from family and acquaintances, but no presents. We had given up such indulgences for the war's duration. It seemed to have been going on for ever.

I recalled the little plane that briefly glowed in the night sky before the searchlights went out. A pale moth, it would surely dash itself to powdery pieces as it fluttered against some fiery object. So fragile, as life was, as I feared the promise of love might prove. But whatever pitiless fate Peter was doomed to be broken by, I vowed I would forever stay constant in my love.

# Eight

M ama recovered her spirits quickly after her shrapnel injury. Or appeared to do so. The wound itself was hideous, the flesh puckering with vivid crimson and a jagged white network of scarring. I saw it quite fresh that first night back at Stakerleys when her négligé fell open as I helped her into bed to await Uncle Millson's applying a fresh dressing. She had sent her personal maid away, perhaps to avoid frightening her at the thought of what a mere civilian might suffer in this vicious war.

It made me burn with anger that any foreign ruler's greed for land and power could wreak such misery on innocents whose rights they totally ignored. Surely such gross inhumanity must finally call destruction down on them, if ever a God existed.

But what justice would there be for the young fighting men who blindly threw their lives away for King and Country? Peter had never spoken of patriotism or sacrifice. He'd taken war on as what life was about for such as himself. He expected hardship, gloried in the new dimension of flying, hoped for nothing – certainly not his nation's thanks. It had seemed as though he set no value on his own life, which for me was the most amazing and precious thing I had ever almost shared in.

I tried to do the same: hope for nothing. And yet I would wake sometimes of a morning knowing I'd been with him in a dream. His essence lingered with me, making the very daylight brighter, warmer; my body sated. It seemed I could reach out and my fingers barely missed brushing his fine hair, pressing on his lips, his flesh.

Ironically, now that Mama was recuperating at home, I was encouraged to spend some time with her talking to the wounded men who were cared for at Stakerleys. But they meant nothing special to me, were mostly a distraction from my painting.

I let it be known that I was working on a portrait of my mother which was to be kept secret until finished. She sat only once for me. After that I made sketches from the magnificent full length of her by John Singer Sargent in the rose drawing-room. Between the two I was able to place her features, but the rest was etched into my memory and I dug it painfully out.

Against a menacing background of greeny greys shot with blue-black, her face in a lurid light was tortured as I'd seen it as she rushed off to find Papa. Her beautiful hair was in disarray, the eyes wide and wild. You could sense tension from the muscles in the neck, and when I reached the torn fabric showing naked shoulders and breast I painted in the gory horror that the fresh wound must have been. Working with passion, I knew it was the finest thing I had ever done.

I had also started a portrait of Peter, and soon realised that it would never be finished. Not that I lacked persistence. It was more that the longer I worked on it the deeper I saw into him and the more I needed to express, yet utterly failed to achieve. Every day I would add more; subtract something; despair; paint over again, and end frustrated. I was miserable at Peter's absence but, angry with myself, mocked my own selfish wretchedness, called myself Mariana of the Moated Grange – *"He cometh not," she said. She said, "I am aweary, aweary. I would that I were dead."* Except that I'd no wish to die. Rather I'd stoutly live on until the war was over and the fighting men returned. Then perhaps, if I were worthy of it, Peter might come home whole and we would meet again.

So the weeks went by and the weather grew mild and I had no expectations. And then there came the Hiring Fair, only by now there were few enough men to hire and a lot of the available work was gone already to the women. Yet it was an excuse for some easing of depression in the village, as everyone who could took a free day and a lift into town, to see the side-shows and get a little drunk.

I went with my aunts. Mildred had organised a charity stall with home-made foodstuffs, knitted garments and part-worn boots, all to raise funds for our troops in France. Isabelle, scorning the "clodhopping yokels", had declined, but changed her mind when Captain de Verville offered to drive us there in the Stakerleys Daimler. This he managed successfully despite loss of his left hand, by having his lame batman sitting alongside to manage the gear lever.

I made short work of losing the aunts once I had deposited my load of daubs, mainly local landscapes, at the crafts stall, and I made for the makeshift smithy where I knew there would be a gathering of my horsey acquaintances. Our village blacksmith was there in his best suit and with a pink rose in his buttonhole, for once a spectator. He raised first his hat and then a beckoning finger as soon as he spotted me worming through the crowd.

"Dan," I said on reaching him, "what's up then?"

He was a hearty red-faced young man who'd taken over from his father, excused war service because of a club foot; and only the most perfect physical specimens, it seemed, were worthy of being blown to pieces by the Huns. I had long regarded him as one of my more sensible village friends, and he'd more than once rescued me from disgrace as a child by riding me home behind him when I'd strayed too far from home ground.

He was affecting to seem unconcerned, but I caught him giving me some sombre sidelong glances while I prattled away in my usual manner. "Come on, Dan," I said finally. "Some little fox is eating at your gizzard. Are you going to tell me about it, or aren't you?"

He flushed an even deeper puce. "I'm not rightly sure as I should," he said, crumpling the brim of his hat between his hams of hands until in mercy I took it off him to straighten the thing out.

"I guess you're scared of me," I said. "A little fellow like you and a great Shire mare like me."

He barked with laughter, setting his fifteen-odd stone of muscle and solid bone ashake. "I guess you'm right, miss, at that, for I've me doubts if it's quite proper what I'm thinking of."

"Shame on you then, for being *im*proper!" And then, since he seemed worse embarrassed than ever, I took his arm and led him away from the crowd. "Now Dan, whatever it is, you have me so intrigued by now that I shall positively sulk if you don't open up."

"Well miss, it's like this. There's a sort of surprise, if so be you'd care to follow me round behind the fodder stack."

Which naturally I did. And there Peter was, waiting, not in uniform but a rough sort of tweed jacket and cycling knicker-bockers.

A dozen notions rushed into my mind at once, one of them being that he was no longer a flier but free of the war, free to go on living out his normal life span, with a chance for me to be sharing in it. But for a long while there was no real thinking, only a marvellous surge of love and together-ness, a oneness such as I could never have imagined. Not that we made love, but simply stared and kissed and stared and held, and felt altogether wonderful at being with each other again.

I knew he felt the same as I. I saw it in his eyes, the intensity of his features, every line of his body which I thought I knew but yet not nearly enough.

"We must talk," he said, still breathless from my smotherings.

"That among other things," I pleaded, pulling him away towards the spinney behind the open field.

He went willingly, but drew me in a slightly new direction and waved ahead. "Your friend Dan has found me a couple of hacks. They're tied up behind that old barn. Will you be missed for a short while?"

We were gone all afternoon, until the sun sank low and the evening chill began. And it seemed only a few minutes. We talked, as he had said we must, giving each other our news, such as it was.

Then came the part that had caused him such soul-searching. We would make love together no more, he said. He knew my age now and it would be quite wrong. There must be nothing wrong between us; only "whatsoever things are true, whatsoever things are honest, just, pure," as Saint Paul said.

"We will wait," he told me, "and in time it will all come about. You see, everything is different now, because of you, because of us. Before, I meant to fly until the end came, and die as decently as I could. But now I have to stay alive because there is so much ahead. I am determined.

"One day I shall come for you, and I'll have made enough of myself so that no one, no man alive, however noble or clever or powerful, will dare to say I'm unworthy. Lucy, I'll never deserve you enough, but by God I'll do my damnedest. Do you believe me?"

And I did. So I promised too. I would wait and be equally good. How could anything go wrong if we were so determined to discipline ourselves for future happiness?

So that I should not be left anchorless we devised a system of correspondence. Peter would write to me every month in an envelope stamped by the NSPCC, so that it appeared to come from one of the charities I was encouraged to support. Peter would obtain these from a friend's mother who worked voluntarily for the Society. This would keep my family from guessing our involvement together. It seemed a cheating thing to do, so to salve my conscience I resolved to enclose in my replies a cheque for the Society, begged off Mama and paid for from my pocket money.

How young we were, how ignorant of the frailty and beastliness of humankind. Now it is a kind of physical pain to remember how we felt then. It is a mercy that we couldn't see ahead.

If we had been less restrained I might so easily have become a voluptuary. But Peter's resolution overpowered my physical need. Because of the ever-present menace of the war I sensed the superstition behind his withdrawal, and neither of us dared put our fear into words lest it had a fatal effect on the outcome. But if we played by the rules, or so we believed, then life would deal fairly with us. Peter would come through unscathed, and finally we'd be together.

Once Peter was sent to France there were weeks when I had no news of him, and then there would be three or four front-line cards arrive together. By then our scheme of using NSPCC stationery had become useless. There was no privacy in the sort of correspondence he was permitted on active duty, but at least in receiving these stereotyped forms I knew he was still alive. And they gave no clue to my family of any more intimate relationship than with any of the villagers or servants who occasionally wrote to me from the war zone.

I poured my deepest feelings into my letters to him and filled pages with the trivia of family and village life, illustrating the pages with little whimsical sketches.

My serious painting seemed the only positive thing in my life then, and quite suddenly it took on a new significance. It came about through that savage picture of Mama wounded by shrapnel.

I had never intended it to be seen, and when Papa enquired how her portrait was coming along I'd said I despaired of getting it right, so I'd painted it over and started a new landscape. He'd made some gallant remark about her beauty confounding the most skilled brush, and we left it there until over a year later when he brought a distinguished war artist back to Stakerleys.

Before I could prevent it they were at the door of my studio, extinguishing their after-luncheon cigars and politely requesting admission. Frank Brangwyn, Associate Royal Academician, almost overwhelmed me. While we talked, Papa moved round the folly lifting out canvases which I had placed with their faces to the walls.

Brangwyn – always fascinated by dramatic subjects – stood a while admiring my amateur copy of Turner's *Eruption of Souffrier*, the volcano spouting crimson against a slatey black sky barred with reflected light.

Our later conversation – about Cézanne, as I recall – was broken into by an explosive protest. Papa stood transfixed with my mother's portrait in his hands and speechless with horror. Not at the agony of the subject, but at my committing such an outrage.

He shook the canvas in my direction and *shouted* – Papa who was always so discreet, so diplomatic – "How *dare* you? This is infamous!"

Brangwyn stood there open-mouthed a second, then went across and firmly took possession of the painting. I saw his face as he turned back towards me. He was impressed, and my heart filled to almost bursting point because he saw what had been in my mind when I threw the paint on.

"But this is good," he said quietly. "This really speaks. What have you called it?"

"*Innocent Victim.*"

"Yes."

His quiet acceptance was enough. Papa was temporarily silenced, although I sensed he felt something near to disgust at how I'd presumed to vulgarise his treasured Eugenie.

But more was to follow. After Brangwyn left Stakerleys, having examined every one of my paintings in turn without further comment, he wrote to Papa from his home in Hammersmith. Although he couldn't take on a further student himself, he felt I might benefit by attending a teacher whom he knew. Because of the war, this artist had left London to work from a studio in Maidenhead, within a reasonable daily drive from Stakerleys.

Despite his shock at the direction my work was taking, Papa allowed Mama to overcome his objections. In August of 1917, with Mrs Langrish chaperoning me like a fussy little tugboat, I sailed into the bohemian lifestyle of Roderick Mainyard.

Physically he was as unlike the expansive Brangwyn as his pictures were the opposite of the Academician's carefully draughted heroic canvases of battles and historic catastrophes. "Roddy" was small, pinched and nervous-looking, but no mouse. Passion exploded from him in fierce distortions of haunting colour. Like Turner before him he concentrated light in circular swirls, and I had never seen anyone before so master the range of blues, able to make them actually hot and thrusting from the canvas, rather than kept coolly receding. Like some well-known continental artists of the time he was a little mad even then, and has since been confined in a mental asylum where he paints away much as before without seeming aware of his changed surroundings.

We were chalk and cheese together, as they say: or more flint and steel really, for we struck sparks off each other and his critical ravings provoked a zesty reaction in me. As personalities we clashed, as my colours clashed. I lived in a riot of primaries just saved from vulgarity by shadows of grey and black with reflections of peach. It seemed to my enthusistic young heart then that I had founded a school of painting all my own.

When Roddy exhibited locally I persuaded him to include some of my works. Seeing them hung together in a separate small salon I was aware of something missing. It took me half a year to discover what it was; and that new element was later the basis of my first professional one-man show in London. It consisted simply of underpainting one section of each picture with the same ominous grey-green plus blue-black which I had used as the background to the contentious portrait of Mama, and then patchily covering it with grainy broken white. This scumbling effect, against the *alla prima* technique elsewhere, was at the same time disturbing yet wildly satisfying.

But at my peak moment, in July of 1918, when at last the tide of war was turning as the American Expeditionary Force added its strength on the Somme and simultaneous advances were made eastward from North Italy and northward from Greece, I was suddenly reduced to my lowest ebb, bitterly disenchanted with myself and my world.

The cause of this was one of Roddy's students, an exceptionally handsome young man whom it had amused me to tease along as though he were a suitor I could pick up and drop as easily as a handkerchief. Unfortunately he saw his role differently and fell passionately in love, or so he later excused it.

One evening as I waited at the studio for Mrs Langrish to arrive in the Stakerleys motor, which had been delayed by floods in Thames Valley, I became aware that, although Roddy had gone out, someone had stayed on in the building with me.

Leonard emerged from behind a model's screen. He took advantage of our being alone. In short, he raped me, for I wanted none of him and fought as fiercely as I could, raking his face and chest with my nails until the blood came. But he was strong and bore me to the floor by sheer weight. I'd no weapon to hand and couldn't throw him off.

As a result of that shaming experience I began his child. It appalled me. I had threatened the wretched boy so fiercely, how my family could destroy him, that he later kept his distance, while not resigning his studentship. But then on discovering my condition I ranted at him and he swore he would "stand by me"; which was the last thing I wanted.

Peter was still out of the country, flying from an airfield

somewhere in France, and anyway I could never have confessed to him in a letter for fear he thought I had been a willing partner in the wretched business. And I felt such guilt, for surely it would be better somehow to have killed the attacker or been killed myself than to let him break me down and so finally have his way.

In bitterly telling Leonard the outcome of his lust I only supposed I must get away and have the child in secret, then give it up for adoption. I saw the poor unborn creature as a mark of shame, and an extension of the boy's vileness. But then I had not reckoned with Mrs Langrish.

I couldn't believe it when they claimed she was his mother. How could anyone so physically handsome be hers? I remembered the other, younger child with its monstrous square head, a blown-up version of her own. How could she have produced this startling Adonis?

But it seemed it was so. Leonard Payne was the son of her first, dead husband; the younger one the outcome of a brief second marriage to a violent drunk. And she loved both her boys, working to support the grandmother's care for Barty as well as providing the fees for Leonard's tuition. Ironically it was through me that she'd heard of Roddy's teaching studio and considered only the best was good enough for her artistically gifted son.

I had always rather pitied the plain but worthy woman. Now I was to encounter her indomitable strength. Without anyone else who might advise me in my agony, I permitted her to override my scruples.

Two months later, before my condition began to show, I spent a night with a nurse she knew. And the following morning, to my further shame, I had the growing baby killed.

It was an amputation, as though I had lost a limb or a part of my mind. Nothing had prepared me for how deeply I would be affected. And, mutilated in spirit, I had barely recovered my physical strength when final news came of Peter.

He had written me down as his next of kin, so it was to me the notification came that Lieutenant Peter Draycott was officially "Killed in Action". And to me the padre wrote with all the slimy inadequacy of condolences. A flier on the same sortie with Peter had reported that no opening parachute had been seen before the plane crashed in flames over enemy territory.

I could not grieve publicly for a man whom nobody knew I'd loved. This must be suppressed together with the other shady secrets of my life. Desperately wretched as I was, it mattered no more that my paintings had begun to sell and were earning occasional good reviews in art publications. My world had shattered like finest glass, and any attempt to pick up the pieces could only cause further painful injury.

While the country wildly rejoiced in peace and victory, I was trapped in a tunnel of despair, lurching from one meaningless occupation to another, silently contemptuous of my family's incomprehension. At that period they must have been deeply concerned about what they saw as my dangerous mental condition. How else could they account for the shredded sheets I left trailing from my bed some mornings, and the explosive violence of my paintings?

It was because of these successful abstracts that Julian came to take over my half-life. He had turned up at my second exhibition at Sussex Street when the red stickers were rapidly appearing on the frames and champagne was freely flowing. He presumed to claim we had met years before, Julian so suavely handsome, the elegant sophisticate.

I assumed even then that my growing reputation was what brought him back to reclaim my acquaintance at the war's end, but there was also the fact of my surname, for I still called myself Sedgwick, reflecting the glitter of a noble background which he'd briefly posed against as a wounded officer.

Whatever his reasons, he found me – apart from my daubing – embittered and with no faith in any meaningful future. For once I permitted circumstances to carry me spiritlessly along, and some fifteen months later, because of his persistence and as a refuge from further deception of my family, I agreed to become first his fiancée and, quite soon afterwards, his wife.

# Nine

M y wartime reminiscences were interrupted by little Eugenie's cooing chuckle. I walked across to peer at her as she lay in the silk-lined crib, and she fell instantly silent staring back; her tiny fists stopped batting at the air.

I willed myself to see Peter in her face, fearing to recognise Julian there. She went on gazing calmly back, being neither, but totally herself.

Next time Mama visited her little granddaughter in the nursery she appeared almost vivacious and said she fancied a morning canter if I would join her. I still felt weak but rather than have her ride alone with a groom, I agreed and asked Mabel to search through the cupboards for my old habit and top hat.

The flared jacket and wrapped skirt hung loose on me as all my Stakerleys clothes did now, but as I tied the stock at my mirror I could see that already the country air was bringing some colour back to my cheeks. Yet nothing more to my memory.

And then, downstairs, when Edwin said, "Lucy, You've no crop; here take mine," something dark stirred in my mind. I reached for its ivory handle fearfully, with a sense of vertigo, knowing – half remembering – something evil. My hands trembled as they took the thing.

I had a sudden vision of a crop raised, slashing pitilessly down again and again, my breath tearing at my throat as I belaboured the loathesome creature shielding his face against the blows. And I, gasping and breathless, hating and hating and hating, filled with utter revulsion for this thing that didn't deserve to live!

Only Edwin was there to see my collapse. I came round to the chatter of glass against my teeth. "Sip a little," he ordered.

Sensibly, it was only water. With brandy I would have vomited. The trembling affected me all over, impossible to control. I felt my brother lift me in his arms, and next I was among the cushions of a sofa.

"This won't do at all," he said severely. "I'll have someone fetch Uncle."

"No," I pleaded. "I'm not ill. It's no more than fear. I just need you to stay with me, to hold on to for a moment."

He hugged me close, on his knees beside me, and the embrace seemed gradually to absorb the tremor until I was able to unlock my fingers from his shoulders.

"Edwin, I'm so sorry."

"But *fear*," he said. "Fear of what, of whom? Not of riding, surely? You were always so daring on horseback."

"A flash of memory," I admitted, trying to sound normal. "Something just came back. Suddenly."

My mind was crowded with horrors. The police were right! I truly had killed my husband. I was a murderess.

"Something very bad?" Edwin probed.

"Hideous. So bad that I refuse to belive it."

His earnest young face mirrored my own horror, but he had believed in me and still wasn't ready for the full truth. "You mustn't deny the reality, Lucy. You'll only suffer more. Concealment's unhealthy."

I laughed wildly. Unhealthy! Such a limp, feeble word. I must suffer the torments of a well-deserved Hell, and Edwin talked in terms of personal hygiene!

"You do need help," he insisted.

"I need love." It was a cry from my heart, not for a brother, but meaning Peter. And Peter had twice abandoned me, vanished without trace when most I needed him.

"There will be no lack of love for you here, Lucy. We all desperately want to help you get well and throw this appalling suspicion off. There will be no blame laid on you by us, whatever has happened in the past. We know you, that you're good and fond and true. We are your family, Lucy. You must let us help."

I turned away. It wounded him, because he wanted so much

to befriend me, to take some of the suffering off my shoulders. But how could I burden him with such a secret as that, which even some part of my brain refused to accept? My only poor hope was to go on denying, to him, to myself, to everyone; to the police above all, because otherwise they'd have me taken out early one chill morning and hanged by the neck until I was dead.

By the time Mama was ready for our ride I had roused myself from the past and recovered my composure enough to join her despite Edwin's protests. He was expected elsewhere with Uncle Millson so we were not obliged to take him along. However, a few minutes after setting out we were overtaken by his friend Clive, who sat on a big grey with confidence.

I had no doubt who had sent him to keep an eye on me and I was accordingly cool, to keep him at arm's length. Mama, with no such notion, chatted with him agreeably. She was arranging a big weekend house party, her first since losing Rupert, and had written to Clive's guardian insisting he should come and join us.

"If all goes well Papa will have arrived back, and this shall be a triple celebration, Lucy, in honour of his return, your baby, and Grandfather's eighty-fifth birthday. So will you let me have names of special friends you would like me to invite? And anyone from Julian's side, of course."

I foresaw enormous embarrassment, if nothing worse. Mama, sheltered abroad from everything unsavoury during her prolonged period of mourning for Rupert, was still unaware that Julian was dead and supposedly at my hands. Among such a gathering she couldn't remain ignorant much longer. Even if everyone could be persuaded not to mention my arrest as a suspect and subsequent release for lack of evidence, yet she would certainly pick up something strange in others' unconscious behaviour towards me.

"I'll think about it," I mumbled. "Perhaps we should keep numbers down in view of Grandfather's frailty."

"Oh, he loves company," she said almost gaily, "even if he can't converse himself. It's quite noticeable, Lucy, how he's really perked up since your return."

"Is the Bishop likely to accept?" I demanded of Clive, to turn the conversation.

"I certainly hope so. He's retired to Hove and finds time lies heavy on his hands without a diocese to run. It must be some time since you both met, Lucy."

Not long enough, I thought. I had briefly considered him for my baby's christening, but now my conscience wasn't up to the encounter. This proposed celebration would be a total disaster. I could never excuse Julian's absence to Mama when everyone else knew all the harrowing details.

"How can I get out of this hole?" I demanded of Clive as he and I took the three horses round to be unsaddled.

"Let's take first things first," he said, "and maybe the rest will take care of itself. The gathering won't be for another seven days. A lot may unravel itself by then."

Such as the police uncovering some solid evidence against me, I thought. Then there would certainly be an end to all this unnatural silence from them. But Clive was so calm, and he at least appeared to believe me innocent.

Didn't he?

He steadied my elbow as I swung down, then handed our reins to the stable boy. "Edwin tells me some glimmerings of memory have already come back. It may distress you, but it's a healthy sign. More are sure to follow now."

"You don't know what it is I remembered," I said hollowly. "Something quite damning. And I've no intention of telling you."

"Nor I of asking." We walked a while in silence. "It could help if you concentrated on memories from a much earlier period which you're sure of. Why don't you send your mind way back, and tell me what's happened to you since we met as children?"

So much; and little to my favour. "I threw your little wood carving in the fire," I said suddenly. "Goodness, I haven't thought of that for years. I really was horrible to you. I suppose it's time I said I was sorry about everything then."

He looked at me with a sad smile. "Are you sorry?"

Unaccountably I found I was crying. "For almost everything

I've ever done. I only wish I could start again and make a
better job of my life. I don't know who I am, or what I'm
about. Do you know I can't even paint now? There's so much
piled up in the way. So many secrets, and not all of them of
my making. It's a house of deceits. Nobody here has ever told
me the whole truth."

If my outburst startled him he didn't show it. I was startled
myself. I found myself blundering along the path, clenched fists
against my mouth, blinded by angry tears.

"How were you deceived?" The truth about what? There's
something specific that troubles you."

I stopped in my tracks and rounded on him angrily. "Wouldn't
it trouble you not to know who you were? Always to be
reminded of who had adopted you, but to be kept ignorant of
who fathered you?"

"You hate his lordship because he isn't your father, then?"

"Hate, no. Resent, more likely."

"Did you ever demand to be told who your father was?"

Pride had prevented me. I couldn't even admit that now. "I
found out for myself, over the years. At least, I discovered his
name and that he was an Italian doctor."

"So did you tell your mother what you had found out, and
discuss it with her?"

We were both speaking more slowly with each deliberate
question and each hesitant answer. Now our feet came to a
stop as we reached a new silence. I knew why there had been
no communication. It was from fear of learning something to
her shame. Family secrets. But Clive was not family, almost a
stranger. I could at least ask his unbiased opinion on something
I'd no experience of.

"There was something wrong with the certificates," I said
haltingly, and then went on to explain.

Clive listened, head on one side, as we again started slowly
walking, and I was grateful that we were side by side so that
he couldn't watch my face. I explained how the names and one
date appeared to have been changed, so that I couldn't believe
what was entered in the documents.

"Do you think," he said at the end, "that it might be

better for you not to know, if someone you love has been a party to confusing the issue? Might it not have been done to protect you?"

"From the truth?"

"From one particular truth."

"You're splitting hairs. Isn't it firmly held by you psychologists that the truth must out, however painful? Do you think that I haven't the courage to face it, because of the shame it may bring me? It could be shame for others too that I am avoiding. But then must I go on all my life uncertain, adding confusion on confusion each time I feel myself at a crossroads?"

He turned to me, stopped and took both my hands in his. "Lucy, I've never thought you a coward, just reluctant to have yourself judged badly. I do understand that this secret is at the base of your uncertainties and you should demystify it. Would you trust me to make discreet inquiries for you? Then you can decide whether or not you confide to the Viscount and your mother that it's a secret no longer?"

"Wouldn't they guess from your questions that you'll be asking on my behalf?"

"There's no need for me to trouble them. There are other ways of finding out, even if it takes a trip to Italy to ensure it."

He had asked if I trusted him. I knew then that I did completely. Despite all my bad experiences with men, here was one I was prepared to believe wished me no ill at all, while making no impossible demands.

We had almost reached the house by now and there was a little crowd on the terrace round Grandfather's wheelchair. I ran towards them, sure that something fearful had happened.

Then I saw the champagne and that everyone was smiling. "Bubbly before lunch?" I called. "What's happened?"

"It's your grandfather," Mama said in a happy rush. "I was telling him about the party I planned and he said – he *said*, 'Splendid, m'dear,' just like he used to."

I handed Clive my top hat and went to kneel beside Grandpapa. He put out his good hand to my head, stroking the tangle of my red curls. "Lucy," he said. It wasn't very distinct and he said nothing else for a day or two, but we had all heard it. So miracles still happened after all.

I hadn't given Clive my answer about trusting him, but he could see that I did. We rode together next day and I began to tell him what my painting had meant to me, how I had seemed to live on a different planet when I immersed myself in form and colour. It was as though another part of my brain came to life. But now that plane of consciousness had gone, paralysed, so that I couldn't touch a brush or pencil.

We tied up our horses, opened up the folly again and turned some of my canvases towards the light. Clive spent a while poring over the portrait of Mother then passed on to Peter's. "Was this your husband?"

"Oh no!"

"I'm sorry, Lucy. I never met him."

"This was someone I loved, secretly."

"And still do, I think."

"Will always love. We would have married but I had news of his death in action. It was then, while I was in despair and my life seemed at an end, that Julian reappeared and seemed to take me over."

"So you married without love."

I sat in one of the wicker armchairs and stared down at my hands. Now that we had reached the subject of the man I believed I had murdered it seemed easier to talk than to keep it all inside.

"Looking back I've puzzled long and often over how I ever came to marry Julian.

"I was seventeen as the war drew to a close, unattached, untravelled, and already gaining some notice for my more vivid canvases. The work I was producing then was savage, because of all the hurt about Peter. I had few friends of my own class, though many among the village families. I had been duly presented to Their Majesties in my virgin white silk and ostrich feathers, but I found the social round of a debutante so trivial. The eligible young men considered suitable to be my dancing and dinner partners were either set on rapidly finding themselves an heiress or determined to remain single while milking dry their popularity as long as youthful charm lasted.

"Yet marrying was a thing a girl did, and at that time I was quite spiritless in opposition, having lost whatever great belief I once had of happy-ever-after.

"I did not love Julian, didn't expect to, and didn't imagine that it would be required of me. I was scarcely aware then of the dynastic aspect either. If anything, since he showed interest in my recent successes, I saw him as a useful adjunct to my artistic career, which was all that was left to me of any worth. He would support me, escort me to functions where society required I should go escorted, help me exhibit and sell my canvases, at other times continue in his role of refined and elegant companion, correct, charming, worldly wise and flatteringly adoring. Or so I imagined.

"He made no physical advances during our courtship. Had he done so I would have been warned and fled at first touch. It seemed that that side of me was frozen. I suppose I never showed him more than a rather glacial respect. Our marriage would be, as I saw it, a formal white-glove arrangement.

"The family encouraged the match, leaving me free to please myself but clearly seeing Julian as a respectable catch, which perhaps he was in view of my fake-Sedgwick origins. Aunt Isabelle in particular urged me not to let such an opportunity escape me. True he had no title at present, but he had hinted at expectations from the French side. Since everything across the Channel was in such chaos immediately post-war, he explained he had not yet resumed connections with his family there. As if it really mattered, when all the French ever did with their aristos was guillotine them.

"We were married quietly in Stakerleys chapel packed with the marble tombs of past Sedgwicks. I wore white with orange blossom and behaved in a mannerly fashion throughout the ceremony, drank a little too much champagne afterwards with my village and arty friends, and slept in the chauffeured car which bore us off to honeymoon at a borrowed manor house in Somerset.

"Julian was icily offended because I demanded a separate

bedroom, since by then I was feeling quite queasy and he looked no better.

"Next morning he called me to book as if he were a public school headmaster and I an erring junior. It seemed that Papa had mentioned too late into our engagement, in Julian's opinion, that I was no true Sedgwick but a child of Mama's first marriage. That old chestnut again!

"I agreed it was true. I asked would it have made any difference if he'd known all along? We'd never taken great account of it ourselves. I was sure there was no intention to defraud him, Mama's blood not being of the proverbial blue but healthy and untainted in any way.

"I remember he stared at me tight-lipped, and for the first time I noticed how his fine nostrils flared and went white when he was angry. Anger was something I'd not encountered in his smooth performances before.

"He then grimly informed me that he'd been assured I'd be treated in every way like my half-brothers, according to provisions made in the Earl's will. If Grandfather died I would be eligible to inherit at twenty-one.

"No one had told me that. It didn't strike me until then that he had also been relying on a generous dowry. Which doubtless Papa had provided. I'd not thought to enquire what the lawyers were arranging between them. Money matters were omitted from my education, there never having been any shortage of that commodity.

"I had wit enough to know we hadn't started off well, and put on a cheerful face to win back his good humour. "It's a glorious day," I pointed out. "Why don't we choose a pair of matched horses and ride out to enjoy the countryside?"

"He turned on me savagely. He didn't actually strike me, but I saw then that he could. He bit his lips under the dark moustache, then without another word strode out of the room.

"I should have remembered that the ex-Hussar didn't ride any more. I guessed it was from fear he should damage his new artificial hand. And that was something I learned I must never remind him of.

"I soon lost any illusions I'd had, but it was less dramatic for the fact that I'd no romantic expectations. Yet I was unprepared for the change in this distinguished officer who had appeared so assured and competent. The early weeks rubbed off his veneer and he was left revealed as petulant and spiteful.

"I wonder if anyone has made a serious study of the psychological value of uniforms? It should be worth a thesis for you at University College. I could even write the synopsis for you.

"Section I: a military uniform earns unquestioning respect. (Of course that's only if one happens to be on the same side. Otherwise we feel antipathy.) Section II: lack of a uniform evokes contempt. (Would you believe that some ignorant girl had given Peter a white feather at the Hiring Fair before we met up, because he'd exchanged his uniform for a jacket and cycling knickers.)

"Then there's dispersal of the myth. Back in civilian dress our fighting men are no longer heroes. Wounds are downgraded to mere injuries, even deficiencies. All civilian gratitude is cancelled.

"Isn't that the way you would set it out, you learned gentlemen who pry into others' minds? Perhaps I'd qualify as part of a case study myself, because although I had thought myself unmoved by those wounded officers at Stakerleys, I was affected after all. At the time I had underestimated the romantic power they exercised, a power arising from proximity and sympathy. Why otherwise all those affairs between them and the nurses; the sudden weddings; the tempestuous partings when they were returned patched-up to the trenches?

"How else could I have found myself married to gallant Captain de Verville who had driven our Daimler with one hand while his batman changed gear alongside? De Verville – whose father, I later learned, signed his name Oliver D. Veal – Julian who before he acquired a Hussar's uniform had learned to 'speak posh' as shopwalker in a gentlemen's outfitters in Dorking, and who, he later rejoiced in informing me, had had my own aunt, Lady Isabelle, for his mistress, enjoying use of her in my studio before I was old enough to take his eye."

I heard a quiet sigh escape Clive. He was such a good listener that I had almost forgotten him as my bitterness poured freely out. It made me pause to check my fit of spleen.

"I know he wasn't the only fake. After the slaughter of Ypres, men had to be found to replace the army's huge losses. A new type was offered commissions and few questions asked about background if only they could fill military requirements. And Julian at times displayed a wild bravado that might well have fired men to follow him; which was how he was made up to Captain on the battlefield.

"Like others he wore an honoured uniform, seemed unquestionably an officer and a gentleman. He played the part admirably, the most charming and sophisticated of them all.

"I never minded the humble father, nor the trade background. He'd earned a living honestly then, and who was I to act the patrician? It was the snobbish pretence I minded, and landing me with yet another undeserved surname.

"He exploded the heroic myth for me. The removal of his uniform left naked a shoddy character underneath. With my family he continued to practise his immaculate manners; with me, after a week or two, he no longer troubled to perform. I soon found that the man I'd married was a bully and a cheat.

"For Julian men and women were two races apart. I realised then that I had always lumped them together as persons. Not identical, nor equal in ability, but complementary, with compatible natures. Both sexes were deserving of the same respect and honest dealing. And while accepting that society had set people into a distinct hierarchy, I'd absorbed the Sedgwick tenet that no decent man should be despised for lack of wealth or position. And similarly no man of rank was worthy of sycophantic grovelling.

"While observing – and deprecating – the opposite attitude in others, I'd never expected to face it across my breakfast table along with the marmalade, or between the sheets at night!"

I'd tried to end on a lighter note and waited for his answering smile, but Clive nodded sombrely. "You came to blame yourself for your position, sharing his deceits, since you wouldn't allow your family to know the truth about your marriage. Worse, after some particular abomination you began to find yourself making excuses for him."

How could Clive possibly know? I nodded. "After one of his rages he would calm down and be so sorry. He'd swear it would never happen again; but it did, over and over. I had to hide away until the bruises faded or else paint my face over. I hate myself now for ever accepting his tearful apologies as genuine."

"I truly strove to like or respect him, and this conflict discharged itself in my ever more hectically vivid paintings. By selling my 'mad' abstracts, still lifes and landscapes, I was able to supplement our allowance from Papa, which was badly eaten into by Julian's losses at cards.

"True, he won small sums from time to time and his debtors had been known to pay in kind. That was how he had acquired the elegant house in Regent's Park that he called our home, but after less than a year of lording it there a legal wrangle forced Julian to return it to the family whose heir he had almost ruined. From there we moved to cramped quarters in Fulham, where we cut the staff down to two and the attic became my studio.

"That was when Stakerleys came back to haunt me. I used to dream of its mellow sun-warmed stone, our gentle Chiltern hills, and in distant wooded valleys a ruddy haze of bare branches lit by the ghostly white of wild cherry in Spring. But most I missed the company of my civil, generous-hearted family. I wanted a real home."

I sat brooding a while and since Clive remained silent I took up the story again. "We had acquaintances in common, but no friends. In public my husband acted as if he were proud of my success, but in private I think he resented it. I found it harder and harder to keep our relationship on a tolerable level, and blamed myself for it. Every criticism of me from childhood, for recklessness and intemperance, came back to haunt me. I was hobbled by guilt. I could never have dreamt of such unhappiness as I had then in my married life."

"His death should have released you, except that now you are afraid you may have killed him."

"Because now it amazes me I didn't do it sooner. And I might have, if Mama hadn't insisted on our rejoining the family so frequently. Here at Stakerleys he had sense enough to behave himself. I could feel human again, but back in London only my work kept me sane."

Now I had reached the most poignant part and was unsure whether to go on. "It was on the second day of an art show at Queen Anne's Gate," I faltered. "I had the greatest shock of my life.

"I was present to encourage sales; but also it mattered to me who saw my paintings, how people reacted, and who would carry them off finally. So I liked to mix with the crowd. I had just come back from luncheon, walked round a bay of canvases and came on a man in a wheelchair.

"There was nothing unusual in that. Many ex-servicemen, wounded and unemployed, came in because there was free entrance to the show. Nothing unusual, except that this was my dear Peter, whom I'd long supposed dead."

I looked across to the portrait in Clive's hands. "I can still feel the great leap of joy and then the bitter realisation that time had moved on to separate us just the same. Peter twisted the chair to wheel it away but I held on and forced him to face me. I said, 'I can't believe that you meant to abandon me.'

"He had been repatriated by the Red Cross first from a prisoner of war camp and then from an orthopaedic hospital, only to hear that I was married and there was no longer any place in my life for him.

"It was untrue: there would always be room. My whole body cried out against the outrage of our being kept apart. We met again, in St James's Park, and talked and talked. I told him how I'd despaired at the official notice of his death and seen no future in life but my painting; and how, abysmally stupid, I'd drifted into marriage with Julian.

"Peter told me he'd wanted to share a little in my success, and so came to see the pictures without any intention of seeking me out.

"I said he could have contacted me earlier through the Red Cross, so that I'd know he was wounded and a prisoner. I would have waited for him. But he denied angrily he could be of any use to me in such a state. It wasn't the wonderful future we'd promised ourselves. 'I've lost the use of my legs, Lucy. I'm no good any more.'

"The dear idiot! It wasn't only from the hips down that I loved him. And, wounded as he was, he was in no way as multilated as I was from my wretched subjection to Julian.

"We met often after that day, secretly at his lodgings and openly at unfashionable restaurants or Music Halls when Julian was at his gaming club. And unsurprisingly our passion was too much to be denied. He was wrong when he claimed he was 'no good any more'. Which is why I have no proof now whose child little Eugenie may be, though in my heart I believe she must be Peter's.

"So I keep asking myself why he has abandoned me now, when I am free again. Can he have been frightened off by the publicity of my arrest and the suspicion of murder levelled against me? Could Peter believe me a murderess?

"Indeed, after my vivid flash of memory, of horsewhipping my husband, can I believe anything else myself? I assume you guessed at something of the sort from whatever Edwin told you I'd remembered."

Clive nodded. "I thought it was sudden guilt of some kind that had upset you. How did the incident end?"

I stared at him. That was the first direct question he'd put to me, and I'd no idea of the answer.

"That hasn't come back to you?"

I shook my head, shivered with sudden cold and put a hand to my temples which had instantly begun to throb.

"It doesn't matter, Lucy." He began restacking my canvases against the wall, his back towards me so that I could recover in private. He made no attempt to take me in his arms for comfort, just offered me his arm in a brotherly way as we went down the folly steps and led our horses back towards the house.

As we walked I dared to tell him what I hadn't confided to anyone: how I'd come awake in that wretched house near Covent Garden, of the dead man on the floor in the next room, and how I'd no memory of what had gone before, even of my little daughter's birth.

"Perhaps," he said gently, "you were mercifully given drugs to stem the pain, and so were asleep for much of the time."

Next day Clive left for Hove to collect his guardian, but in fact the Bishop was to arrive alone by hired car. He was as gentle with me as ever, but I had no inkling of whether he'd been warned how things stood between me and Mama. Clive, he told us, had been obliged to return to University College Hospital on a matter of some urgency.

As the days passed and Grandfather's birthday came closer I found myself resenting whatever emergency had delayed Clive in London. I felt abandoned afresh, since again I had nobody who knew the torments of my mind, and I bitterly resolved never to confide in anyone again.

# CLIVE

# Ten

I went looking for Professor Garland and found him in the morgue, dissecting the corpse of a three-year-old child rescued too late from a lodging house fire in Russell Street. The Professor's pink, balding crown looked flushed in its ring of black hair, and when he glanced up his brows were a single dark line, the mouth tight like a drawstring purse.

"One of five cadavers," he said tersely. "Have you come to lend a hand, Clive?"

"All children?" I asked appalled, aware that the normally cool academic had barely recovered from loss of his own young son from diphtheria.

"Four below the age of ten, plus their pregnant mother."

I stripped off my jacket, fetched a rubber apron and went to wash my hands. I stayed with Garland for the two bodies that remained, replacing the mortuary assistant, an insensitive blatherer who at present would be a strain on the other man's temper.

We worked in comparative silence except for remarks the Professor threw over his shoulder to a note-taking policeman.

Nothing sinister was revealed: the burns were consistent with circumstances at the site of the fire, where a paraffin stove had been found overturned near the charred remains of a truckle bed. It appeared that one of the stove's rear supports had been broken and an empty gin bottle shoved under, leaving it unsteady. The little family had all slept together while the mother huddled in a straw-stuffed armchair nearby. Death in all cases was from asphyxiation. The children were poorly nourished in general but had full stomachs. The woman, covered in old bruises, had drunk a quantity of alcohol but eaten barely any food. As ever,

131

the skills on hand would never have been needed with a little more charity earlier on. So frequently reminded of our capital's social shortcomings, I was filled with dull anger.

The morgue assistant was left to stitch the last body.

"Poor Law cases," said the Professor. "Our students need more experience with children, so I am obliged to send them to the Anatomy Department. Not the woman, though, poor creature. She's known indignity enough. God knows what trials and torments brought her to such a pass. There's no wedding ring, but under all that carbon she'd done her best to stay decently clean.

"Clive, if you've still the stomach for it, I suggest we take a cab to my club and I'll repay your efforts in kind."

Over lunch at St James's I found it easy enough to broach the subject uppermost in my mind. "Do you get a lot of burns cases, Professor?"

He grunted. "Even one would be too many. Mostly they're from house fires, caused through negligence. About the same number as of bludgeonings, I suppose. Knifings are more often from the East End, near the docks." He seemed prepared to drop the subject, but I pressed on.

"How about fire-death from car crashes?"

The Professor was about to light a cigar and paused, the match in his hand burning down until he shook the flame out with a sharp exclamation. "Not so many. With the persistence of horse-drawn carts among the motor traffic, most accidents happen at low speeds. So principally we find damage to limbs and heads, with fewer deaths and rarely conflagrations. But I have a feeling you've a specific case in mind, Clive. Am I right?"

"You are. Two or three weeks back there was such a death. A Captain Julian de Verville, wartime Hussar and now a gentleman of leisure. It was thought his car struck a tree out in Cricklewood and took fire."

"I didn't handle that, being away in Wiltshire at the time. You'd need to ask Peabody." Garland's voice was cold, confirming for me a reputed rivalry between the two experts.

"But if the victim's family were to request a second post-mortem, would you be prepared to take it on?"

I didn't miss the brief gleam that lit Garland's eyes. His voice had almost a chuckle in it as he replied. "Catch Peabody out in a bluff, eh? Is that it? What do you know about the case, Clive?"

"Not enough, and that's the truth. Apparently it has the police baffled. Although they made an early arrest they stopped short of charging their suspect with murder. Since then both she and they have been lying low."

"*She?* So there's a woman involved? And apparently not an accident after all? If you have a personal interest in the death, Clive, I prefer not to know it. You understand? I have to stay free of suspected partiality. The more so if I'm to challenge any findings by my respected colleague."

"I understand perfectly. In this I'm a mere bystander."

"You mentioned a family interest. So who is this party?"

"My one-time guardian, Bishop Malcolm, godfather to the victim's widow and acting on her behalf. Would you enter the lists for him, sir?"

The Professor gave a wry smile. "As an anti-clerical agnostic, I'd gladly offer my services to such an admirable debater. He has a damn sight more horse-sense in him than many a High Court Judge in the Lords. In fact, lad, it was initially through his reflected glory that I took you on. And a quite exceptionally acceptable student I've found you, if the truth's only known. It's a pity, though, that your mind's set on all this psycho-nonsense instead of a decent skill like surgery."

It wasn't only good food and wine that were responsible for the mellowing of the Pathology Professor. His nose was up and aquiver like a hound's at the sound of the View Halloo. The prospect of outwitting his younger rival in their shared expertise had put new life into the man.

On quitting my one-time tutor on the steps of the club, I made for New Scotland Yard to seek an appointment with the Commissioner for the Metropolitan Police. He had already received a letter from the Bishop's hands in which the Home Secretary recommended the bearer to receive all assistance in researching the police case against Lucy de Verville, née Sedgwick, in the matter of her husband's suspected murder.

Lucy's stepfather, telegraphing from abroad, had also intervened without any positive benefit, the police then reacting with a bristly stubbornness against interference from on high. Beyond allowing the Viscount's representative a brief visit to Lucy while she was held for interrogation, they had volunteered no help one way or the other. As a result, although they had allowed her to go, the shadow of suspicion still hung over her. It was regrettable that the family had not been informed of her release, and so had lost touch when she was spirited away.

It appeared to me that my own technical experience could be used to probe any medical chink in the case still being built against her. At least my qualifications might justify inquiry into it, and so I'd discover exactly what evidence they held to implicate her.

Sir Arnold was not that day at his desk, but an appointment was made for Clive Malcolm, MB Ch.B. to see him at 11.30 next morning. With a modicum of optimism I next set off on a tour by cab of all the London hospitals accepting maternity cases, but none of them had records of anyone recently admitted who answered to red-haired Lucy's description. This was a real setback, for the countless private establishments offering similar services – quite apart from the unofficial back-street midwives available – made the task of tracing little Eugenie's birthplace almost insurmountable. As a last resort I dropped off in Fulham and rang at the door of the last-known de Verville address, in a residential street a few doors past a corner dairy and a newsagent.

I waited some time, then as I was about to give up and walk away I heard a heavy tread on the inside stairs. A bolt was drawn and the door opened to reveal a squat, middle-aged woman whom I took at first to be a cleaner. Her hair was a pepper-and-salt bird's-nest and she wore a grubby apron over a checked gingham dress. The woman took a step backwards as if caught off her guard. "Who're you then?" she demanded roughly.

"I'm looking for lodgings and they told me you had a vacancy here."

Her small eyes screwed with suspicion. "Who's *they*?"

"Your neighbour." I sketched a vague wave in the direction of the newsagent's. It seemed to satisfy her, then a look of sly calculation replaced the earlier suspicion. "Lodgings? That depends," she said warningly.

"I'll pay a fortnight in advance, if the room suits me."

The offer seemed to have half won her over, but a habit of wariness still made her grudging. "It'll not be what suits you, but what suits me, young fellow. I don't want no cardsharps or drunkards or loudmouths to 'ave to clear up after."

"You would hardly know I was here." I tried her with a boyish smile, and as a final temptation, "I'm a medical student and I keep my nose in my books if I'm left alone to it."

"Well, so long as that's all you sticks your nose in, I s'pose it'll be all right."

She turned and stomped upstairs leaning heavily on the handrail. Despite her advertised aversion to drunkards I recognised the gin on her breath. But what had alerted me to make a bid for entry was the sight of what swung on a cord from her waist. Cleaners wouldn't normally carry scissors. But nurses did.

At some past time this old wreck had worked on the wards of a hospital, and long-held habits died hard. I'd bet my boots she did the odd job still and either helped babies enter the world or made sure they never did.

"There's a choice of two," she said ungraciously, allowing me to squeeze past her bulk into the front, double-bedded room where bulky furniture was covered in dust sheets. A large Victorian bay window was darkened by half-opened slats of venetian blinds.

I walked in and pulled back the sheet on a serpentine chest of drawers in rosewood. There had been the pair to it in a room at Stakerleys, so it seemed this had been the marital bedroom of the de Vervilles, furnished with pieces from Lucy's family. If any personal possessions of hers remained they would surely be in here; but all the same I said, "I'd like to see the other."

She showed me a slightly smaller room at the far end of the passage, passing open doors which revealed untidy interiors, one with an unmade bed undoubtedly her own, another a sitting-room.

We entered the smaller bedroom. Yes, I decided, pulling open a wardrobe door on the floor of which lay a pair of stretchers for a man's riding boots, one broken, this had recently been used by a man and someone had removed all his possessions of any use.

So, I wondered, had Lucy stayed hidden in this house for the birth, attended only by the crone? In such unhygienic hands it would be a miracle that mother and child had survived.

I nodded to the woman. "I'll take the front room."

"It'll cost you more. And you get all your meals out. I'm not wearing meself out over cooking, nor risking a fire in your bedroom."

We settled it between us, I explaining that I'd fetch my bags later that evening. "The owners," I said, "are they away for long?"

It threw her for a moment. Had she really believed I'd take her for the lady of the house?

"Gone abroad," she decided on the spur of the moment. "That's to say, she's abroad and 'e's recently dead."

"Nothing infectious, I hope?"

"Lord no. Unless getting your 'ead stove in is catching." She seemed vastly amused at it. No love lost between herself and her past employer then.

I went back to the front room and raised the blinds on the quiet street. I pulled off one or two more dust sheets but there was no chance to search then because the woman still stood in the doorway watching.

"What am I to call you?" I asked. "My name's Malcolm."

"I'm Mrs Pearce, with a he-hay. Emily Pearce."

I stared a moment, unused to having my spelling done for me. "Oh, I see. Yes."

"Well, 'adn't you best go get your bags then, and leave me to make up your bed, Malcolm?" Already she was patronising me. Perhaps it was as well she should go on thinking I'd given her my forename. I might not care to be identified later.

"Right then, Mrs P," I said perkily. It seemed to strike the right note, for she leered familiarly back at me, more than satisfied with the unexpected windfall that had come her way.

"You don't get no key of your own," she warned me finally, "so don't go coming back at all hours making me wait up late."

I attempted to look duly chastened, went off to collect some things from my lodgings in Bloomsbury, and to telephone the Bishop at Stakerleys with a progress report.

He later gave me a full account of that evening and I was able to picture him and Lucy together.

It happened that Lucy, trapped at the piano to accompany her mother's rich contralto in Delilah's lament, observed from the corner of her eye Hadrill's discreet whisper to him and his own response. She would have heard the telephone ring and guessed I would be reporting to my guardian. She appeared impatient to have a word too, to discover if I was on my way back.

The Bishop was talking with me for a considerable time, but she was still prevented from joining him because Geoffrey insisted she remain for a four-hand arrangement of some Schumann pieces with her Aunt Mildred. Then she was needed to turn the pages for Edwin's clarinet solo.

Before they were through, the Bishop had returned and was being served a brandy, no doubt looking thoughtful, scarcely an indication that any news he'd received was very good. Lucy was left free to surmise that perhaps it hadn't been me calling after all. The Clive who had departed so abruptly could have cleared his mind of all Stakerley matters and be about his own private business.

When good-nights were being said and the family broke up, she became aware of the Bishop lingering with a cigar on the terrace outside until the drawing-room had cleared but for herself. He came in again quietly and indicated a chair. "Can you spare me a moment, Lucy?"

"Of course, Bishop."

"Don't look so apprehensive, my dear. Clive and I have few secrets from each other and he has confided some of your worries to me, since he was prevented from staying to comfort you himself. There are things I should like to talk over with you, although there is no reason on earth why you should agree to discuss them with me. You are perfectly within reason to tell me to mind my own business."

"I hope I'd never be so rude. I'm sure you're concerned for the good of my soul." Perhaps it had sounded more sardonic than she'd intended. She softened it by adding, "Papa had good sense when you were asked to be my godfather."

He smiled in reminiscence. "Such a lovely little girl. I wonder if you can recall your christening, Lucy? You were barely four."

"I seem to have a memory of candles and a smell of herbs; looking up at you and then my face running with water. It must have been in the chapel here at Stakerleys. It's strange it wasn't performed when I was a baby."

"Because you were born in a Catholic country. Which was my good fortune, otherwise I might not have received that privilege. Doubtless you remember your wedding better, in which also I was allowed to take part."

"Strange to say, I can hardly recall anything I did that day once they'd dressed me up and I stood waiting for Papa to lead me up the aisle. It's quite a blur. Just isolated scenes come back, like pictures in a book. The whole day went so fast."

"That's often the case, as I understand. With funerals too. The words so weighty, but it's as though they mean nothing. They flow over one and it's like a dream." He had taken her hand in his and it seemed natural for her to sit at his feet and listen, as so many times before as a child. The question when it came was unexpected.

"Did you love your husband, Lucy?"

She found it impossible to answer. Whichever way, it seemed to choke her.

"Lucy?" He bent forward to look in her eyes.

"There are – there must be – many different kinds of love. Aren't there?"

"And yours?"

"Deep love, no. And nothing romantic. But, after a while, I couldn't help . . ."

"Yes?"

"Pitying him." She said it in a voice of wonder, as though it hadn't struck her before. "That's a kind of love, I suppose. The feeling for humanity."

"Loving-kindness, yes. Although he was brutal to you, even evil?"

"He made me very unhappy, yes. But he was my husband, after all. For better or worse. And then, it kept coming back to me how the war itself had been so evil. I couldn't know the whole measure

138

of it, couldn't imagine what it would do to a man. Day in, day out, and asleep too, one's never-ending nightmare, the fear of being killed, of having to kill others, strangers who'd done one no wrong."

She was suddenly stiff with anger. "Julian had been a shop-walker, for God's sake, in a gentlemen's outfitter's. He'd kept his fine hands clean. What had a man like that to do with wholesale murder? And don't say war's not murder. That's a legalistic quibble. You'd have to deny a part of yourself, ever to believe war could be just or holy.

"Imagine Julian exposed to all that, poor benighted soul who believed in nothing. Sadly, not even in himself. He was a bully, but he wasn't strong. Underneath, he was weak and vain and self-indulgent. And now he's dead.

"I had never lived so close to anyone before. Even with my parents there had been some distance between, some intervening person: a servant, a governess. I discovered . . ."

She stayed silent a while, forcing herself to see the needed admissions ahead. "I discovered that a man can have two persons inside his head, one of them still a child, uncertain and vulnerable."

"And the other person wouldn't admit to this child's existence?"

"Denied him, yes. And had to be cruel and insensitive to compensate; to prove himself truly a man. I lived with both of them alternately, and it changed me, pitying the child and fearing the man, never knowing which one I was to face next."

The Bishop had spent some time lost in thought. When he spoke it was as if he explained to himself. "Most of us function at several levels. Circumstances swing us from one to another, so that it can sometimes seem we have numerous persons living together and warring for expression under our skull."

"That's true in my case. I've changed utterly, once so rash and independent, and now I don't dare admit to the shame of how he used me. I was reduced to shivering indecision. Can you understand that?"

"I understand how suffering abuse can make one feel somehow responsible, guilty even. And so one goes on accepting, enduring, trying to believe the abuser every time he pleads for pardon and promises the evil things will never happen again. I can see too how you would feel obliged to cover the truth and put a bold face on for the outside world. But there remains one puzzle I cannot explain to myself."

She had stared back at him, as if hoping for some miracle of revelation.

"The puzzle is why suddenly on that one day such a person could no longer go on accepting and forgiving. Why, Lucy? If you did attack him, something new happened to turn the practised martyr to aggressor. What was it?"

"I don't know. I must have been out of my mind. And I think I've been a little out of it ever since. There's no other explanation."

"Unless something so unendurable happened that your memory has mercifuly wiped it all out."

"Then don't force me to remember! Please, *please.*" She got to her feet, fists tight closed against her chest. "Oh, what's keeping Clive? Why doesn't he come back? When he's here it helps me be less afraid. You can't imagine what a coward I've become. It's the thought of what I must have done, and then its consequences; being arrested again; more questionings; and being forced to confess to what I can't remember. Then, finally, if I'm found guilty, being condemned to—"

She felt his hands pulling at her wrists, then shaking her firmly. "Lucy, stop. How can I have been so insensitive? But I had to be sure, don't you see? I had to have it from your own lips that you don't remember what happened to your husband.

"Listen. From what I've learned of his dealings I am convinced that there are others who had reason to wish him out of their lives. Some perhaps without scruples, who would not have hesitated to attack him and, perhaps finding they had gone too far, take his body away and set the car alight, hoping to disguise the manner of his death. Nothing will convince me that this is something you could be capable of, however extreme your mental agony. Lucy, I believe in you, as anyone who knows you must do."

She looked at him with madly staring eyes. "But do you know

what the worst is? Mama has no idea even that he's dead. They all kept it from her, sending her off with friends to Germany while she was grieving over Rupert. She will have to be told. She must know, but I can't do it. I can't."

"Will you trust me to tell her then?"

"Not now. Let her have another night's peaceful sleep. And if you could wait until after Grandfather's birthday? Just another three days. Unless the police come first."

Which he agreed to.

So I had the best part of three days to discover what I could and to get back to Stakerleys.

I had fairly high hopes of my coming appointment with the Police Commissioner. Sir Arnold Bascombe had been a career soldier and it was evident from his stiff, Brigadier mien, the clipped moustache, the challenge in pale blue eyes which had seen too much and liked little of it. Invalided out of the Royal Artillery and decorated with a Military Cross, he'd been considered ideal for the senior Metropolitan Police desk and the social ceremonial that went with it. He took with him a distinct scorn for any who had avoided serving their country in uniform and was prepared to make short shrift of this young whippersnapper's attempt at interference.

"So," he said, eyeing me distantly, "you are a medical man, have spent the last – what, seven? – eight years at your studies, eh?"

"With a break of twenty months," I agreed. "If you wish to check my credentials . . ."

"It's no concern of mine, Dr Malcolm, how you followed your career in wartime."

"Except that you are prejudiced against me as a civilian. The twenty months I spoke of was spent as a naval surgeon at sea. I was released from my commission only to follow a further course at University College in the treatment of shell-shocked ex-servicemen."

The Commissioner's granite face showed the briefest flicker of scorn at the mention of shell-shock. Yes, I recognised, this was one of those officers who'd had "deserters" shot out of hand.

I'd get nowhere with him at the humanitarian level. I must seek compromise.

"I appreciate that your time must be spent on more important matters than the case I've been asked to look into. Perhaps there is some less senior officer who could see me on this matter?"

"That is what I had in mind, Dr Malcolm." The Commissioner pressed a bell on his desk and stood up, bowing stiffly. When the sergeant came in to lead me away, Sir Arnold was at the window with his ramrod back turned, looking down on the silvery Thames.

# Eleven

Sergeant Bradley, red-faced and overweight, had none of his superior's prejudices. He had a constable fetch enamel mugs of steaming tea and set out the documents of the case alongside.

"Poor lady," he said. "I never saw anything like it. It was like she never knew where she was or what month of the year it was. Some of them, Lord, you'd never believe the screaming and swearing and caterwauling. But not her. She just sat there, shaking her head and staring. Barely seemed to know what we was going on about."

"Shocked," I offered.

"Shocked right out of her mind. Couldn't get nowhere with her. If we'd had brass-bound proof we'd never have got her to court. Unfit to plead, that's what."

"So you gave up?"

The sergeant paused. "We don't close a case that easy. It stays open till more evidence comes to light; and it will, given time."

"Do you believe she killed her husband?"

Bradley narrowed his eyes until they almost disappeared in the fatty creases of his round face. "Seems likely. Took a haxe to him. Caught him off guard. But she'd not have managed the rest without help, being in the state she was. Expecting, I mean. We heard de Verville was a big fellow, too heavy for her to lift and get into the car, with her a little slip of a thing. No, there was someone else in it with her. A man. Give her her head and in the end—" He leered at me. "In the end she'll lead us to him."

He kept his forearm over the papers on the table between us as if some sudden wind might burst in and blow them away. Or as if I were an examination cheat and might dart a glance at his answers.

"Can you tell me why she was a suspect in the first place?"

"No secret in that. Housekeeper heard them rowing just before. Screaming at him, she was, threatening to kill him. And the haxe gone missing straight after."

"And the car, did you find traces of her in it?"

"No traces of anything. Couldn't tell it from burnt toast, the way we found it. Just hitting the tree wouldn't have set the tank off, according to the fire officer. Must've been drenched in petrol. Had to be deliberate. She'd had that much sense in protecting herself."

"Or someone else had. Do you know if she can drive?"

"Not his Bentley. He never allowed anyone else behind the wheel. Always drove with his manservant alongside. But we've witnesses that she used to drive other cars, in the country, when she stayed with her parents."

"Is there anything that made you doubt she was responsible? Anything at all?"

Bradley shook his head and, recognising that this was the end of his questioning, rose to his feet. "There's just one thing *I*'d like to ask *you*, sir, while you're here."

"Certainly. What is it?"

"Where were you, sir, on the evening and night of July thirteenth?"

Well, I should have been prepared for police suspicion. It was the nature of the beast. I searched my memory, came up with a fortunate dinner engagement with two colleagues which had been prolonged into the early hours while we argued a case of hysterical paralysis. I gave the particulars and the men's addresses in Pimlico and Ealing, then left – unexpectedly with a summary he provided of the police findings.

Because I was personally involved in the case I restrained my impatience and kept clear of the post-mortem set up for the following morning. Professor Garland had no difficulty in obtaining access to the refrigerated remains since Sir Arnold had notified the authorities that a further investigation was to take place. Certain that they had identified the right suspect, the police would be keen to gather as much further medical information as possible.

It was more the Home Secretary's signature than my own intervention that had speeded matters. But perhaps, too, the police themselves had some doubts about the thoroughness of Peabody's earlier examination.

Newspaper accounts of de Verville's death had given no details beyond two facts: that both car and body were badly burnt and the circumstances were considered suspicious. It was Sergeant Bradley who had mentioned an axe to me, and Mrs Pearce had volunteered the crude information that the man's head had been "stove in", when she denied my suggestion about death from an infection.

She had seemed quite sure of this fact and had not elaborated it with any gossipy exaggeration. I believed that unless – improbably – she had access to police files, she had acquired that knowledge from evidence discovered in her presence. Which suggested that sufficient of the dead man's blood was found inside the house to rule out his driving the car away himself.

It should be possible to find out from Mrs Pearce exactly where Lucy had been at the time and why suspicion had been levelled at her, but no solid proof found to bear it out. However, that question must be left to another day, for fear of alerting the woman by seeming over-inquisitive for an uninvolved stranger. Nevertheless I was determined to get her talking freely and to search diligently for any evidence in the room I was to rent.

As a doctor I knew well how difficult it was to remove all traces of blood, and Mrs Pearce struck me as a half-hearted cleaner or overseer. If my suspicions were correct I was almost certain I would find some residue on floors, carpets or walls.

At Scotland Yard one useful fact had emerged from my interview with Sergeant Bradley. It was that no weapon had been discovered which might have caused the fatal injury, although one exhibit held there was the ivory-handled riding crop belonging to the dead man's wife.

I had had it from Lucy herself that she'd drawn blood when she used it on her husband, but it was highly unlikely that such a lashing could provide the quantity of blood the police needed for their theory. And there had been no mention of anyone's bloodstained clothing being discovered at the house.

Somewhere in her room there could be the riding habit Lucy had probably been wearing during her attack.

I contrived to meet Mrs Pearce on the stairs when I brought in my bags and enquired casually whether there were horses for hire as I sometimes fancied a ride in the park.

"Oh Lor', yes," she said, adding that Madam had ridden almost every day and used a livery firm a short walk away.

"Not Mr – er, whatsit?"

"Mr de V? Never, on account of some wartime injury. Had a very distinguished military career, did Mr de V."

Yet those had certainly been stretchers for a gentleman's riding boots I'd seen in the bottom of the smaller bedroom's cupboard. And one had been broken, so why hadn't they been thrown away? I should have to get round to the subject when Mrs Pearce was more accustomed to me and at ease. Meanwhile I could purchase newspapers and tobacco from the newsagent next door, drop into my conversation the fact of where I was lodging and see what gossip bobbed up to the surface.

"Nasty business there," the newsagent told me with relish. Clearly de Verville's murder had been the highlight of his otherwise uneventful life.

"Can't say I'd fancy moving in where a thing like that's just happened. Doesn't do much for the neighbourhood neither, though I'll admit paper sales shot up while it made hot news like."

"You'd have known them quite well?" I insinuated.

"Saw them about, but they weren't locals, any of them. That Mrs Pearce is a sad old woman. Don't know why she stays on unless she's got expectations from the family."

"What family would that be?"

"*Mrs* de V's, I should think. She was a real lady, you could tell, despite being a bit of an artist. Very pleasant when we'd meet on the street. Which was more than her old man was. If she did up and do him in, nobody hereabouts would blame her."

"Did they have any children?"

"No. Funny that, though. The lady was expecting, but she still went riding two or three days a week. Took her husband's man as groom most times, but not towards the end. He'd go off to the King's Head drinking instead. We thought she'd paid him off to keep out of her way. My missus was just saying as how she must've had the baby by now."

I paid in advance for a week's papers to be delivered, and strolled off to catch a bus for Gower Street. Professor Garland should have finished his post-mortem even if the results weren't yet officially to hand.

Travelling on the upper deck, I watched the bustling London scene below and mulled over the little I'd just learned. The groom was a new element in the case. Lucy had mentioned two servants; which could mean this man and Mrs Pearce. It was probably he who'd left behind the broken boot stretchers when he cleared his things on leaving. If the man could be found he might prove a witness to some of the happenings in the murder house. Or even an alternative suspect.

The Professor was in his office, having just dismissed a chastened-looking student who nevertheless rolled his eyes wryly on recognising me as we passed. "He's on the top of his form," the young man murmured, "or else I'd have been rusticated."

And indeed Professor Garland was almost purring as he signed off his handwritten report and leaned back to remove his spectacles. "Well Clive, what kind of rabbit are you expecting me to draw out of the hat?"

"As spectacular a one as you can."

"Then I trust you'll not be entirely disappointed. The cause of death was as reported: a deep wound to the occiput effected by some heavy and sharp instrument with a convex edge, such as an axe or a meat cleaver. I should add that it was delivered from behind and above, implying that the killer stood while the victim was seated with his back turned."

"And unaware?"

"Most likely. One hopes so." The Professor took a gold half-hunter from his breast pocket, scowled at it and rose abruptly. "I'm afraid I must leave you, dear boy; I'm expected elsewhere twenty minutes ago. But make yourself at home. This copy is for you. I have others for official purposes. I think, from what you've told me, you should find reassurance in its findings. This is not, my experience tells me, a woman's crime in any way. And most certainly –" he paused and looked arch – "not a *lady*'s." With a throaty chuckle he bustled from the office.

The document which I read through twice was long and detailed. Professor Garland had had the good fortune to discover the organs and entrails, packaged separately, as well preserved as the cadaver. Using these he had amplified Dr Peabody's findings, dwelling on the stomach contents and general condition of the deceased which had been lightly touched on earlier, due perhaps to the charred state of the body and the obvious cause of death.

On my second reading I reflected that, thorough as I knew the Professor to be, there were aspects of his report that beggared belief. In particular, one expected detail was missing, and two were unaccountably added.

I helped myself to a paper-clip from the desk tray and attached the new report to my notes on the police interview, which I took from my pocket and smoothed out on one knee. Taken together they hinted at a crime more complex and more foul than the unpremeditated assault I had at first supposed. As it stood, there would be no comfort in any explanation I could offer Lucy.

There was more to be dug out at the Fulham house, and in addition I must discover where Lucy and the baby had been taken after the birth.

I called in at my Bloomsbury lodgings to pick up some medical books on my way back to Fulham and Mrs Pearce, for whom I purchased a half pint of gin and two bottles of Chianti. This evening, I promised myself, she should fill in as many of the missing pieces of the puzzle as she'd had access to.

It was the old midwife who raised the subject herself as we sat drinking in the upstairs sitting-room after I'd polished off the hot steak pie I'd taken in for my supper.

"I see you went ordering newspapers along the road," she said sourly. "And what vicious stories had that lot to tell you?"

"That there'd been a suspected murder here, but the police had changed their minds about it."

Mrs Pearce grunted and clasped her fat hands round the cup of gin. "Waiting to pounce, that's what they are. I don't know why they 'aven't 'ad 'er up in court already. 'Eard 'er meself,

I did, threatening to kill 'im. Out of 'er mind, shouting and swearing like a madwoman. And 'er usually so mealy-mouthed you wouldn't think butter would melt. Still, it stands to reason she 'ad some evil depths if you'd seen the things she used to paint up there." She nodded darkly and thrust a thumb in the direction of the ceiling.

"Yes, the newsagent mentioned she was an artist. Did she leave any of her work behind?"

Mrs Pearce sniffed. "Nothing that looks worth anything. But 'Uggett said—" She broke off, darting me a sly look. "Well, we'll 'ave to see about that. Since the master's dead and she'll likely go to prison, who's left to want 'er stuff anyway?"

"How about family, his or hers? Some relative must have been found to identify the body."

"There wasn't no family. Not on 'is side. That's why I 'ad to do it."

"It must have been awful for you. I heard he'd been badly burnt."

"I've seen worse in me life. But like you say, 'is skin was all black and shrivelled." She reached for the bottle and refilled her cup. "Wouldn't 'ave known 'im but for 'is watch and fancy cufflinks. And that cornelian ring 'e always wore."

"You said he'd a head injury. Could that have come from the accident, when the car crashed?"

"Didn't 'ave to. She'd done it 'ere, 'adn't she? Blood everywhere downstairs, like a slaughter'ouse. And then she'd loaded 'im into 'is car that night while I was away, driven 'im off and crashed it to make it look like an accident. That's what I told the police, and that's why they come for 'er, and 'er expecting the baby any day. 'Ad me 'ands full when they let 'er out again, because what she'd done brought the baby on early and I 'ad to deliver it right away."

"What a nightmare for you. Did you manage it all alone?"

"No, me gentleman friend . . ." She looked at me blearily, suddenly suspicious.

"I told you," I said cheerfully, "I'm a medical student. This sort of thing interests me. I get to wondering how I'd have managed myself."

"Like most fancy doctors," she said bitterly. "Leave it to us midwives."

She had half-finished the gin and was now on the red wine. Another sentence or two, I guessed, and she would switch off like a gas tap. "Time I got down to my books," I said regretfully. "I'll say good-night, Mrs Pearce. Don't bother to wake me in the morning. I may sleep in late."

I closed my door noisily and set it silently ajar again. I heard her chair scrape on the board floor, a lavatory flushed, and scrabbling movements as she barged her way to bed, mumbling under her breath. The only distinct words I caught were, "'Uggett, you bastard. Just wait till I catch up . . ."

Huggett, I thought: possibly the man she'd called "me gentleman friend", and the second servant in the house, who acted as Lucy's groom.

Could I assume Huggett was also the man who had deposited Lucy at the squalid house where she'd woken up? And was he also the dead man she'd found on the floor in the next room?

If so, why had he abducted Lucy to hold her there in a drugged state? The police had released her for present lack of evidence, but they could call her back at any time. So had Huggett meant Lucy to be seen as fleeing her guilt perhaps? But I received a strong whiff of venality from the sly Mrs Pearce. Were she and her "gentleman friend" in league to obtain monetary gain over Lucy's disappearance? And, in that case, from whom?

These were questions I'd follow up tomorrow; but for the moment, once I'd made certain the woman was soundly asleep, I intended examining the rooms on the ground floor, where, presumably, the de Vervilles had mostly lived.

There were five doors off the square hall; three of them locked, plus a cloakroom and kitchen. The locks were old-fashioned and large, offering ample scope for my set of old medical tools, the dental probe of which proved most efficacious. The front drawing-room was elaborately furnished with oversized pieces which had evidently come from a larger residence. The draperies and seat covers were in good order, but the room itself had faded gold wallpaper with dark rectangles where pictures had once hung. Those that remained were characterless works, nothing

that could have come from Lucy's hands. The bureau held little
of interest except unpaid bills and casual notes addressed to de
Verville and signed with initials. I assumed they were from his
gambling acquaintances setting up meetings. One dated recently
carried the request that he should "get H to see to it promptly,
or you'll be in a hellish situation".

Could H be Mrs Pearce's Huggett? It wasn't clear what he was
to "see to", although the earlier sentence had mentioned money
and "she'll have to make provision if all else fails." I felt a shiver
of horror as I connected it with Lucy's present dilemma. If de
Verville had been pressed for payment of outstanding debts it
could be supposed he would apply to his wife for assistance.
And if she had tired of his repeated demands draining whatever
she made from selling her pictures, was she to be handled
roughly by her husband's man until she agreed? Even in her
delicate state?

Mrs Pearce had given no consideration to her physical condition when she spoke of Lucy packing her husband's body in
his car and driving it off to set fire to it in a faked accident.
She had assumed Lucy was fit, since she was still riding several
times a week, although this might have been her excuse to slip
away and meet her lover, Peter.

But the police had discussed the unlikelihood of Lucy, small
and pregnant, manhandling a big man like her husband. So who
might they have lit upon as her helper?

If by some means they had discovered Peter's existence, his
wheelchair confinement would have ruled him out. So perhaps
they sought some other unknown lover, and my own intervention
now might be offering them a possible suspect, despite the alibi
I'd offered.

I smiled grimly. Perhaps they had been aware of H's presence
on the scene, whether identified as Huggett or not. For myself
I was becoming more certain every moment that Huggett was
indeed involved in the murder, colluding with another who could
in no way be Lucy.

I rose from my seat on a *chaise-longue* and covered it again
with its dust sheet. It struck me as curious that the nurse-
housekeeper, a disorganised worker, should take such great care

151

of a dead man's possessions; unless she expected to reap some future gain from it.

I went through the archway, under claret-and-gold swagged brocade and velvet, to the dining-room which was reasonably large and gave on to a wooden-floored verandah hung with creeping plants and roses on a white-painted trellis. Looking out, I imagined Lucy there busy among the pots with a trowel and gardening gloves, but she had not been present for me in any of the other rooms. She wouldn't have cared for this house, so much pretentiousness crammed into a little space. No, Lucy would have been in her element upstairs in the attics smelling of turpentine and linseed oil, busy with her soul-healing pictures.

The third locked door yielded up a morning-room converted to a gentlemen's smoker. Nothing feminine remained among the dark leather chairs worn to pale streaks by legs carelessly flung over arms, and tipsily hung hunting prints against blotched wallpaper. I remembered then that Lucy's writing-desk had been set up in her bedroom, leaving this little snug as alien territory.

A brown leather chesterfield was wedged along the shorter wall at a jutting angle. Elsewhere the arrangement had an empty space and its incongruity struck me. I pulled the chesterfield forward and its wheels fouled a hidden edge of carpet where a piece had been cut away. Behind where the chesterfield had stood there were arcs of stain thrown across the wallpaper, dark brown shading into near-black.

This was where the killing had taken place. The missing stretch of carpet would have been taken by the police to match against the blood of the cadaver. And, as I had foreseen, Mrs Pearce had failed to arrange for a charwoman to clean off the wall.

The downstairs cloakroom, which also contained a plumbed iron bath, had a few outer garments hanging from a hook-board, and a cupboard containing a single pair of men's town shoes. Julian had had dapper tastes. A velvet-collared overcoat too was of good quality, as it should be with his experience of outfitting.

Just the kitchen remained to be searched, and because Mrs Pearce made do upstairs, little appeared to have been changed here since her employers had left. There were even up-ended saucepans left to drain in the sink after the daily girl had washed up. A dresser held almost a full service of Meissen chinaware and on top of a table was a quantity of polished silver which had never been put away. I counted cutlery for seven. The last meal prepared here had been a formal one with guests. I would need to find out who was present and whether Lucy had been of their number.

It seemed I'd learned nothing of value from my clandestine visit; but rather than be downhearted I continued patiently to search. And finally, on a high shelf, I found a cardboard box sealed with string.

Standing on a stool I observed that the lid was clean although on the shelf where it stood dust was thick enough to write your name in. I lifted the box down and cut the string through with a kitchen knife. Then I took out the contents and lined the little bottles up along the draining-board.

There was no need to remove the corks and sniff. To a medical man it was clear from the scrawls on their labels what they contained: among them iodine, ether, laudanum and morphine. Which Mrs Pearce would have made good use of, delivering the baby and keeping Lucy in a semi-comatose state until she could be transported elsewhere in the company of the man she'd awoken to discover dead.

So had that been Huggett? But if so, Mrs Pearce couldn't have been involved in his later death, because she'd been muttering what she'd do to him when she caught up with him. And if she didn't know where he had ended up, who did? Apart from the luckless Lucy?

It was clear that the next thing I must look for was the squalid house near Covent Garden where Lucy had finally returned to consciousness.

# Twelve

Next morning I was up early, determined to make good use of the last full day left before I must return to Stakerleys. Tomorrow was the Earl's eighty-fifth birthday and my absence would be remarked on.

From the university office I borrowed a map of central London which was used in checking student lodgings. Then, dressed roughly and wearing a stout pair of walking boots, I set out to scour the neighbourhood of Covent Garden. Having questioned Lucy closely about the area where she had regained consciousness I had hopes of eventually locating the house. Whatever her drugged condition had been until then, it seemed that once properly awake she had been painfully aware of every detail around her, observing with an artist's eye.

I started from the market itself and identified a doorway like the one where she had spent the night with her new companion, Mabel. From there I could see the portico of the church. It checked with the direction Lucy had described. So far so good, but beyond that point I had a choice of three hundred and sixty degrees to work outwards, with no clue as to which street to follow.

It was unlikely that anyone here among the already milling crowds of porters and buyers would remember a woman and baby who had taken temporary shelter days ago. Even at this hour of the morning there were vagrants still haunting the place and no one gave them a second glance.

But Mabel, having lost a child of her own, had been specially aware of Lucy because of the baby. Of course I should have spoken to her before this. It was possible she could have helped in my search.

In Maiden Lane I noticed the doors to Rules restaurant ajar and

154

a sound of whistling as two young men briskly set about preparing the dining rooms for luncheon. "Sorry, sir," one began as my shadow fell over them, then he saw the guinea in my hand.

"Telephone?" I asked. "I have a brief inquiry to make to a country number near Aylesbury."

The two youngsters looked at each other. One rubbed his hand down his aproned thigh. The other took the coin and examined it carefully. "I'll have a see," he offered.

He disappeared briefly to put his head round an interior door and beckon me in. "Best be nippy," he said. "His nibs is due back in five minutes. Jest gorn to order the veggies."

I was fortunate in having Hadrill's assistant take the call since the old man's faulty hearing would have made a long-drawn business of it. Even then it appeared that the household boasted two Mabels and Lucy's nursemaid was barely known to the senior footman.

At length she was on the line, breathless and nervous, but with her wits about her. "Yes, sir, I did see her arrive," she was able to tell me. "She came into Henrietta Street out of Bedford Street, but I've no idea where she was before that."

"Thank you, Mabel. That's probably saved me hours of searching. I'd be grateful if you don't mention this conversation to your mistress until I've seen her again. By which time I hope to have some useful information for her."

"Very good, sir. I'll be really mum, sir."

I stepped back into the sunshine and headed south towards the Embankment. Mindful that Lucy said she'd gone alternately right and left and had crossed a broad, brightly lit street with considerable traffic, I guessed she must have come from somewhere in that jumble of narrow ways near Villiers Street.

Once I'd crossed the Strand the smart vehicles disappeared and ancient buildings huddled close. I felt I almost smelled the place Lucy had spoken of, yet there were so many crowded little houses almost identically wretched. On my left a cafe window shrouded by grubby net curtains displayed a handwritten card with the single ill-spelt word "Breckfasts". I pushed the door open, entered to the tinkle of a bell and ordered tea with kippers and brown bread.

There were eight or nine men in there seated at padded benches against the walls, elbows on tables among the crockery. It could have been a country inn the way all conversation ended as the stranger came in. I was conscious of watchful eyes taking in every detail of my dress and I was glad I'd chosen an old collarless blue shirt with a faded handkerchief choker. These worthies would shut up like clams with anyone they thought was police, and I might need to ask questions. The only trouble was: what questions? I bent to the business of boning my kippers and noisily slurping the strong tea.

Gradually the growling conversations resumed, the scraping and filling of stale pipes, punctuated by assenting grunts or argumentative protests. And in the end I had no need to ask anything because the weasely little man at the next rickety table had a copy of the morning paper and suddenly exploded, "Ere, there's a bit in 'ere about that dead bloke."

In London there were dead blokes aplenty, as my morgue visits proved, but the chances were that this was a local one.

"They got the woman what done 'im?"

"Nah. Jest the perlice are followin' a new line of hinquiry. Some 'opes. It's poked away 'ere in the corner. If they was reelly on to somethink it'd be on the front page."

"I reckon that's the last we'll 'ear of it," said his companion. "Pore ol' bugger nobody's gonna miss."

I vainly searched my pockets for shillings but had to get change for another guinea, thanked the wizened grandfather by the till and went out to clear my lungs of the smoke-laden atmosphere. There was a boy selling newpapers on the corner of the Strand and I bought a copy of the one they'd been reading in the cafe. At the foot of page five I found a short paragraph about the body found twelve days back at a house in Cuts Alley.

The police claim of a new line of inquiry sounded vague to say the least. I doubted the report was anything more than a journalist's attempt to fill an empty space. But the gem of information it did give was the dead man's name: Hugh Jarrett. Not Huggett, but not a long way off it either. It might of course be someone totally unconnected with Lucy, but if you were called

Hugh Jarrett and didn't want that fact widely known, wouldn't Huggett be a handy sort of alternative?

In Charing Cross station I waited for a public telephone to come free and rang the number of Professor Garland's office. His secretary answered. "Mrs Pettifer," I begged, "I wonder if you would do me a great favour?"

"Of course, Dr Malcolm, you've only to ask. If it's in my power, that is."

There was neither a Huggett nor a Jarrett among the cadavers the Professor had worked on for the past two weeks. So it appeared that Dr Peabody must have dealt with this case too, unless it had progressed no farther than a confirmation of death given on the scene by the police surgeon.

"Would you like me to pursue it?" the motherly lady offered. "I usually find the police quite helpful when I check on inquests. Let me try. I'll leave any results for you downstairs with the porter."

Cuts Alley was close by the arches under the railway lines as they ran out to cross the Thames, but as the newspaper had mentioned no number it was left to me to identify the house.

"You wanna look out," a man shouted as he passed with a bundle of copper pipes bouncing over one shoulder, and as I stepped back I barely missed a basinful of slops thrown from an upper window. A sad stream of brown water and potato peel trickled to join the rest of the ordure in the gutter. I looked up to confront an impish-faced woman grinning down on me.

"Is this the house the murder was at?" I asked impulsively.

"Not yet it ain't, but there's always 'ope," the woman replied with feeling, then burst into laughter at her own wit. "My ole man's ripe for it any day 'e comes 'ome the way 'e did larse nigh'." She leaned confidentially over the sill. "Wot murder's that then? You doan mean ol' Jarrett, do you? That wasn't no murder. Them newspipers got it all wrong as usual. Always stirring up trouble, they are."

"What happened to him?"

"You wanna come in, ducks, and I'll tell you all abaht i'."

I grinned back. "Maybe I'm safer out here."

She screeched cheerfully again. "It was 'is lungs. Awful state they was in. Got hisself gassed in the war, poor devil. E'd bin warned, but 'e musta overdone it. Been workin' for some toff up west, or so we 'eard. Then suddenly 'e's brought 'ome some fancy woman and 'er kid. Coupla days later 'e got took bad and when 'e started coughing up blood she upped and scarpered. They found 'im stretched out stiff on the bedroom floor. Only thirty-nine 'e was, but they all went young, them Jarretts. All 'ad great big muscles, but rotten right through inside."

It didn't bother her that she'd already laid blame at the door of the Germans. But I was inclined to believe her version of the death rather than the stabbing Lucy had served up. Lucy's mind was confused, and as victim of past violence she'd assumed too much at sight of the blood.

Whether the state of Jarrett's lungs was partly inherited or a direct consequence of gassing, in this quarter of London it would have been readily accepted as a natural consumptive death, a disease the Public Health authorities were at pains to eliminate. With no family to consult, and little possibility of payment for the services, a coroner could understandably have dispensed with the costs of inquest or post-mortem.

"So where was he buried?" I asked my informant.

"Oh, there wasn't no funeral. Nobody to pay for it, see? Council dustcart, I guess." She squawked again. Accustomed to the black humour of some of my terminal patients, I recognised the cheerful despair of those totally without means or family. She would take no thought for her own body after death because she was fully taken up with keeping it in one piece in life. I held up a florin which had come in my change from the cafe. Anything more would have made her suspicious. "Thanks for your help," I told her. "I'll leave it on the doorstep."

There was no doubt in my mind where the body would have gone, and might still be, at least in part. The fate of vagrants and debtors was to end on the slab of a dissecting room at the probing hands of students such as I had once been. The question was which teaching faculty had claimed Jarrett: Charing Cross or King's College farther up the Strand.

When I finally ran the body to earth, or rather to table, I found that although the lower limbs had already been removed and the neck opened from behind the right ear almost to the clavicle with its intricacies exposed, it was possible to lay the triangular flap of skin back and the face appeared almost untouched. A member of the Anatomy Department staff provided me with a camera, and I took away with me three plates which, exposed, could settle whether the dead man was indeed Huggett or not.

Again I was indebted to Professor Garland's forensic science department for development of the photographs. That evening, with copies of profile and full face, I returned to my new lodgings and prepared to interview Mrs Pearce with the gloves off.

To wash away the dust and distresses of the day I took a bath in the downstairs cloakroom. As I shivered, sponging on the cold water – the geyser refusing to function – I thought of Lucy in this cramped space. Where my hands stank of formaldehyde hers would have carried traces of the pigment, turpentine and linseed oil which she'd used in her painting. Hardly romantic, yet I caught myself picturing the delectable outline of her naked silhouette against the white-tiled wall.

I envisaged difficulties in approaching her with my findings. They could only increase her grief even while they eased her sense of guilt. She would need great courage to get through the next few days without regressing further into the defences of amnesia.

But before then I must tackle Mrs Pearce, and in her case I must be brutal, finesse being useless. I wondered how deep her feelings for Huggett could have been – her gentleman friend, as she'd called him.

Lying half-submerged, I reviewed the little I knew of the man: de Verville's servant, meant to accompany Lucy when she rode, but in the later days probably accepting her payment to stay away.

Had he always gone drinking as the newsagent supposed, or did curiosity compel him to follow and see where she went, discover with whom she had made a rendezvous? I believed that was what he had done, and that he'd carried back news of his discovery to his master. So at what point had de Verville revealed to Lucy that he knew about her lover? And what had happened then?

By Lucy's own admission she had drawn blood, taking her riding crop to belabour her husband's face and hands. Yet shouldn't the other way about have been more expected – the husband beating the faithless wife? So had de Verville managed to restrain his anger at that point, out of consideration that the child was almost due – the child he might still believe to be his own?

Perhaps he had known he could do her more damage with his tongue. He had threatened . . . Yes, that was when Lucy's mind snapped. That was when she had lost control and Mrs Pearce had heard her screaming that she would kill him. Because of what he threatened to do. Or had already done.

It was just after that that Lucy's memory had been wiped away.

I thought I understood now, but I still couldn't see what part Huggett had been meant to play later.

Strange how often surnames had been changed. These labels we carry; how crucial they are to how others see us. It is a reflection on modern society.

There was my own, altered by deed poll to please my kind guardian, although it still left me uneasy to have slighted my dead father in this. Then from early childhood Lucy had chafed under her stepfather's surname instead of the Italian Gabrieli which was apparently her birthright. And thirdly her husband had faked a new name for himself out of snobbery, because he was ashamed of his humble background and had social ambitions. He had chosen a Norman name with a hint of nobility. And, overloaded with wartime preoccupations, a good regiment had accepted it unquestioned.

But Jarrett? A servant and a social nobody: why had he needed an alias, unless he was a known criminal? Huggett was the assumed name, because didn't his neighbours remember him as one of the Jarrett family? All muscles, but rotten inside, the woman had said of them.

So had Jarrett taken a new name to deceive de Verville, or Mrs Pearce, or both, or someone else? I had a strange feeling that the dead man was somehow at the centre of the murder mystery, and the only way I could get to resolve it would be through the only remaining person capable of remembering.

Mrs Pearce was vital to my quest. I must confront her boldly, show her the morgue photographs and, while she was off-balance, demand to know who the dead man was.

Because of my investigations I had forgotten to eat at midday. Now I visited the nearby pie shop again and brought back sufficient for two. This time there was no drink. I didn't want the woman falling back on Dutch courage.

The aroma of hot steak and kidney brought her to the door of her sitting-room. I laid down the wrapped offering.

"Brought some grub in," I said matily. "Enough for us both for supper. But first there's something I want you to look at." I placed the two photographs side by side on her table.

There was no doubt about her reaction. "Why it's . . ." she began, then stopped open-mouthed. One hand went to her ample bosom as she took in the closed eyes and grim features. "Oh my gawd, my gawd! E's dead, ain't 'e?"

"I'm afraid so. It's your friend Huggett, isn't it?"

"Silly bastard, I warned 'im. I said there was sumpthink wrong about it. People don't give you a fortune for nothink, but 'e was so cocksure, thought the world was gonna be 'is oyster. Well, 'e never lived to get it, did 'e? So what'll 'appen to all that money now, then?"

"Heaven only knows," I sympathised, hiding my puzzlement. "But are you sure he never got it?"

"Well, 'ow could 'e? She ain't dead yet, is she? And not likely to be for bloody years if she gets off scot-free." Momentarily forgetful who I was, she was letting slip more than was wise of her plottings with Huggett.

I saw my knuckles whiten on the food wrappings, but I held on to my anger and began to look around for plates. As yet the woman seemed unaware that she had given herself away. Her first concern was one of greed. It hadn't even occurred to her to ask how "Huggett" had died.

I turned to find her eyeing me narrowly. "'Ow did you come by them photos?"

"I told you. I'm a medical student. The body turned up at the morgue and I recognised the name," I lied.

Fortunately she seemed to accept that and reached for a chair to sink back on. "Lor', I'm knocked all of a heap."

161

"He was a rather special friend, I think. It's been a terrible shock for you, Mrs Pearce," I sympathised.

"I need a drink," she said scrabbling to stand again. "I suppose you 'aven't . . . ?"

"A bottle? I'm afraid not."

"Neh mind. I got one put away. For celebrating like. Well, there won't be no need for that now." She went across to a low cupboard, knelt and removed some tins to retrieve a bottle of rum from behind them. "This is what 'e liked best. Not what I go for meself, but it was goin' to be a treat for 'im, when 'e got back."

So she had known he was to be away. But had she known he had Lucy in his care (if continual narcosis could be described as "care")? Almost certainly, since Mrs Pearce had been the source of the drugs the man was using. But she had expected him back before now, else why those muttered threats of yesterday? Whatever should have triggered off his return had never happened, and his morphine supplies for Lucy had been running low. Which was how she began recovering her senses while he suffered his final haemorrhage from the lungs.

"It was tuberculosis he died from," I said sombrely. "Did you realise he was so ill?"

"Knew 'e'd got TB," she grumbled. "'E was coughing up blood a week or two back. We knew it would 'appen. Jest a matter of time. Only 'e wasn't supposed to snuff it so quick."

*We*, I thought. So I must revise my first idea of Pearce and Huggett in control, to a plot with "Huggett" playing a crucial part but finally expendable. So much for Mrs Pearce's supposed fondness for the man!

"So it leaves you in a bit of a pickle," I suggested mildly. "If there's to be no money, I mean."

Mrs Pearce sat slumped at the table, brooding. "Mebbe. Mebbe not." She drained her glass and reached to pour another.

I continued to unpack the pies and allowed their succulence to tempt her nostrils. "Can't be helped, I suppose. Here, Mrs P, let's eat up. You've got to keep your strength up. You can't be expected to guess what would happen."

"No, I couldn't. But it makes you wonder if 'e did."

The way she emphasised the word made it clear she didn't mean the dead man. I felt I was missing something here. "So what's to be done?"

Mrs Pearce waddled across the room, pulled two plates from a rack and plonked them on the table with a handful of cutlery. "That remains to be seen," she said as if to herself. "Only all I know is it's me wot's got the upper 'and still."

"How's that then?"

She stared at me with little, embedded blackcurrant eyes, her mouth pursed in mean triumph. "Well, there's only me knows where 'er will is."

We ate without more ado, both occupied with our private thoughts, but I felt the savoury pie would stick in my gullet.

*"Her" will*: that must mean Lucy's. She was expected to die, presumably at the hangman's hands for the murder of her husband. And someone – the dead "Huggett"? – was supposed to benefit as legatee.

It was as though the woman could read my mind. "To my devoted servant, Samuel 'Uggett," she jeered, gulping again at the rum, "all the residue of my estate."

"But he can't inherit. He's dead," I reminded her.

"Well, is 'e? *Is 'e*?"

I didn't understand any of it; especially since the woman was assuming Lucy had a fortune to leave, which she hadn't. Apart from her effects in this house and a few paintings at Stakerleys, Lucy hadn't any estate to speak of.

Then I remembered: she would come of age next year. And British criminal justice, like the mills of God, ground slowly.

Lucy could inherit from her grandfather before she was found guilty and sentenced – once the old man had died. The elderly, paralysed Earl, who was powerless to defend himself.

It was suddenly imperative that I should return to Stakerleys at once.

# Thirteen

M y train was due in at Great Missenden at 9.30 a.m., but even as Forbes drove out of Stakerleys' main gates to collect me a black saloon had approached and turned in. The chauffeur had a swift glimpse of a uniformed driver with a flat cap and two dark-suited men in the rear.

Like all the staff at Stakerleys he was aware of the threat still hanging over Miss Lucy since her husband's murder. The return of the county police could only mean further shocks for the family.

The London train was three minutes late pulling in, and by then Forbes was fuming that further delay might prevent his getting back to the house before disaster struck. What disaster was uncertain, nor was it clear how he might help to divert it, but he felt frustrated, torn between performing a mundane duty and an urge to protect.

The chauffeur's greeting as I swung out of the train was as warm as ever but I detected some strain in his manner. "Have all the guests arrived for the celebration?" I asked.

"You're the last, sir. The London company arrived yesterday morning, and Mrs Fellowes from St Leonards in the evening."

"Good." I looked across at him. There was certainly something disturbing the man. He seemed torn between habitual discretion and a compulsion to unburden himself. After a moment's hesitation he added, "And on my way here I just passed some uninvited visitors." He closed his lips firmly on the words. Maybe it was out of order, but since I always chose to ride alongside him instead of in the back, perhaps he felt it put us on more equal terms.

"Uninvited? Who then?"

"Inspector Cummins and a colleague, I think, sir."

"How far ahead of us are they?"

"Twenty minutes, sir. Maybe a little less."

"Let's hope they're being kept waiting. Can you step on it, Forbes? I need to beat them to it."

The Daimler leapt forward as Forbes' spirits seemed to rise, secure in the belief now that he'd been right to speak out of turn.

On our arrival the police were still with Viscount Crowthorne in the study, since Hadrill had considered it proper to keep them cooling their heels a while before his master was informed.

"Lady Crowthorne? Mrs de Verville?" I asked.

"The ladies are still at breakfast, sir. There is a place laid for you. I'll have Jolly take your bag."

"Would you ask Lady Crowthorne if I might have a word with her in private first?"

At least the women hadn't been alerted to the officers' presence, unless word had reached them through the lesser servants, but I couldn't risk Eugenie's learning all the grim details in one burst without some prior warning. At least I could ensure she knew as much as Lucy did, before there were further revelations.

If Hadrill found the request strange he gave no indication. "Very good, sir. Would you care to wait in the smoking-room? There are some callers in the study, sir."

"So I understand."

The old man's eyes met mine briefly and his voice quavered slightly as he said, "I'll fetch her ladyship at once."

"Clive," Eugenie cried in delight on coming in. "Why such secrecy? Hadrill wouldn't say who my visitor was."

I kissed her cheek and kept her hand in mine. "I needed to speak to you for a moment alone."

She leaned back to scan my face, recognising the seriousness in my voice. "Is it about Julian?"

"Do you know, then?"

"I could see something was very wrong with Lucy. I was afraid she and Julian had fallen out and decided to part, so I asked your guardian whether he had any knowledge of it."

"And what did the Bishop tell you?"

"That they had parted, quite finally. I didn't understand at first, then he explained, gently of course, that Julian was dead, viciously killed by some unknown hand. Poor Lucy, she's being so brave. And because she hadn't told me herself I felt I didn't dare mention it until she was ready. But what news is there?"

"It's complicated," I said. "Since you know the bare bones of it now, I think everyone should be together to hear what I've just found out. I may have been forestalled by the police themselves. I understand they're with your husband at this moment. Let's warn Lucy they're here, so that everyone is prepared."

We joined Lucy at the breakfast table and I was grateful we should be uninterrupted, all the guests enjoying tables set up in their rooms.

"I thought you'd deserted us," Lucy accused me.

"You knew I would be back. I'd promised you."

"I don't set great store by promises." She was being deliberately awkward but I knew she wished to punish me for my absence. Perhaps that was encouraging in a way, but time-wasting, a quibble which at present we couldn't indulge in.

"Lucy, there are some policemen with your papa. Exactly what they've come about I'm not sure, but it may be in connection with some facts I've unearthed in London over the past three days. Or it may be on account of their own investigations, but I think you should be warned . . ."

The door from the hall opened abruptly and I was too late. The three men stood there unannounced. Frowning, Lord Crowthorne motioned the other two forward. "Eugenie, Lucy, these gentlemen are from the Buckinghamshire police force: Inspector Cummins and Sergeant Watt. Clive, my boy, it's good to see you again."

He turned to the two policemen. "Gentlemen, you may have met my wife and daughter. May I present Dr Clive Malcolm, a friend of the family."

"A pleasure, sir," said the Inspector, dismissing the women with a single glance and a nod, then advancing on me with pursed lips and a fiercely bristling moustache. "Heard a great deal about you, Dr Malcolm. Seems you've been setting a cat among the pigeons for our colleagues up in London."

"I take it the Metropolitan Police have been in touch."

166

"They have indeed."

"You're very prompt to act on their information."

"Strike while the iron's hot, sir. An admirable motto, to my mind." At last Cummins took stock of the two women and fixed his gaze on Lucy. "I take it I am addressing Mrs de Verville, ma'am?"

"Yes." Her voice was little above a whisper.

"You must be congratulated, ma'am. You have some good friends. Or one special one at least. Doubtless you've been told by Dr Malcolm himself what he's found out about the matter you were earlier questioned on."

Eugenie, alarmed by the man's suggestive tone, moved forward between them. "Inspector, Sergeant, please sit down. Let us all be comfortable and civilised. It seems there's quite a long story to come out. One I've only lately learned of."

Cummins rocked on his heels, the centre of everyone's attention. "It needn't take all that long, milady. You see, the long and the short of it is—"

"—that Lucy can't be accused of murdering her husband," I put in tersely, "because he isn't dead at all."

"Lucy?" Eugenie demanded shrilly. "How could Lucy ever be suspected . . . ? But Julian not dead. The Bishop told me that he was. Clive, just a moment ago you let me go on thinking that. I don't understand at all."

"I'm sorry," I had to admit. "I'd hoped to sort this out a little better in my own time, but these gentlemen have called my hand. Perhaps I should leave them to explain everything." I broke off as Hadrill entered, followed by a footman with fresh tea, hot rolls and crockery for the newcomers.

With a show of unimpressed stolidity the inspector allowed himself to be seated at the table while nodding his sergeant to remain at his back. "Now ma'am," he addressed Eugenie. "Milady, that is. Without distressing you ladies with the unpleasant details, I have to report that a second post-mortem on the body of the supposed Julian de Verville has caused the Metropolitan Police to revise their original opinion."

"So there *is* a body?" Eugenie asked faintly. "Someone was actually murdered?"

"That is so, milady."

"But it has to be Julian," Lucy said abruptly. "Mrs Pearce, the housekeeper, identified him."

"You will remember, ma'am, that the car was set fire to. It was not possible to identify the dead person in it from his facial features. The housekeeper did, however, recognise certain articles found with the body, namely his dress ring, watch . . ." Cummins hesitated, reaching in his breast pocket for papers of confirmation.

"And cufflinks," I supplied.

"And cufflinks," Cummins echoed.

"The cornelian ring?" Lucy queried. "He would never take it off. He thought it was lucky, because he'd won it at cards. Though it didn't seem to be very effective."

"He was lucky enough on this occasion," the Inspector insisted with grim humour, "inasmuch as it wasn't him got murdered."

"Then who . . . ?" Viscount Crowthorne demanded, seeming at last to come out of a daze.

"That we don't yet know, my lord. But doubtless the Metropolitan force are pursuing that question at this very moment."

"Are you saying that Julian – my husband – is still alive?" Lucy clutched at the table edge.

"Exactly that, ma'am. And if any of you has any doubt about the body not being his, I'll leave it to the medical gentleman here to explain how we know."

They all turned to face me. "Very simply," I said, "no one had thought to inform the surgeon who performed the first postmortem that de Verville had an artificial left hand. Despite the state of the body it was clear that the dead man had had both intact."

"This raises some very disturbing possibilities," said Crowthorne grimly, "which would be better considered elsewhere."

"No." Lucy put out a hand to detain the Inspector who had begun to rise. "If the body wore those things of Julian's, either they were taken from him by force or—"

"Or he was a party to the deceit," Cummins nodded. "And if that was the case, why hasn't he come forward since to refute the suspicions levelled against his wife?

168

"It is the opinion of the Metropolitan Police, ladies and gentlemen, that Mr de Verville was most probably responsible for the killing, and intended the full blame to fall squarely on the lady and so save his own neck."

"But now Lucy is entirely exonerated," Eugenie breathed with relief.

"Unless, milady, it can be proved that she was an accessory before or after the fact. Acting in collusion, as it might be. In which case it will be made much clearer when the villain is apprehended and can make a statement on the matter."

"When it will be his word against mine," Lucy said in disgust. "I can tell you now: I know nothing of this murder or of my husband's low-life companions. For a moment just then I believed I was cleared of all suspicion, but it seems if you can't reach the real culprit you will make the most of anyone you can."

She rose spiritedly. "Mama, Papa, Clive, please excuse me. I've heard enough of this." And darting a scornful glance at the senior policeman, she left the room.

When the Inspector and his shadow had driven off it left the family in disarray. "I don't know what to advise," the Viscount apologised. "I've been away too long. You should have told me how serious things had become. I feel this is partly my fault. Clive, it is you we must thank for this latest development, I believe. Really I find it difficult to see whether you bring more good news than bad. Is there any comfort you can give, since apparently Julian's survival is small matter for rejoicing."

"Exactly, sir. And I must emphasise how important it is now that Mrs de Verville should be offered every available measure of protection. Also Earl Sedgwick, because to my mind he is possibly another intended victim of the same vicious plot."

"My father? How on earth is he involved?"

So I explained as far as I could how Huggett, otherwise Hugh Jarrett, had figured in the case. "As de Verville's man he was almost certainly implicated in the murder which actually took place at the house in Fulham, before the car 'accident' was rigged.

"So far I've been unable to discover where Lucy was at the time. It is even possible that she overheard or glimpsed something

169

of what was going on. The shock of it, together with the injury to her head, could account for her amnesia.

"When the police arrested her following Mrs Pearce's accusation that she overheard a quarrel and Lucy threatening to kill her husband, she was traumatised and incapable of making a coherent statement. They were eventually obliged to let her go, for lack of evidence.

"Lucy returned to the house and went into labour soon after, which provided an excuse to keep her heavily sedated and unaware of what was going on. The housekeeper, who was a one-time nurse, acted as midwife, and the child was delivered safely.

"It rests with the police to find out what happened next, but we know that only a matter of days later Lucy woke up in the house where the servant Huggett lodged, her mind much clearer since the man's supply of drugs had apparently dried up. The baby was healthy but subdued, since she also had been semi-comatose through ingesting her mother's milk. The man Huggett addressed Lucy by name so that at least she remembered who she was and her recent trouble with the police; but nothing else he said made sense to her. He died, of natural causes, shortly after.

"Because he had suffered a severe pulmonary haemorrhage and Lucy had somehow come in contact with the blood she wrongly assumed he had been stabbed and that suspicion must again fall on her. She took the child and, frail as she was, fled the place, encountered Mabel who befriended her, and eventually reached the sanctuary of your Belgravia house. The rest, sir, you will have heard from Edwin."

"This is quite appalling. But my father, what is the danger to him that you spoke of?"

"The motive is one of financial greed. I understand that Lucy was to benefit from her grandfather's will, equally with her half-brothers?"

"A third of the unentailed part of his estate, shared with Edwin and poor Rupert. That was so originally. Recently the will has been amended so that she receives exactly a half of the money set apart from the entailed estate."

"And a will exists – whether forged or with a signature

extracted under duress – which purports to be Lucy's. It leaves everything she owns to her 'faithful and devoted servant Samuel Huggett'. I believe that with Lucy a supposed widow there would be no challenge to such a will."

Eugenie looked puzzled. "Except on behalf of her child. But there would be little enough for Lucy to leave, beyond her paintings and a few personal effects. She told me she had used her allowance to the full and it would cease immediately on her death."

"I think you will find it was Julian who used it to the full, with considerable debts to be settled and many still outstanding."

Viscount Crowthorne looked grim. "Indeed? She should have confided in me. I would have made an alternative arrangement for her."

I waved a dismissive hand. "that is history now, sir. But it is crucial that she should revoke the false will by signing a new one as quickly as possible. Otherwise I could fear for her life. And for her baby's."

Eugenie made a gesture of repugnance. "I cannot believe—"

"Oh, believe, your ladyship. We are dealing with a man who has murdered once and would find it easier a second time. Lucy was intended to be a victim at the law's hands, hanged for the supposed murder of her husband. Since it's now impossible, thank God, a further plan must be activated against her."

"But if this man Huggett's dead, how can he still threaten her?" Eugenie demanded.

"He was only a pawn in the game. His real name was Jarrett, and I believe he invented the other to pass on to his master. Julian de Verville, assumed dead, would adopt the new identity and so in due course inherit from his 'master's widow'. And I dread to think how the child's rights would be dealt with. It's true that de Verville wouldn't be satisfied with the little that Lucy has to leave at present. It was intended that she should inherit from her grandfather before her execution."

"That's hideous! How could the man be so evil and we never suspected?"

"Not even Lucy dreamed of treachery like this, and she'd few illusions left. The truth is that evil can grow like moss, gradually, and no one ever thinks to measure exactly how far it's reached."

The viscount turned back from the window where he had stood with lowered head and fists clenched against his sides. "The man must be found at once. He'll have no idea that Lucy's been warned he's alive. He could strike at any time against either her or my father. We must protect them both."

"We've no clue to where he might be lying up," I said. "But something Mrs Pearce let out makes me sure he must return to the Fulham house. She either holds, or knows the whereabouts of, the will with Lucy's supposed signature. De Verville will need to get his hands on it when he's set himself up as the new Huggett, and I'd swear the woman won't let him get away with it unless she receives a partner's share of the benefits. Which puts her too in danger, because the man has gone too far by now to tolerate any opposition.

"I've informed the London police of the situation. They were reluctant at first to believe me, but they have agreed to set a man to keep watch on the house from one across the road. And as soon as I have had a private word with Lucy and paid my respects to his lordship I shall return there, where I've been lodging for the past three days."

"We can't let you take that risk. Leave it to the police at that end, and we will get someone experienced to keep an eye on things down here."

"There's no risk in it. The woman trusts me. Believe me, I can be impressively devious and deceptive myself when the need arises. But there is one thing I would ask of you both."

"Anything at all," Eugenie promised fervently.

"I have further distressing news for Lucy. It concerns the man who was left for dead in place of de Verville. He was a close friend of hers, someone she has secretly loved for years, from before her marriage; but she believed him killed in the war."

"How can you be sure it was he, if the body's face was so badly disfigured by burns?"

"In the same way that we were able to eliminate de Verville. Through his war wounds. The first man from his missing hand; the other by a severe injury to the spine which had left him a cripple in a wheelchair. I believe that de Verville was informed of this man's existence and that Lucy was clandestinely meeting him. De Verville feared she would leave him, and his source of income would dry up, so he laid plans to prevent it.

"Somehow he must have tricked his victim into visiting the house, perhaps by an urgent request written in what appeared to be Lucy's hand. There he chose his opportunity and struck. The man was attacked from behind as he sat helpless in his wheelchair: a coward's crime, and one Lucy will grieve over all her life.

"But now I must break this sad news to her. Will you go to her when I leave? Will you help her to get through the day at her grandfather's side and be there if she finds it all too much?"

Eugenie's eyes had filled with tears. "Is there no end to this suffering? My poor darling. Of course we will be there for her. But take care, Clive. None of us would be able to bear it if anything happened to you as well."

I was told later that Eugenie found Lucy with Mabel and the baby. "It's time I spent more time with your little namesake," Lucy had said with false gaiety. "Poor Mabel. Do you know, Mama, that she was up half the night walking the floor with my wailing child. Colic, she says, and indeed there are the most alarming gurglings going on inside. You wouldn't believe it. Anyway I'm insisting Mabel should go and lie down. We can manage quite well ourselves, can't we?"

"Certainly we can. Off you go, Mabel, and rest. Baby has a bonnet on, so we'll take her a promenade round the gardens in her carriage. But first, Lucy, Clive would like a quick word with you. I'm afraid he has to return to London by the mid-day train."

"How very disagreeable of him. I'm not sure I want to have a word with him however quick. And what word anyway? Honestly, I never thought we should find that he'd been in league with the police."

"He has been at great pains to help us, Lucy. How dare you be so ungrateful."

"Should I thank him for finding out my husband's still alive?" She shuddered theatrically.

"Alive and still a danger to us all. Remember that. And but

for the proof Clive has insisted on digging out, you could still be a suspect for what that fiendish man has done."

"Oh, I know. I know. I'm sorry, truly, Mama." She seemed to have relented. "But Clive irks me; so sure of himself, so shrewd. It makes me look and feel inadequate."

"Yes, you must find that a quite galling novelty." Eugenie considered her sardonically, then smiled. "I think I discern the true cause of your pique. It's his leaving so soon after he arrived. You see it as a rebuff. Believe me, it's nothing of the sort. His insistence on speaking with you should be proof of that. So tidy yourself up and don't waste either his time or your own. You'll find him in the morning-room."

# LUCY

# Fourteen

I found my hands trembling, which was ridiculous. For one mad moment I was back inside the child in the green plaid dress, standing by the mirror in Mama's boudoir. Her maid was about to discover me in forbidden territory and I had to get rid of the boy.

Why couldn't Clive be some new acquaintance, and not forever reminding me of that long-standing guilt? Admittedly it had been his own idea to escape by the window, but I'd pushed him into it when I shut him behind the curtains. He'd clearly been avoiding trouble for me.

I might have killed him; did actually cause that injury to his leg which still showed at times in a slight limp. Every sighting of him now served to shame me. I wished he would leave me alone.

And yet it infuriated me when he did.

So what was he to vex me with now, that I couldn't have heard in my parents' presence? Wasn't I confused enough, over Julian dead one moment with myself suspected of his killing, and then suddenly everything reversed: Julian very much alive and planning my destruction? Because that was what lay behind the news he'd brought.

And something stirring darkly in my clouded memory was warning me, threatening to emerge and confound me further. Clive had the power to force its recall. A mind-manipulator: I was right to fear him.

I stood outside the door, waiting for my courage to return. Whether he had heard my approach or somehow sensed my waves of apprehension through its panels, it was suddenly open and he was there leading me by the hand over to a sunny window-seat.

He was frighteningly gentle. It made me more fearful and

abrasive. "Do you expect my forgiveness for walking out on me the minute I'd unburdened myself to you?"

"Forgive? There's no cause for either of us to forgive the other. Aren't we friends? Let's just accept each other as we are.

"Lucy, I'm obliged to go back to London immediately. It's essential I should be there when de Verville surfaces. So I must be briefer than I wish in breaking further distressing news to you. You will need to be very brave. It concerns the dead man we took at first for your husband."

A terrible shuddering went through me as though I had known in advance what he must say. And yes, I did. Some part of me had known all along, and I had refused to believe.

"*Peter,*" I said, and the single word seemed to swell in my throat so that I couldn't breathe. The sunlight danced in a million dazzling motes and then was totally eclipsed.

I came to in Clive's arms, the heathery smell of his jacket against my nostrils as he held me close.

"Lie still a moment," he urged as I fought to sit upright. "You must rush nothing now. Just allow your mind to find its own way back."

I hung on, my fingers hooked into him, clinging as though I would drown if I let go. The shuddering went on and on, so that my words were distorted. "I remember," I mumbled.

"I saw him. Dead, in his wheelchair. The awful wound gaping; his face and shoulders covered in fresh blood. In our house. I knew at once that Julian had done it. And then he came in, his shirt sleeves rolled up and his hands still wet from washing. He confronted me, and he laughed. How could I ever have forgotten the way he laughed then? He was evil. A madman."

I pulled myself upright, vibrant now with rising anger. I fought against hysteria to give a rational account.

"It had started as an ordinary day. The baby wasn't due for another three weeks, so I'd gone out riding. But Peter hadn't been in the park where we always met.

"I left my horse in a friend's care and went to his rooms. He wasn't there either. His landlady said he'd taken a cab in a terrible hurry as if some frightful disaster had struck.

"I didn't know what to think. I went home and Huggett tried

to prevent me going indoors, but I pushed past. That's how I – came on it."

"I went for Julian with my riding crop and I got in a few blows before he wrenched it from me. His face was cut and bleeding but his terrible eyes still mocked me. He threw me across the room and my head struck something. The mantelpiece, I think.

"I could hear his voice going on and on, ranting at me, but I couldn't make out the words. And then there was nothing."

Clive nodded. "You fainted. Which was when your mind blanked out, as a result of physical and mental injury. It meant that later, during the police interrogation, you truly could not explain what had happened. And after that, Mrs Pearce kept you befuddled with drugs so that you were never fully conscious; not even of giving birth. Many would think you fortunate in that."

"With drugs? I think you must be right. But Eugenie, my baby – will she have suffered from that? How awful if she should be left affected."

"She isn't, I'm sure. She seems perfectly normal. Perhaps you found her unusually good at first, listless and lethargic, but I've heard what a lusty cry she has now. There's nothing wrong with her at all."

"Only with me, now that such bitter memories have come back."

"You've remembered the worst," Clive said, still holding me. "It's over now."

"Never over. How can I live with it, remembering for always? Oh, Peter! Peter, you never deserved such an end!"

"He couldn't have known," Clive insisted. "He must have been tricked into thinking you were at the house and needed him. The single blow was delivered from behind when he was totally unaware."

"But he's finished. Gone. You can't understand."

"Understand, no. But I can feel the loss with you."

Perhaps in some strange manner he could. I dared then to confess to him a fear I'd refused to face fully before: that Peter had waited only for our child to be born and then—

"Despite our love, and being so often together, it wasn't enough for him," I admitted. "He used to insist he was useless and

179

finished. In a way he thought of himself as already dead. He was just another whom that devilish war had ruined, taken away all his trust in life. The only thing he still believed in was that everything must end in disaster. And all the time I was pouring out my love, offering myself, yet it made no real difference.

"He looked to be the same man I had always loved, but inside there was this terrible blackness eating him away. For a while I believed I could help heal him, but it wasn't to be."

I looked up at Clive's face and thought I saw saw tears in his eyes. "How can I help?" he asked.

I pushed him off me. "Find Julian," I said savagely with my whole heart. "See that he's brought to justice. I want him to suffer all the long delays and humiliations of the law, and finally come face to face with death and know just how wicked he's been. Nothing less will ever burn all the hate out of me."

Clive nodded sombrely. "Lucy, you realise he meant you to be found guilty of his own murder?"

"Yes, I see now he must have. He wished me dead."

"I have to warn you that he may still intend that, even if you're not found guilty of any crime. If we can't catch him in London he may try to get to you here."

"I'll be on my guard, and safe enough anyway with so many friends around to help me. It's you who will be in danger when you go after him. Please take the greatest care."

Out on the sunlit terrace Forbes was standing uneasily by, waiting to drive him to the station, yet Clive still found time to congratulate Grandfather, pass him some little gift and shake the Bishop's hand. Then with a wave for us all he was gone.

My mind was in a turmoil, so many emotions mixed together. And shamefully one was relief. It was as though a great burden had been lifted off my shoulders and I could walk tall again. Or as tall as my five feet three inches allowed. And, you see, I could joke again, feeble though the effort was from lack of practice.

Yet now I knew for sure that Peter was no more. There was this irreplaceable part of myself gone with him, a hideous chasm.

I avoided my mother who was clearly expecting to comfort me, and ran away to the folly. Locked inside I could grieve in private with only the imperfect, forever unfinished, portrait of Peter for company.

When I emerged the midday light dazzled me. In the face of such evil how could the treacherous sky stay so innocently blue?

But then it wasn't my sorrow that mattered. It was Grandfather's day, and nothing must be allowed to spoil it. I tidied myself and went to join his guests.

By late afternoon he had retired and the visitors began to thin in the gardens. Only thirty of us remained for the cold buffet which was arranged to leave the staff free for their own evening celebration in the marquee. As family, Mildred, Geoffrey, Edwin and I did the little serving that was required; then when the village band appeared and struck up we left them to it.

"What a day it's been," Mama whispered, hugging me. "We shall quite understand if you wish to retire early."

But there were still guests to entertain and to distract me from thinking. I must have lived up to my reputation for wildness that night for I romped through every dance and went to bed in the early hours, my head spinning from too much champagne.

Next day I knew that I must get away from Stakerleys and its poignant memories if I was to keep my poor brains together. Grandmama Fellowes had only two more days with us and I decided to escort her back to St Leonards where I could hope for some peace and to catch up with events. It meant leaving little Eugenie behind, but she was in excellent hands, accustomed by now to a bottle, and it was a time when I could barely endure looking at her for seeing Peter in her wide-spaced eyes. I told myself I was not running away from pain, just taking a deep breath before I faced it fully.

Naturally there was opposition to my going, because at Grandmama's I would have less protection if Julian should come seeking me. But I made the point that it was to Stakerleys he'd come first, expecting to find me, and there the police could arrest him. We had visited St Leonards only once together shortly after we married, and it would never occur to him that I'd choose to stay there with my straitlaced grandmother.

So, accepting the proviso that I should take a companion, I

invited Mrs Langrish who was now retired and lived in Aylesbury. Her little encephalitic son had died in the previous year and she shared a cottage with her widowed mother who was quite capable of caring for herself when left alone.

The wretched older son had soon tired of the sparse rewards his painting brought in and was now a potter working somewhere in Devon. Mrs Langrish spoke of him with fond pride, as if totally forgetful of how distasteful I must find any mention of him at all.

She had aged since losing Barty. All her sharp edges seemed to have been rounded off and blurred. She was forgetful at times and soon tired physically, so I was confident she would opt out of the cliff walks we had enjoyed before. The prospect of long half-days on my own comforted me.

Papa wanted Forbes to stay on with us, but I insisted he should return by train and I would retain the Lanchester for our own use, having accustomed myself to driving it at Stakerleys. Since Mama too had long been a competent driver she was able to persuade him, adding that it would keep my mind occupied if nothing more, and there were two other motors at home for family use.

Grandmama Fellowes had not mellowed with age. Where Mrs Langrish had softened she had sharpened, a commoner who increasingly acted the duchess on the strength of her only daughter joining the aristocracy. Twice weekly she held a little court of her own attended mainly by card-playing local widowed ladies who discussed servants interminably and revered her edicts concerning dress.

It never occurred to her that her own career as a successful tailoress could permanently set her on a lower rung in the social hierarchy. I found it droll that she chose never to mention Grandfather's onetime profession of master printer, deeming it somehow more vulgar. However, I seconded her robust assumption that in the present climate almost anyone could climb to great heights through competence and will-power alone. It was a post-war novelty gradually taking off, but Grandmama seemed to have assumed it from birth, at least in the case of her own connections.

I was determined to throw myself wholeheartedly into Sussex

seaside life, or at least convince others I did so while keeping my tears for private moments.

On the sea front, near the foot of London Road, was a quite splendid ladies' hairdressing saloon from which intriguing scents escaped as we passed. I observed the ladies who sailed out, elegant as Egyptian deities, with bobbed or shingled heads under cloche hats, or even bare-headed. In contrast my tangle of red curls branded me as old-fashioned, a sort of pre-Raphaelite model, such as Rossetti might have used.

By Grandmama's telephone I booked an appointment and eventually was waved through gauzy cubicle curtains to discover mysterious rites far beyond the mundane services of a personal maid.

I allowed myself to be persuaded to a moderate length. The coiffeur posed and primped like a mannequin, but he knew what he was about. If the hair was cut only to shoulder length, then for evening it could still be swept up and secured Empire-fashion in a top-comb with a little cascade of curls dropping behind.

So without a single regret I abandoned the thick ropes of red curls snaking over the salon floor and walked out lighter-headed.

And then, already mesmerised by mirrors, I noticed the photographer's studio next door: "Warschawski". Nothing for it then but I must go and have the new me immortalised in monochrome.

Appearing different on the outside, I felt transformed within, liberated as an insect must feel freed from its chrysalis. It gave me the boldness to ring Clive at my old house at Fulham to enquire how he was faring.

I stayed my hand until a minute or so before five when Mrs Langrish was still out shopping and Grandmama would be occupied with her visitors.

As I waited, hearing the distant ringing, I pictured him crossing the tiled floor of the hall, picking up the instrument. If Mrs Pearce answered I would say nothing and simply replace the receiver. But it would be Clive, had to be Clive.

"Hello." The deep voice was metallically distorted.

"It's Lucy."

"Lucy!" Only a single word, but now the tone made it unmistakable. Not Clive at all. But Julian.

Julian who wasn't dead. Julian who wanted *me* dead.

# Fifteen

I should have expected that. Where else would Julian surface but in his own home? For some reason I had thought he would be lying low for longer, perhaps even go abroad and create a false background for his new identity. Yet he had only to disguise himself to feel safe, if he didn't yet realise that it was himself, not me, that the police were now interested in.

The constable supposedly keeping watch from the house opposite must have missed his arrival.

But, with Julian returned home, where was Clive now? Mrs Pearce could hardly explain him away as a lodger when she had no sanction to let out any rooms. Had he managed to get away before Julian arrived?

Or had there been a confrontation? "Find Julian," I had ordered him. And sent him into danger once again. How unthinkingly stupid, and unnecessary when the police must already be at pains to find Peter's killer. And yet somehow Julian had eluded them and regained his home without being recognised. Had he drastically changed his appearance in taking on the name of his dead manservant?

In which case he could well have come across Clive unprepared. As Peter had been. Oh God, no! I couldn't bear that I'd sent that good man to his death. A second time! Why must I always be so headstrong? It seemed I was fated to be his evil genius. I should have foreseen their meeting and that Julian could take extreme measures with anyone threatening his safety.

In this stunned state I was slow to take in Mrs Langrish's condition as she walked unsteadily in and sank on to a sofa, still in her outdoor clothes. Her unfashionable straw hat was askew and her hair dropping from its pins. Her face bore the

185

undisguised tracks of tears, but that was nothing to the wetness of her summer shoes and the dragging skirts soaked right up above the knees.

"You've been in the sea," I exclaimed in horror.

She turned her head towards me, but I wasn't sure she saw me. "I stood there a while," she said in a monotone. "Down by the water. With my memories."

I didn't have to ask of what. She had been remembering that previous time we'd been to St Leonards, when I was a child. Her mother had brought little Barty to play on the sands. And now the poor child was dead.

How could I have been so insensitive as not to realise the pain such memories would bring?

"Oh, my dear," I said, and went to sit close, taking her cold hand in mine. "I'm so very, very sorry."

"I found the waves had come washing in and my feet were wet, my ankles," she said in the same lost voice.

"And then what point was there in staying dry? So I walked on. Farther in."

"Dear God, no." I said, taking her by both shoulders. "You don't mean that. You would surely never mean—?"

She seemed not to notice me. "There was this man. He came splashing up and he pulled me away. Such a fuss. All those people gawking. They found the address from a letter in my handbag. Someone called a cab." She nodded slowly. "The man put me in it."

At last she became aware of my hands gripping her and she tried to free herself, but her voice was still empty. "Quite a rough man. One of those trippers, from London. With his trouser legs rolled up to paddle. He had hairy feet and his skin had caught the sun. But kind. He meant to be kind."

"And I haven't been," I admitted. "My dear Mrs Langrish—"

Her laugh was like a short bark. "Why should you be kind to me? It's not your business to be kind. Your sort don't expect to do more than pay us to serve you."

The sudden bitterness was gone as swiftly as it had shown. She looked at me, focused now, and seemed again to be the governess, explaining the way things were.

"I'm Mrs Langrish to you: always shall be. I don't suppose you ever even heard my first name, let alone wished to use it. It would be improper." She managed a crooked smile. "Do you know what that man called me?"

"No."

"Ma. He called me Ma. As if I belonged to him."

It was a moment when words could do no good. I simply lifted her to her feet and supported her upstairs. She sat quite passive as I ran her a hot bath and peeled off the damp clothes. I led her naked to the warm water and sponged her with my special soap. And wept with her.

As I helped her out at the end and folded a towel round her she stared hard at me and demanded, "Child, what on earth have you done with your lovely hair? Oh, it's quite ruined!"

I hugged her and gave a poor sort of laugh. "This is the new Lucy. I hope you'll find her quite different."

Then while she settled to sleep with the blinds lowered I went downstairs and telephoned my grandmother's doctor. When I'd explained the circumstances and that Mrs Langrish was resting quietly he promised to call in next morning. It would give the lady a chance to regain her mental equilibrium before he examined her.

My next call was to London, considering a warning to the police preferable to alarming the family at home. It took a while for me to reach the sergeant who had spoken with Clive because I had never heard his name, but eventually I passed on the message that my husband could be found at the Fulham address. On being questioned as to the time I had rung the house and identified his voice, I had to admit to being tardy about reporting it.

"There was a family emergency here," I explained. "Almost a case of life and death. I was forced to deal with that first. No, it has nothing to do with the other case; a purely medical matter."

The brief contact with Julian, even by telephone, had unsettled me. To still my unease I had to remind myself that at least he had no idea where I had rung him from.

I made excuses for Mrs Langrish to my grandmother at dinner, stomped out a few Schumann pieces on the pianola for her and went to bed early.

Strange how one's mind continues to work even in sleep. I awoke abruptly at a little after four and her name was on my tongue: Laura. As clearly as if she spoke then, I heard again her mother's sharp tone correcting my assumption that she was Barty's nurse. "No, a grandmother. Which is much the same thing, wouldn't you say, Laura?"

Laura, Laura, Laura. I made a promise to myself not to forget it again.

By breakfast-time Mrs Langrish – Laura – was quite rational, but uncertain how to face me. She had put up shutters between us, and behind them appeared defensive and apologetic in turns. When the doctor arrived – a pink-faced gentleman with a white goatee beard and pince-nez – she submitted to an examination while attempting to conceal she was affronted.

He questioned her to ascertain her state of mind, but she was admitting nothing, adamant that she had recovered from her "momentary absent-mindedness".

How consistently, desperately, everyone hides the truth. Secrets again: covering up to save one's face and others' feelings. That was what I had constantly felt about Stakerleys: all of us concealing our inner selves from those on different levels of the hierarchy – children from parents; parents from children, who could only guess at their intimate affairs through eavesdropping; the family from servants, and certainly vice versa. Yet all speculating and wondering, concerned but hiding it under decent reticence.

Yet doctors were an exception. Inhabiting a social layer entirely to themselves, they contrived, by subtlety or bullying, to penetrate the strata and pull out the secrets. As Uncle Millson did in his quiet way.

It struck me suddenly that he must be privy to the innermost secrets of all the household, and most of the village. Why had I never approached him in my search to find out who I truly was?

This Dr Baumann of my grandmother's was just such a one. As I looked at him, light reflecting off his spectacles hid his eyes, but I knew he'd missed nothing.

"I thought I might drive her home if she's fit enough," I suggested, after we had closed the door on his patient.

"A return to familiar surroundings," he considered, "could ease the melancholia. Rest, and the companionship of someone she trusts completely. I should prefer not to prescribe any medication for fear she becomes dependent."

"She lives with her widowed mother. They seem to understand each other well."

"Then take her, my dear. The simplest remedies are often the best, I find. She should manage a short journey well enough." He waited for me to provide further information.

"To Aylesbury. The car's a comfortable saloon."

"And she has confidence in your driving?"

"I believe so."

He patted my hand. "Look after yourself too."

I watched from the window as he took the seat beside, not behind, his driver who barely acknowledged his return, staying seated and folding away his newspaper with evident regret.

It was a little tableau that stayed sharply in my mind and which I knew I should one day paint. Not so much a double portrait as a whimsical social comment.

We set out shortly before eleven, to follow the same route by which Forbes had brought us down, and again stopping for lunch at Guildford. As Laura clearly preferred to travel in silence, taking in the countryside through which we drove, I had ample time to mull things over in my mind. My main concern was still Clive and I was quietly dismayed that last night had brought no message from him. Surely he would have been in touch with Papa by now and would have learned how to reach me. Of the police I'd no such expectations. They see themselves as existing to extract information, not volunteer it.

I cheered myself with the thought that Papa's discretion could have made him withhold my whereabouts even from so staunch an ally as Clive. It was ingrained in his diplomat's nature to give nothing away that could be used against his cause.

And this brought me again to considering how others' secrecy foiled me in so many moves I would make, as though ignorance guaranteed safety and the truth could do damage.

I must really confront the family when I returned, perhaps through the offices of kind Dr Millson, my distant uncle through

Mama's second marriage and that later one of her elder stepsister-in-law. (How complicated these relationships were; and my own request so simple – just to know who my father was!)

I spent as little time as possible at Aylesbury once I had delivered Laura into her mother's stoic hands. With Stakerleys so near, I longed to make a diversion and see my little Eugenie again, hug her close and promise that soon life would be all sunshine and flowers for us both, but I had promised not to deviate from the plans I'd first outlined to Papa. It was bad enough that I had taken on this journey, so that if they telephoned St Leonards it might worry them I wasn't where I'd said I would be.

I stayed only to change my bodice, which I was constantly having to do, and so always carried a spare one. Just the thought of little Eugenie had brought the milk flowing and soaked almost through to my dress. She might be quite ready to change to a bottle, but evidently I was not.

I completed the return journey without a break, left the car for Grandmama's man to put away and found a single place had been set for me at table with a cold fricassé of turkey, a half bottle of claret and two of Cook's special chocolate éclairs.

There was no message on the notepad by the telephone and my grandmother was out at some friend's. She returned just before eleven, barely remarked on my presence and declared she was exhausted and going straight to bed.

Half way up the stairs she paused. "Oh, you had a visitor, Lucy. A young man."

"So long as it wasn't Julian." To Grandmama anyone under fifty was "young".

"No, I think I would have recognised your husband, Lucy, for all that it's so long since he came here. Now, what was the young man's name? He said he would leave his card in the hall, but he must have forgotten when he left."

"Would his name be Clive? Clive Malcolm?"

"The Bishop's boy? Good gracious, no. I'd recognise him in a flash." She put a hand to her brow, shook her head. "No, it's completely gone. But I'm sure he will call again. He seemed quite persistent."

It sounded ominous. "What was he like? Tall, dark, with a

moustache?" Having so recently heard his voice, I feared it might yet be Julian.

"Tall, yes, and quite charming, but cleanshaven and with really fair hair. And spectacles, I think. Yes, certainly spectacles. I remember thinking what a pity. He was so good-looking otherwise."

That description made it nobody or anybody. It left me wondering how on earth the man had discovered I was here. It implied surely that he'd been sent by the family, so there was nothing to worry about. I would have asked Grandmama about their conversation together, but she had already gone on up, leaving me to lock up and extinguish the lights.

There was too the possibility that some local busybody had become aware of my presence and recent notoriety. He could even be a reporter wishing to ask impertinent questions (though pertinent to him). In that case I should be out if he called tomorrow, and Grandmama's maid should be instructed to tell him so.

Despite my uneasiness about this man and the worry over Clive, I felt a distinct relief at being free of my guardian. Laura's mother telephoned after breakfast to report that her daughter seemed a little brighter but full of remorse for having let me down. I made the necessary social noises and sent my heartfelt good wishes to Laura herself.

After that there was a sense of emptiness which I recognised would be followed by an increasing and irresistible restlessness; then the upsurge of a powerful drive to start working.

Was I so far removed from the recent sad circumstances that I was ready to lose myself in painting again?

There was a bulky envelope addressed in Mama's hand by my breakfast plate, a short note enclosing an unopened letter to "Miss Lucy Sedgwick" and with a half-familiar crest on the reverse of the envelope.

Inside I found a deckle-edged invitation from the Carter-Ravenscroft Gallery for Modern Art to exhibit from three to five watercolours or oil canvases at their November show of the Cougan School of abstract painting.

Was I a Couganist? I didn't think so, but the offer was useful, coming when I must begin to look again to the future and build on the reputation I already had. The professional reputation; not the police-suspect one.

Because of family restrictions and then the war, I had missed out on the proverbial Artist's Life according to the Paris model – a hugger-mugger sharing of communal rooms and beds and theories, with hours of convivial carousing in Left Bank café society where ideas are passionately espoused and loudly declaimed without necessarily being believed in.

From outside it had struck me as exciting, amusing and more than slightly false: a sort of anti-convention which became itself a convention. But then I am almost a loner; self-absorbed, as I'd been accused as a child.

Cougan, however, had spent years in Paris and on the Riviera, mixing with the *Fauvistes*, copies of whose brilliancy I admired, and we shared the same dislike of Cubist intellectualism, preferring to paint from the heart.

I wrote back immediately expressing how I felt: that there were similarities of style but my abstracts were in substance different from Cougan's, growing from my own turmoils and doubts and passing passions. I painted what I must. It emerged. Simply that. Nevertheless I should be pleased to exhibit three works in November. It would give me ample time to paint something new.

I felt an instant need to go out and look, and look and look, saturating my mind wih shapes of living things to transform by my own experience.

I had brought nothing with me but a suitcase containing clothes, books and shoes. Now I was in great haste to find an art shop and buy pencils and sketch pad.

With my new short hair, I rushed out bareheaded and revelled in the soft touch of rain which started gently drizzling from a sea mist. What a new sense of freedom that gave, to be uncaring of appearance or weather. I felt a true bohemian.

I gave little heed to what Grandmama's maid called after me: that yesterday's gentleman had turned up again asking for me and that she'd done as she was told. Nor was I particularly aware of anyone lingering in the church doorway as I passed on foot. If I had been, I might have thought the figure was sheltering from the drizzle.

I spent the morning on the promenade and shingle, sketching ripples patterning the sands, individual pebbles on the beach, the curves of active human bodies, gauzy skirts mischievously whipped by a freshening breeze as the sun broke through, the weird outline of black-hooded Bath chairs pulled by ancient, bowed men, with less ancient dowagers cosily enthroned within. There was almost everything there I needed: harmony, movement, humour. But no wild drama. For that I must go through to Hastings Old Town and watch waves hurling themselves on the cliff face off Rockanore.

It is a curious coastal formation, beaten by south-westerly winds up-Channel. Hastings Old Town lies in an old river bed, deep between two sudden hills. Its shoreline is gently shelving and well suited to beach landings, but the East Hill cliffs rise sheer from the sea with a narrow strip of rocks below, which shows only at low tide.

As you approach from the St Leonards end you pass the Fishmarket with its tall black wooden huts in which the nets are hung to dry and to be mended. Where the boats come in, the pebbles are strewn with fish guttings which gulls sweep savagely to scavenge. The road, running past the Fishmarket, is crowded in early morning by barrows, and vans loading with fish for inland.

At its extremity the high-beached shingle is built up by south-westerly tides against the final groyne. Then, abruptly, the concrete ends. You can go no farther. Beyond a safety railing the quay drops vertically to deep water swirling uneasily, greasily, below, sucked off as the waves recede, only to be churned and come crashing back in a great wall of foam against the chalk and sandstone verticals above.

Primaeval and dangerous, this viewing point has always excited me. However calm the sea elsewhere, here it is a witch's cauldron of seething malevolence. The scents of salt and seaweed and gentle rotting are wildly stimulating. In rougher weather the adventurous watcher is drenched with spray.

By now it was just after noon. The frenetic activity of the

fishmongers and their motor transport had lessened and ceased. Far behind me, little groups still lingered round the whelk stalls, but most had gone indoors to prepare their midday meal. I fancied I could smell hot bacon and fish pie flavoured with onions.

Leaving the human normality behind me, I concentrated on the magnificent power of the sea, totally absorbed as I strove to catch and reproduce a line, a shape, instantly there and instantly gone, never to be repeated the same.

I was unaware of anyone else in the world, until weirdly the hair on my neck seemed to stiffen erect.

Across the edge of the parapet my shadow had lengthened as if it were instantly evening. I saw from the corner of my eye a sharp change of outline as one edge of it snaked out like an arm with a great lumpy hand at its end.

Instinctively I recoiled from the presence behind. The rock struck, not my head but my nearer shoulder. For an instant the pain was immense and then I felt myself lifted, had a brief glimpse of the hate-distorted face under the straw-coloured hair, Julian's demon eyes behind tortoiseshell spectacle frames.

He held me a long moment out over the water, and then he hurled me. I fell, turning over and over, into the thrashing cold of the sea.

# Sixteen

The shock as I struck water brought me to my senses. As I plunged down I was dragged out by the strong undertow streaking back from the breaking of a massive wave. I knew I must go with it and strike through the battering of the following wave building above, able even at this depth to hurl me, thundering against the cliff face.

Swimming once when the red flags were hoisted, I had suffered buffeting by the sea before, although never so violent. I remembered then squaring up to plunge through the walls of water as they swung at me, but now wave after wave bore me further down under them.

It was like giving birth. Strange that at last I could remember it: fearful pulsing forces thrusting against my will. But this time, instead of yielding and flowing with them, I must fight them to survive.

I knew that the tow was fiercest on the surface, but I had to come up to breathe. My lungs were empty, straining for air. There had been no chance of drawing breath as I fell.

My feet touched sharp rock and I was drawn forward on my knees. At last there was something solid to get a purchase on. I judged the moment as the water shuddered from the impact of a giant wave and then, against the dragging bulk of my clothes, I thrust upwards.

I seemed barely to move. The circle of dim light above grew no clearer. My lungs were bursting. Everything was happening so slowly, dreamlike. The fear gripped me that my senses were already slipping away, but then I knew my accelerated mind merely made the outside world seem to go slowly. There was time enough for a drowning woman's past life to flash through her brain as she expired!

195

But I wasn't drowning, wouldn't drown, refused to. And here suddenly was a brief burst of sunlight and heaving sky. Two great gulps of air and I saw the next wall of water curving towards me, a white fringe of foam breaking like a sneer along its edge. And I dived, felt it pass over, tearing at me, but I was through, ready for the next. And there came a flash of ridiculous memory: attending the Grand National with Julian: all those poor horses straining at their fences.

As my strokes began to flag it seemed that each attack of the waves was less powerful now. I guessed I was several yards farther out than the point at which I'd been hurled in. But I must strike out ten times as far to reach calmer water where I could safely swim round the groyne to the raised beach where the fishing boats came in.

One of the flow patterns I had been sketching was the way water raced faster along the edge of the groyne even between waves. It would be folly to try and take refuge near it yet.

My skirts were dragging at my thighs, tangling themselves between my knees. The raincoat put on against the earlier drizzle loaded my agonising shoulder, and my one good arm was numbing from its efforts. Too long in London, I was out of practice at swimming, and still not fully recovered from the birth. For a brief moment I lost faith, believed I might not ever round the point of the groyne.

As I surfaced again, gasping in a mist of spray, I heard the high, lost cry of a gull.

It was like my baby on waking hungry. A new surge of energy filled me. And now failure was impossible. I knew I would return to her.

I made for where the groyne was just submerged and slithered over its bruising granite, slid into shallower water, dragged myself forward on my knees and the waves now were only teasing but still they rolled me on my face. I lay at last on wet shingle, hidden from the road by a ramp of larger pebbles built up by some earlier high tide. And beyond that would be the beached fishing boats and tall black net huts. I could lie here unseen, a sad pile of rags, until my energy returned.

But then what?

I prayed that Julian would have gone. Surely after seeing me plunge in injured, he would stay only a moment to ensure I didn't resurface? He would need to disappear then before anyone recalled seeing him at the scene of the "accident".

But who was there to see?

Then a sharp image came back of a woman in dark green some way off behind him, cowering as though something unthinkable was happening. A witness! When eventually I reached the police I would insist they find her. And I must give them the new description of my husband: clean-shaven, with horn-rimmed spectacles and straw-thatch hair.

The sun had gone in again and the rain returned. Luckily the tide was on the turn, just ebbing, so there was no need to move from where I lay. My shivering had stopped and I began to feel warm, dangerously almost comfortable and immeasurably tired. I closed my eyes for a moment.

In my dream brutal hands were shaking me, a rough voice growling obscenities. I knew if I hung on tight he couldn't throw me back in the water. Not without going over himself. I dug in my nails and screamed in his face.

But no, this was still the beach, and they weren't obscenities.

"Wake up! Wake up, missy," the old man begged, shaking me again.

"Thank God," I told him fervently.

He leaned away. "That I do," he informed me piously. "And so *you* should. Whatever possessed you to do a wicked thing like that?"

I sat up, furious. "I didn't wade in. I was thrown. Off the point there." I waved towards the Rockanore edge.

He shook his head. "Here, you're all bleeding."

"He struck me with a rock," I shouted; or tried to shout. My voice came out as a croak. But then I was past words and burst into a flood of tears. Not wet enough?

At least I was found. I could cope with whatever came next.

I was taken in a car to the police station at Hastings town centre, just behind the Town Hall, and there bandaged by their surgeon and given a fresh blanket to replace the oily one the old fisherman had put round me. Over strong hot tea loaded with sugar I told my story. There was some telephoning to London and to Stakerleys, so finally they believed me and tempered their rough kindness with a sort of awe.

When it came to describing the woman in green who witnessed the attack I found myself hesitating. She had been too far away for me to have seen her face properly, and yet I seemed to know the features. This must be because I'd seen her elsewhere and closer. I have this habit of making snap portraits of people in my mind, and doing it almost automatically.

She belonged to today; I was sure of that. I could have glimpsed her at the Old Town Fishmarket, or along the promenade.

No, surely it had been before then, soon after I left my grandmother's house on foot; then again at Warschawski's shop window where I'd paused, struck by my own photograph on display. I'd seen the woman's reflection behind mine in the glass. She had high cheekbones, dark eyes, a wide mouth and an olive complexion. Striking enough to make a good model.

It was the third and final time I glimpsed her that she had stood some way off and watched as Julian try to kill me.

"I believe that woman could have been following me," I told the police. "You should be looking for a couple, not a man on his own." And I gave them the best description I could.

It wasn't long before I learned that I need not have worried over Clive's safety.

At the Fulham house he had eavesdropped one end of a telephone conversation which ended with Mrs Pearce coming to find him in a hurry. "You'll 'ave to leave, young Malcolm," she said brusquely. "The master's on 'is way back. Due 'ere any minute, and I didn't let on we 'ad a lodger."

So he had allowed her to pack him off, and went to keep an eye on the house from beyond the newsagent's.

A taxi cab had drawn up and the driver began to unload cases from it while the tall passenger, his head covered by a straw boater, ran up the steps and let himself in with a key. His cabbie, having pressed the doorbell to ask for payment, was kept waiting for several minutes, impatient at first, and then resigned since the meter was still running.

Eventually the tall man hurriedly returned, re-engaged the cab and ordered the luggage to be restowed.

The abrupt change of plan was baffling. Clive was on foot and cabs were quite a rarity in that street. Since pursuit was impossible, Clive decided to face up to Mrs Pearce again with the excuse of having left something behind in his hurried departure. And the silly woman, quite flurried by that point, let out that de Verville had been in the house only a couple of seconds when the telephone rang and he was called away once again.

"Does that mean I get my room back?" Clive demanded.

"I can't say," she snapped. "'E's gone down to the coast after 'is wife."

"Just a jiffy," Clive perked up. "I thought you told me he was dead, got himself murdered or something."

Mrs Pearce scowled. "This one's 'is brother, that's 'oo," she said on the spur of the moment. "'E's took the 'ouse over now. Next of kin, see?"

Clive saw only too well, and didn't care for the idea of de Verville's sudden seaside jaunt. He made two telephone calls himself from the nearby sub-Post Office: one to keep the police abreast of developments, but the first to Papa at the House of Lords to demand whether I was staying with Grandmama at St Leonards.

Unfortunately Papa was in the Chamber speaking at the time on a Government bill, and a further call to Stakerleys failed to produce Mama.

Clive managed to pick up a cab in Old Brompton Road, was dropped at the House of Lords and gained an interview with Papa. There he learned that I was, as he'd feared, with Mrs Fellowes and Mrs Langrish at St Leonards.

He intended to catch the next train down, but on paying off the cab outside Charing Cross station had the great good luck to see de Verville again, this time accompanied by a handsome dark-haired woman, taking the cab ahead which had just been vacated.

The man now seemed to have no luggage of his own but was handing in a single suitcase with a lady's brolly strapped on the side. They entered the cab and were driven off.

Clive withheld the fare from his own cabbie, explaining there was a change of plan. He was to follow the cab in front and draw up near to wherever it stopped.

It was a short journey, to a hotel in Earls Court. Clive sat on for five minutes after the other two had gone in, then, out of breath as if he had been hurrying, followed and asked at the reception desk for his friend Major Brooke whom he believed he had just missed.

"I'm sorry, sir," the receptionist said, "but we have no Major Brooke staying here. The gentleman you saw come in must have been Mr Veal."

The registration book lay open on the desk, and reading it upside down Clive saw the last entry, the main word of which began with an extravagantly decorative V. He recognized Veal as the name I had mentioned as de Verville's original, so it seemed the man was to stay there overnight. Before the name he made out the words Mr and Mrs. So it appeared that de Verville had signed in the woman as his wife.

There were two possibilities. Either she was the "wife" he had told Mrs Pearce he was off to see, and she had travelled to Charing Cross from the coast, making unnecessary de Verville's fetching her, or he was indeed intending to go to St Leonards but was delaying the visit because of this other companion.

In either case Clive believed he could safely leave his own journey until next day and spend the evening on a pressing piece of business in the Medical Faculty of UCL.

In this he was mistaken. We learned later that Julian had left the hotel half an hour after he arrived, had taken a train to Warrior Square station and called on Mrs Fellowes to check that I was still there. His woman friend had followed next morning and joined him in tracking me down.

The reason Julian knew of my whereabouts was simple, as he sneeringly told the police later. It was due to stupidity on my part, because when I rang Fulham, hoping to speak with Clive, I had mistaken his voice through the instrument's distortion, and I'd given my name. Then, unnoticed by me because I was so accustomed to the sound, my grandmother's ormolu clock in the hall had chimed five, after a little Mozartian trill. On the single occasion Julian had visited St Leonards with me, that was one of Grandmama's treasures he had observed and coveted. He recognised its notes and so knew where to find me.

There is no knowing what would have happened if I had been at home either time that he called. I cannot believe he would have risked killing me there and then, even disguised as he was. But who knows? I think already he was barely in control of his mind.

As it was, I played again into his hands, leading him and his companion to where I would be at his mercy and the sea's.

Clive was no more than half an hour behind them, and it horrified him that if I had not been so strong a swimmer, or not managed to deflect the blow meant for my head, he would have arrived too late.

The police had rung Grandmama to explain my dilemma and she called Clive to the telephone to speak with them. It was he who arrived with an assortment of dry clothes and a lawyer in tow to help with my statement.

There was quite a hubbub in the corridors outside as we were ushered out by a different door. This, apparently, was to avoid our coming face to face with Julian and the woman, who had been arrested trying to board a train for London.

At Grandmama's they insisted I should eat a late lunch and then sleep for a while in the afternoon. By the time I was dressed again Clive had brought round the little Sunbeam which he had hired to drive down in.

Despite my grandmother's warnings that I was far from fit enough to go out that evening, Clive pressed his case for taking me on a mystery tour.

He drove inland through Silverhill to the Harrow and turned eastwards along the Ridge, past St Helens and into Ore. The rain had cleared, leaving wispy cloud and a melon slice of moon with a sprinkling of paler stars. As we descended towards the Old Town of Hastings the sea was ultramarine with purple shadows, stacked up to the horizon.

Clive looked sideways at me and smiled. I knew then where he was taking me and why.

We parked at the very edge of Rockanore. Clive got out to open my door but I was there before him. I could feel, almost hear, my heart pounding as I relived that moment when Julian stood over me, struck, and lifted me like a limp rag doll.

"Going back to a place where you were happy can often be a disappointment," Clive said evenly. "But going back to a place of fear is part of the cure."

"I'm not afraid any more," I told him, watching successive waves break on the cliff. Twelve hours after the incident, the tide was almost at the same high level.

"I just want to be sure nothing of the sort will happen to me again."

He put his arms round me, one hand cautiously below the injured shoulder, and he kissed me. It more than made up for the rest of the day.

"So what would you have me do now?" he asked as I stayed silent.

I considered. It was a moment for boldness. "You could perhaps propose marriage?" I suggested.

He didn't answer; simply looked at me gravely.

"Or perhaps we don't know each other well enough." It seemed only proper to offer him a way out.

"I'd rather wait," he said, "until you are quite sure who you are."

"And how on earth is that going to happen?"

"Come back to Stakerleys with me. There's something there I want to show you."

"Something in my own home that I've not seen before?"

"Seen many times, I'm sure, but perhaps not noticed." And he would say nothing more then, but wrapped my cloak round me and walked me back to the car.

# Seventeen

It was small for a Gainsborough but there was no mistaking the master's hand. It revealed itself in the pose, the texture of fabrics, the contrasted values, the grading of cool and warm colours.

She sat in semi-profile against the trunk of an oak, chin raised so that the large-brimmed, ostrich-feathered hat shaded only the area of the brow. Her eyes were the blue of a periwinkle and her curly hair fair with gold highlights. Against this the dappled silver-grey of a satin dress extended to her knees where one delicate hand lay on the head of a small silky dog.

Perhaps if the portrait had a fault it was over-pretty, yet the child's air of independence saved it from sentimentality. I say "child", but she would have been fifteen or sixteen: a woman in those days when the chrysalis stage was curtailed or even denied.

"Who is she?" I asked.

Clive moistened a finger on his tongue and rubbed at the plaque on the lower edge of the frame, which had taken on a coppery patina. I peered at it and made out the name: Miss Caroline Sedgwick. No date. I had to guess at the mid-seventeen hundreds.

She had escaped the elongated features I was familiar with in the present male side and in dear, sheep-faced Aunt Mildred. Her face was more rounded, the chin lightly dimpled like Aunt Isabelle's. Yes, the same ancestor had left his, or her, mark on them both.

"How many generations back, do you suppose?" I asked Clive.

"From your Papa? Six, perhaps seven." He sounded amused.

I turned to look at him and his eyes were bright with something like mischief.

"I see a likeness," I admitted.

"To?"

"Aunt Isabelle."

"Who else?"

And then it struck me. But for the colouring I could have been looking in a mirror. Give the portrait red hair and green eyes, then this could have been me five years back.

"Ah," Clive said. I was conscious of him watching me and moving closer behind so that I felt his body supporting mine. "Now you have it, Lucy."

"Myself. But this likeness would imply that I *am* a Sedgwick, or else closely related. With their blue blood in my veins after all."

"I've never doubted it since I first saw this picture two years back, when I visited with my guardian and was given this room. I questioned the Bishop, because I'd understood you were from your mother's first marriage."

"And he admitted it? That I was a bastard? Papa's child by Mama before ever they were married?"

I walked apart from him and stood by the window looking down over Grandfather's rose garden, my mind awash with so many half-thoughts. I remembered the story of how Papa had once fleetingly called on Isabelle in Egypt on his way home from the Far East, and Mama had been her paid travelling companion then. It was the summer before I was born. That must have been when—

"You still haven't worked it all out, Lucy." Now Clive's voice had taken on a note of sympathy.

Why sympathy, when I had recovered both parents I'd assumed were mine as a very small child? What did it matter that I wasn't legitimate? It only meant I had missed a title.

"Look again. At the colouring, which was what first struck you."

I did as he said. So at last the appalling truth broke on me. I saw but would not believe. It was the very likeness I had first recognised, and it accounted for so much. Now I was furious with Clive for showing me the picture, that at one stroke he had deprived me of *both* parents.

"*Isabelle*'s daughter? You want me to accept that *she* was my mother?"

"Is, Lucy. She *is* your mother. It has been a well-kept secret within the family all your life."

"But why? I don't understand why she has never acknowledged me."

"Why not ask her?" he said; and I knew that I was compelled to.

It was a terrible interview, each of us at times incoherent, crying with anger, bitterly laughing. Two of a kind, I was thinking. How could I ever doubt she was my mother?

Clive had left us to it from the beginning, but I was aware of him not far off, ready for when I emerged.

I had flounced out of Stakerleys, escaping from the wretched portrait, and flung myself into the little car he had hired. But he firmly held the door open again and insisted on taking the wheel himself.

"Insurance," he warned me. "It doesn't cover your driving." At least he didn't challenge my ability with the injured shoulder.

All our way down to Kent I seethed within, able to speak only briefly, barely aware of the late summer countryside we drove through. I could see only my own point of view, the betrayal and the long deceit. It never occurred to me that Isabelle could have a reasonable motive for what she had done. Much less that she herself had suffered from her decision.

Clive held me back as the maid opened the door at our ring. "Gently," he said. "Not your bull-at-a-fence act."

"No act," I assured him with black humour. But he had said the right thing. I was able to walk past Geoffrey as he welcomed us, and plant myself silently in front of my mother.

She guessed at once from my expression. One hand went to her mouth and her eyes flickered closed. "Oh, my God," she whispered. "I knew one day it would come to this."

Geoffrey came between us, the welcome still slowly fading in

Clare Curzon

his eyes. "Lucy, what is it? And for heaven's sake what have you done to yourself?"

I had forgotten the sling which served to rest my shoulder.

"A final embrace from my husband," I said bitterly. "From Julian, whom you pressed me to marry, Isabelle, if I remember rightly. Julian, who was your lover immediately before I accepted him."

"What do you want with me?" She was still pretending, but she knew well enough that her past had finally caught up.

"To be told who my father was. If ever you were certain of that."

Her face flushed with colour, then went deadly pale. "Lucy," she faltered, "who told you?"

"I found out for myself. No one needed to betray you. They have all been totally loyal, all these years, lying and implying, because you were ashamed to acknowledge me, your bastard."

Now she came back fighting, almost spitting with anger. "You can have no idea how it was. In those days in a family like ours one had to be so respectable, above suspicion like Caesar's wife. The Old Queen was still alive. She'd have had me crucified socially.

"I was only twenty. As you are now. And I'd been a widow just a few weeks too long. My grandfather, the then Earl, would have cut me off without enough to live on. And who would have married me then? I had to go abroad and hide what had happened. My reputation—"

"False reputation. You lumbered your paid companion with your baby, forged documents to make it seem the birth was legitimate. Who was this Italian doctor you must have bribed to marry her? Does it mean that when Eugenie married Papa – I mean your brother – that the marriage was bigamous?"

It took a long time to get the complicated story sorted, but there Geoffrey, dear patient Geoffrey, was able to restrain us and fill in the missing pieces. He knew everything; had known before he married Isabelle; married her from devotion, not pity.

The doctor, Gabrieli, whose name I had adapted for my own baby, was no more than the one who had attended the birth and provided the false papers. He'd been better at doctoring them than at attending Isabelle, for he botched the job and ruined her for ever having more children.

A corrupt forger who would do anything for money. What a fool I'd been to imagine so much that was noble about him! The one Eugenie had been pushed into marrying was called Facci, an elderly peasant on his deathbed. So at least by the time Eugenie married into the Sedgwick clan she had been honestly an Italian's widow, as she claimed.

"Why did she agree to it?" I demanded.

"Because she loved you on sight. It was she who called you Lucia. I had named you Margherita after the nurse who helped at the delivery. And I had Eugenie named as the mother. Once she had you she refused to give you up."

As if that mattered for the moment. There was only one thing I would demand she confess to me now. "You haven't answered my question. Who was my father?"

"It's better you shouldn't know."

A new horror gripped me. What kind of demon was he then? A criminal? A killer? Had I that sort of blood in my veins?

"I think you're wrong, Isabelle," Geoffrey insisted gently. "What harm can it do? And she has a right to know."

Nevertheless, sniffing and sobbing, she held out until later. Then, after she had changed her dress and tidied her face she brought me a little pasteboard programme with a florid Scottish character depicted on the cover. It portayed Macbeth, and inside was the photograph of the man whose passion had swept Isabelle, newly widowed, off her feet. Robert Grainger, the red-haired Victorian dramatic actor.

Standing there with the programme in my hand I remembered another; how when I was a child of nine I had fallen in love with an opera singer whose name I could scarcely remember. It was ironic. Surely the Greeks' gods would have howled with laughter at us.

I was cooler by then and agreed to stay overnight, and they were happy to have us there. Perhaps I should have rung Stakerleys to explain how much I had learned, but it seemed too difficult for me just then. In any case I must face Eugenie and the viscount in person when I told them. And humbly thank them for their good care of me all these years, my kind uncle by blood and aunt by marriage. I would always privately mourn them as parents.

With so many of my relations reversing their positions, and my half-brother Edwin now become my cousin, no one seemed to have remained constant, except Clive.

I was exhausted by emotion as much as by the earlier physical assault, but I had just energy enough to get me to Clive's bed after the household had settled to silence.

He made room for me as if he had expected the visit. For a while we lay passive in each other's arms before he stroked my hair from my face and tenderly asked, "If you're quite certain, Lucy?"

And I was.

# Eighteen

S o many things remained to be sorted out in the next few days that I had little time to consider what my intentions were over contacting my father. Isabelle had reckoned that he would be well over seventy by now, and since there had been no stage news of him for several years, perhaps he was dead.

Fortunately I was saved travelling to Hastings again because the Sussex police arranged for further statements to be taken from me at Stakerleys. But the Metropolitan Police insisted that both Clive and I come to Scotland Yard for questioning about the final developments at Fulham.

Julian had been taken to London and already been charged with Peter's murder, with Mrs Pearce as an Accessory Before and After the Fact. Also a case of Attempted Murder was being prepared in respect of the attack on myself.

No charge had yet been made against Edith, the woman in green, who was being questioned about Julian's murderous attack at Rockanore.

She was expected to produce a marriage certificate to prove that as Edith Montgomery, nurse, she had secretly become Mrs Julian Veal shortly after tending him at base hospital in 1916. Aware of his false alternative name, how far she had gone in collusion over his making a bigamous marriage with me, and the intended acquisition of Grandfather's legacy was still uncertain.

She appeared to be a person of some determination, but I remembered her expression of horror as I glimpsed her over Julian's head before he threw me in the sea, and I hoped she might have been so appalled as to finally give evidence against him. It would be worth her while to lessen the capital charge against herself. Remembering my own nightmare thoughts of the death sentence, I could not bear to think of such a young woman ending in that way. As for Julian's ultimate fate, I set my face resolutely against pity, content to leave it with the law to take its course.

I was still conscious of being watched. Now that the police had left me in peace it was the family and my friends who seemed to hedge me in however differently, tiptoeing around my feelings. I grew increasingly irritated with everyone's concern and was determined to break away, leave Stakerleys and start out on something quite new. At the same time I had nowhere to go and could not yet settle to the new work I had too readily agreed to supply for the Cougan exhibition.

My chance arrived when Papa's inquiries into my real father's whereabouts came up with the name of his one-time theatrical agent. He would give out no information by telephone, so I went to see him in his London office.

He was an extraordinary man, immensely fat, so that he could sit only at a distance from the front of his laden desk. His arms were barely long enough to reach the nearest sheets of information, and his secretary was obliged to stand at his side holding his glass of Madeira, of which he insisted on having a glass poured for me too.

You would have thought he interviewed me with a mind to finding me an opening in some future dramatic production, but I assumed this was purely from habit, so I humoured him until such time as he was willing to give me the information I needed. This, when it came, consisted only of a London address where the agent, Mr Vincent Addams, had last communicated with him. It had been to send on the offer of an audition at the Abbey Theatre in Dublin for a play by Eugene O'Neill. Mr Addams had later received a picture postcard of the River Liffey on which Grainger had scrawled, "I will strut no more, but live."

"What does that mean?" I asked.

"Shakespeare's poor player that struts and frets his hour upon the stage and then is heard no more. You know it surely?"

"Wasn't that 'the way to dusty death'? But after the quote this Robert Grainger wrote that he would *live*."

"Ah." The agent slumped further in his chair, chins bedded on massive chest. "So what was life become for the poor fellow by that point? To research the new 'e' in whisky no doubt, for he'd been much given to scotch. That and a succession of less and less satisfactory women."

"Do you think then that he stayed on in Ireland? Went to earth there?"

"*Went to earth* in one or the other sense of the phrase, yes. I am sorry, Miss Sedgwick, but beyond that surmise I have nothing to offer you. For the world at large, Robert Grainger, actor, is no more."

However, refusing to be put off, I booked a passage to Dublin and restarted inquiries there. The family was opposed to it, of course, insisting that someone else should be employed to do the detective work and horrified that I was determined to go unaccompanied. But by now it seemed unlikely that any discoveries made would be to my father's credit and I preferred not to share the coming shame.

I left Papa the name of the hotel I had booked into and promised to keep in touch by telephone.

At the Abbey Theatre no one in management was able – or willing – to give me any information at all, but a cleaner, wrinkled and kindly, told me where to find the man who had briefly been Robert Grainger's dresser during his last few abysmal performances there.

I tracked the man down to the bar stool where he was customarily to be found and, ignoring the curiosity of other drinkers at my breaking into a male preserve, plied him with Jameson's until his tongue loosened enough to admit that the actor had gone west and then north into County Londonderry, where he was thought to have spent his last earnings on buying a derelict farmhouse on the road out to Claudy. From there he had refused to be prised, and ignored all demands for repayment of debts incurred back in Dublin.

It was hardly encouraging, but having come so far I was not to be put off. I took a train to Belfast and another to Londonderry where I put up at an hotel hard by the Guildhall, booking in for three nights. Over that time I expected to find and confront my father. What sort of welcome I should receive was beyond present imagination.

There was some difficulty at first in hiring a car, since it appeared that here women were seen as a danger behind the wheel except in open farmland. So eventually I settled to be driven by an enthusiastic twenty-year-old mechanic who took his indisputable half of the road in the middle. The one advantage of this mode of transport was that it left me free to take in the countryside, which, under an immense sky, was like no other that I had ever seen.

We twice missed the turn on the Claudy road because the rocky track, once suited to farm carts, had grassed over. There were no hedges here to delineate the fields but the whole flat landscape was devoted to peat. The diggings lay in straight, prune-black horizontals with pools of sullen water between which glinted with an oily, opalescent sheen. It was eerie and miserable under the sporadic rain.

As we approached the farmhouse – a low-lying single-storeyed building, once white but now looking as if the wash had been mixed with cow dung, the unexpected happened. The sun blazed through. A sudden half-rainbow showed ahead and then a reflection of it above the other. The young man driving tooted his horn and informed me, between closed teeth in the Ulster manner, that a double rainbow was lucky and came often. I began to feel that the place had some magic to it.

A woman was standing in the open doorway, one hand on the wooden jamb, the other fist on an out-thrust hip. No, she said, scowling, himself wasn't at home. She'd tell him so, she would, when he got back. And who should she say the fine lady was?

"His daughter, Lucy Sedgwick," I said shortly, turned on my heel and went back to where Billy, in reverse, was attempting to extract the car from a boggy patch of vivid green.

It was only fair, I thought, that the man should have some chance to draw breath before meeting his own issue that he'd no idea existed. And draw breath was something he well might manage, to judge by the solid snores that had reached me from behind the woman on guard.

We returned next afternoon, parking closer to the road to save sinking in up to the axles. It had given up raining. I ordered Billy to stay with the car and he nodded agreement. "With the engine runnen," he promised, "so's you can get away quick."

It wasn't encouraging, but this time the woman was making some show of sweeping the threshold with a hazel broom as I approached. I saw, but could not hear, her call back over one shoulder, and a moment later an elderly man appeared in the doorway, legs astraddle in an heroic pose. He slowly raised his right arm in a kingly greeting. I wondered wryly what fate he would decree for the bearer of bad news.

"Welcome, child," he greeted me. "It's taken you long enough to find me."

I took it for bravado, but he calmly claimed that all along he had been aware of my existence.

"And did nothing?"

"What should I do?" His eyes were wide and round with assumed innocence. "A poor player at the castle gate."

"If you'd loved my mother you would have married her." Such depraved indifference, taking advantage of poor, silly Isabelle.

"Marry?" His voice rose in a bull-like roar. The whiskey hadn't killed off all his histrionic art. The voice then plummeted. Wounded to the core, he sounded. "She'd have none of it."

Well, at least Isabelle had started to show some sense at that point. How could she ever have been taken in by such a mountebank? But then, I had to remind myself, he had been at the peak of his powers, playing Lear, Macbeth, Coriolanus. Isabelle was newly widowed, at the same age as myself now, and God knows we women are not made of stone.

He bowed low, gestured to head and heart then graciously to the cabin's interior. Now he was an Islamic sheikh offering the hospitality of his bedouin tent.

I felt obliged to enter. A pity, because the light was dimmer inside and I wanted to study every line of his face and be sure there was nothing of me in it. Yet there was, of course, starting at the top with his grizzled red raggle-taggle hair and beard. If I could only penetrate the wrinkles round his sunken eyes I would find the iris among the broken veins, green as my own.

"And now you have nothing to say," he remarked shrewdly.

"So many questions, but they have dissolved on your tongue. So let me take up the tale by asking whether you have ambitions to walk the boards and bend the ear of the multitudes yourself."

"None," I said tersely, half-hating him. "I'd rather dazzle their eyes. I paint."

"Ah, but you have a way with words. Not my way, but something less –" he struck a chin-stroking attitude of wisdom – "less exquisite. You are a vicious symptom of the modern disease. Your children will end grunting monosyllables. Nevertheless people will understand them."

He flung back his head and declaimed, "'We are the music makers,/ We are the dreamers of dreams,/ Wandering by lone sea-breakers/ And sitting by desolate streams; /World-losers and world-forsakers,/On whom the pale moon gleams:/We are the movers and shakers/Of the world for ever, it seems./For each age is a dream that is dying,/Or one that is coming to birth."

"You won't have heard that before, because England has yet to appreciate there's more to Ireland than potatoes. Ode by O'Shaughnessy. 1844 to 1881." He smiled wickedly. "Rather good, don't y'know," he added in over-refined English gentility.

"So that's what we are," I responded. "I'd often wondered." And then I was impatient with him, because now I knew he only played the mountebank. He was still capable of more.

"Why do you waste your gifts here in obscurity?"

"I had to come here, if only to learn one thing," he said slowly. There was a hint of irony in the tone, as if he recognised the portentousness of what he would say and mocked himself. "I have learned that creativity is an illusion. The most we do is copy or rearrange. We observe, comprehend, reproduce: I the actor, you the artist."

"You mustn't diminish your achievement . . ."

"No, child. Can you truly tell me you have ever produced what was not a shadow of something there before?"

I thought about my blazing abstracts, burnt out of my living heart. Everything in me shouted to refute what he claimed. And yet, if I considered . . .

"We are simply channels. That is all. Life appears through us, uses us. We purify its passage, or else we pollute it with our less pristine selves so it is transmuted. For a time we leave a mark; no more. But we do not create."

"Whatever it is you do, you once did it supremely well. Why cheat the world of more?"

"I doubt if I owe the world more than I've already paid. Whereas you, child, have a long future ahead. I shouldn't seek to tarnish it. And I am humbled that you troubled to find me. Only go now, it's enough. Your youth upstages me and I take that badly." He made shooing gestures, smiling to expose yellowed teeth. "Your coach awaits, and the munchkin grows anxious."

"Nonsense," I told him. "Suddenly I remember all the things I wanted to know, so find me somewhere to sit down and let us really talk."

We did, until it grew almost too dark to see each other. "I'll come back tomorrow," I promised.

"Must I over-act you offstage? No, go like Orpheus, but never look back. Remember me as a cold-hearted villain who thought of no one but himself. And go off equally free."

We stood together at the door as the sun hovered on the horizon. He was silent a while, gazing out over the reflected crimson and black of the bog land. The wind stirred the forked beard on his out-thrust chin, and I thought of Lear the madman. I wasn't entirely sure he was playing the part.

Then he spoke simply, turning to smile at me. "This is where I was born. I came back to die. Something we all do at the last. I wanted to do it as myself, if only I could find me."

I looked at him and loved him with all my fierce being, the being his passion had brought about. And I understood that we had been on the same road, I a long way behind. But I had caught up. We had found more than ourselves, acknowledging each other.

At times there have been people who thought me mad. Maybe I have been. I had needed to know where it came from.

I did as ordered. I walked away from my father without so much as ever having touched his hand. Distant as we had always been, and respecting the fact. I stumbled along the rocky track where the last green had dissolved into grey.

The peat bogs extended in black bars ahead and the dying sun shot flame through the sullen horizontals, turning the stagnant water to the colour of blood.

From such drama had he come. Of such was I made too. I was consumed by the passion of the place and the knowledge that he had sired me.

I was halfway to the car when he called after me. "Lucy! Child, where are you going?" Tragedy personified. Lear again, but I was no Cordelia: he had forbidden it. His mocking laughter followed me.

"I'm going home." I never turned my head, but let the tugging wind carry my shouted words back. Whether he heard them or not hardly mattered. The important thing was the warmth in my heart. I walked on in the blood-red of sunset and its black-barred reflections in water across the bog.

I rejoined Billy in the waiting car and we drove in silence back to the town. Towards my other family, to my child. And, perhaps, to Clive.